April 19, 2006

Legacy of Atwater .

Debra Morgan

*It's your abilities that count,
not your disabilities.*

Debra Morgan

PublishAmerica
Baltimore

First printing

At the specific preference of the author, PublishAmerica allowed this work to remain exactly as the author intended, verbatim, without editorial input.

ISBN: 1-4241-1965-0
PUBLISHED BY PUBLISHAMERICA, LLLP
www.publishamerica.com
Baltimore

Printed in the United States of America

Dedication

To my father, Edgar Silas Clements, who taught me the art of Storytelling. To my seven brothers for letting me know exactly how boys think. To my mother Dorothy, who put up with us. And to my daughter Kelly, who is my best editor.

Acknowledgements

To my first real writing teacher, Mary Kettredge. And Madison Memorial Physical Therapy, who inspired me to come up with some real gruesome ideas for the storyline. They know who they are and why.

Prologue

Sixty years ago, the Clan Lands of the Green Crescent, were over run by the Warriors of the Bloodstone Cult of Cerebrus. These pagan worshipers of the Blood-red Mother Stone enslaved the inhabitants and demanded offerings. Not just of crops and precious metals, but slaves.

The Bloodstone Cult believed they had been given the right to rule the world because of their ability to use the Bloodstones to do magic. The Bloodstone Wizards had great power, but only at the cost of blood, not their blood. They used the blood of slaves.

The Clan Lands had to give tribute to them year after year, including their children, to be carried off to be slaves of the Bloodstone Wizards of Cerebrus.

Forty years ago, Atwater rebelled, discovered the use of silver, and led the fight that drove the Bloodstones out of the Green Crescent. Other then a few scattered raids, they lived in un-easy peace.

1

Hania cracked his eyes open and glared at the tent's canvas ceiling. *It's your own fault. When are you going to learn?*

With the charley horse's first twinge he remembered that he had not taken the dolomite often enough. He stretched the leg out hoping he could stop the muscle from cramping. No such luck. He gasped as the leg pulled up tight even as he tried to relax it.

The battle lost, he struggled to sit up and started rubbing the knot of muscle popping out of his right calf. Gritting his teeth, he rubbed and kneaded it trying to force the muscle into submission. He did it quietly. No need wake anyone else. Not even Skelly, who shared the tent with him.

His hands dropped to the sleeping mat. It wasn't working. He would have to get up and walk it out. With a sigh, Hania got to his knees and crawled out of the tent, it was still dark. Now the bottom of his foot was starting to cramp up as well; glaring at his foot he reached down and slapped at it. *Sure, have some sympathy pain. Why not? I was only trying to sleep.*

He crawled over to the lichen-splotched boulder they had pitched the tent behind. Turning his back to it, he placed his hands on the rough surface; then pushing up with his hands and pushing back with his good leg, he stood.

He paused to catch his breath. *I hate this trial. I hate hurting all the time ... being tired all the time.* It was only late at night with no one around that he allowed Hesutu, the illness that plagued his father's Clan, to get to him.

Closing his eyes, he prayed to the Great Spirit, to help him handle it. *Give me peace; give me knowledge of what to do. Help me get through it.* Looking up he smiled; it was not as late as he had thought. He could still get enough sleep. The full moon was just inching over the Bald Cypress trees to the east.

He straightened his bad leg, preparing to put weight on it. As he rocked onto it, he had to bite his lip to keep from crying out. *Deep breaths, take slow deep breaths.*

Hania did not want to alert the other boys to his problem. They would ship him off, back to Atwater. They did not want him or Skelly along on this, their Manhood Trip.

The Manhood Trip was a leftover from the Pagan past. It had been changed from a drug induced Vision Quest into a survival trip, a rite of passage from boyhood to adult. They had to make tools, catch their own food, and craft a boat or raft to return them over Grassy Lake back to the village of Atwater. They were supposed to learn to rely on each other.

Instead, they divided into two camps. Skelly and Hania in one; Chval, Dreogan, Tesar, and Barra were in the other.

Hania limped around the boulder to one of the few trees, a young Red Maple, growing on the boulder-strewn hill. He relieved his bladder. If any of the four boys from Chval's camp saw him, they would think that was the reason for the nighttime stroll.

Finished he headed for the tent and his interrupted rest. He stopped. Something was wrong; he listened for what it was, not moving. Had the Hesutu affected his hearing? No, he could hear was his own breathing and Skelly's snores. He paused, head cocked, in the moonlight. It wasn't something he heard…it was what he didn't.

No sound of rodents foraging for food on the forest floor. No snap of wing as an owl fought for air after a successful snatch. No soft flutter of bat wing overhead. No sound of crickets or beetles calling for mates.

There has to be a predator. There was sign of it…what else could cause such silence? The fishing spears Skelly had made leaned against a nearby boulder, points up. Hania's hand inched towards them. Soon the smooth shaft of one was firm in his grip.

Turning, he peered into the shadows. The moon was bright enough to show shadowed hues of the colors around him. He hunted for the eye shines of night hunters. He searched for cats, big cats, a puma, or jaguar; they alone could cause this stillness. No eyes shined back.

He sniffed for a skunk. No, the only thing he could smell was his own urine and the earthy smell of springtime on the lake.

Puzzled, he looked down the hill to where the other boys had pitched their tents. He blinked his eyes. *Did I see what I just saw?* As he stepped back his foot slipped on the wet leaves and he sat down hard on his rump, a rock biting into his hip.

Hania scrambled to his feet using the tree and fishing spear for support. He paused, giving himself time to think. *You're making too much noise.* He held

10

his breath and peaked around the trunk. *Am I dreaming? If it is a dream, I'm having a nightmare.*

He backed into the tent, ignoring the pain in his leg, foot, and hip. Slowing his breathing, he crouched next to Skelly.

As he clamped his hand over Skelly's mouth cutting off a snore, he leaned close. "Please don't make a sound."

"Am I allowed to breathe?" Skelly mumbled against Hania's hand. Dark brown eyes looked up at him waiting for an explanation.

"Bloodstone Warriors!" Hania felt Skelly stiffen as his own heart pounded hard in his chest. He could feel the panic constrict his muscles and thoughts. He took another deep breath, fighting for control. Everything he had ever heard about the Bloodstones was racing through his mind. *Where should we go?*

"Gather everything you can take." Hania snatched his hand away from Skelly's face. "We'll hide in the caves for now…figure out where to go from there."

He searched through his supplies. As a potion-maker he carried small amounts of everything you could need and more. *Oh please be in here…please!* His pack contained a wilderness kit and he dug though it's pockets. It should be in here. It was, a small bottle of silver paint. He grabbed it and smeared a band around his head and handed it to Skelly.

He motioned for Skelly to do the same. Skelly copied Hania, but his eyes were demanding answers.

Swift and quiet, Hania and Skelly stuffed everything they could into Skelly's backpack. Skelly even ducked outside to grab the rest of the fishing spears; they were the only weapons they had, except their hunting knives. Then they packed up the bedrolls and tied them to Hania's pack. Taking his knife, Hania slit an opening in the tent's back wall.

"Is your father going to be pleased with you putting a back door in his new tent?" Skelly asked, as they crawled through the hole. It tore even bigger when Skelly yanked his enormous backpack through.

They heard yells of panic. Hania slipped and dropped the coil of rope he was carrying; he had to reach back into the tent to retrieve it. He hated dropping things…just another part of having Hesutu. *You don't have time to drop things, concentrate on holding on! You must make your hands work!*

He looked down at his hands. They were green from crawling through the grass to the boulder. He rubbed them hard up and down the back of his leggings. Can't have the green rubbing off on the stones…marking the climb…leading the way to the caves.

"What's going on?" Skelly grabbed Hania, spinning him around. "Are you sure it's Bloodstone Warriors?"

"Yes, I saw the Bloodstones…in the moonlight…gleaming on their breastplates." He shivered. The others, judging from the sounds, were being dragged from their tents. *Block it out! You have to concentrate on what has to be done now.* He slipped the coil of rope under his arm and over his head. That should keep it from falling again.

"Come on!" Hania yanked on Skelly's muscular arm; they had to get out of sight fast. He stepped onto the nearest rock outcropping. "Don't leave any footprints." Hania started to climb towards the nearest entrance to the caves.

Skelly trailing, glanced often in the camp's direction. "I feel like a coward." He hissed at Hania.

"We can't help them, we don't have the right weapons." Hania stretched out for the next handhold, the cliff still warm from the sun.

"You're right. What we have is crude and not silvered." Skelly scrambled up even with Hania who was already trembling with fatigue and pushed him up onto a ledge where they could both rest.

Hania waited for Skelly to climb up and slide over next to him. "How many of them are there?" He handed him the spyglass from the wilderness kit.

Skelly peered down into the camp, panning the area. "Five. No, six. I see four Warriors, a man, and a boy."

Hania closed his eyes and took several deep gulps of air. Quit shaking, he ordered his arms and legs; they didn't listen.

"That's odd." Skelly shifted on the ledge.

"What's odd?" Hania opened his eyes and looked at Skelly, who was leaning out, looking south.

"There's a pathway of stones heading into the swamp. How did they do that?"

Hania grabbed the spyglass. "Where?"

Skelly pointed south then leaned back so Hania could get an eye on it. "Towards the swamp."

Hania stared. It was a bridge. It was a stone bridge floating on the water! And it was heading…straight as an arrow…into the swamp.

"They have become more powerful…or more practiced." Hania leaned his head against the warmth of the cliff. "How did they raise a pathway like that?"

"It's something new." Skelly rose and pulled Hania to his feet. "What do we do now?"

"Let me think…the Bloodstone Cult. The Atwater Clan led the fight against them in the Great War." Hania climbed to the next ledge and started along it. "But I've never heard of an attack this far over land. They've always used ships to come into the heart of the Clan Lands."

"I wish I knew more about the Great War. I've just started that part of my schooling. Maps and battles…things like that." Skelly said as they reached the opening to the secret caverns of Manhood Island.

"I am also learning some of it…ways to fight the power they use to rule…interrupt their control of everyone." Hania stepped through the opening into the dark, his hand brushing along the rough cavern wall as he tested his footing on the slanted floor.

"The Bloodstone Warriors?" Skelly asked as he followed.

"No." Hania said. "Their leaders, the Stone Born Wizards, the ones that can use the Bloodstones." They were now deep enough into the caverns that Hania felt it was safe to light a torch.

He spun Skelly around and reached up to pull a torch and flint out of the pack. The torch flared up, throwing flickering shadows against the walls.

Hania looked up at Skelly's face, the torchlight accenting the tension. Skelly was a tall, muscular young man, with chiseled features and black wavy hair. If it weren't for the Lise, he would be of much interest to the young ladies of Atwater. But like Hania, he was doomed by disease to bachelorhood.

Skelly was studying to become a historian. Hania was sure he knew some things he didn't. "Tell me everything you know."

Skelly looked down. "The Bloodstones swept over the Green Crescent lands and took control. We were powerless against them. They made us chattel…we were slave herds, to be culled as they wished. We had to give them tribute every year."

On and on Skelly talked as he drew a map in the floor's soft dust, his hands gesturing in the air at key points. Most of it Hania already knew. But none of it explained how the Bloodstones were able manipulate the stones to create the pathway.

Hania started to pace. What was it about the stones in the swamp? *There was a clue in them…think…it has to do with silver.*

Skelly quit talking. He had reached the part where the Atwater clan had rebelled against the Bloodstone Cult's rule.

"If I remember correctly," Hania stopped and leaned against the uneven tunnel wall, "It went badly. They were driven back though Atwater until they were confined in the temple…all their arrows were gone…swords and spears, useless. Weren't they contemplating committing suicide rather than becoming slaves? How many were left at that point?"

"63 children, 68 women, and 93 men. Some of the women had escaped into the hills with their children. Some had been captured, held in pens next to the docks…just like animals." Skelly's face looked grim, he blinked and a tear escaped, sliding down one of his long lashes.

"Go on."

"The Chieftain, in desperation took down one of the gilded silver arrows from the wall. They were the only weapons they had left."

"And?" Hania prodded, he had a vague recollection, vague wasn't enough now.

"He shot the Bloodstone Wizard right in the heart…it killed him." Skelly looked up at Hania. "They had found the Bloodstone's weakness."

"Then they defeated them." Hania leaned against the cavern's wall and looked over at Skelly.

"They grabbed up every gilded weapon in sight and tore out of the temple into the middle of the Bloodstone Warriors. It was like wolves in a flock of sheep. The Bloodstones fled back to their ship. So fast that they even left the ones they had captured on the docks. Never to be seen again at Atwater."

"Silver. The only thing that works against them." Hania slid down and sat in the dust. That's it…the stones in the path…are free of silver.

Skelly slid down next to him. "Other than a few raids on the unprotected, they have left us alone."

"This makes us one of their raids." Hania stuck a twig into Manhood Island. "What about the others?"

"One that I know of; a family fishing or something here." Skelly stuck a twig into the sea, just off Whitewater. "It was about 5 years ago. They were in the ship building business…my father knew them. Knew them well."

"And twenty years ago a group of maidens were taken from near Bainbridge, here." Hania pushed in his own twig, and then leaned back studying the map they had made. "One of them escaped and returned."

"This is the farthest they have come into the Green Crescent since the war." Skelly touched the twig on Manhood Island. "They're getting bolder."

But Hania's mind was on the Bainbridge maidens his father had told him about. One had been his father's cousin…gone…never to return. The one that came back had been younger and she came back after four years time. She had escaped not from a camp of slavers, but from Cerebrus, itself.

Cerebrus. The name was enough to make you shutter. His Grandfather had told him tales of that place, the City/State of the Bloodstones. And his father said the maiden that had returned told the people of Bainbridge things that had caused them to double their fortifications. Now it was the most secure clan in all the Green Crescent.

It was from her they had learned of the Sleep Spell and how to stop it. At least the healers knew.

And then there were the prophecies.

Skelly was shaking Hania. "I said, 'What are we going to do?'"

"Sorry, I was thinking." He blinked up at Skelly, his mind blank. "The weapons?"

"They're in the armory." Skelly gestured in the general direction of Atwater.

Hania nodded. "How far along is Tesar's raft?" Tesar, the group's eager beaver builder, had dropped an Ash he was felling right into Hania and Skelly's cook fire yesterday. Encouraged no doubt by Dreogan, the group's prankster.

"Umm, finished, tied up next to the dock I think." Skelly nodded his head. "Go for help! The men in the village, they'll know how to fight the Bloodstones."

"We must alert them." Hania nodded.

We're going to be heroes! What a way to end a Manhood trip! Edging back out to the cave's entrance, they checked on what the Bloodstones were doing. A slave pen had been constructed and the boys were inside.

There was something odd about the slave pen. He stared at it. Stone? It was made of stone, not wood. But how did it get there? Tall, thin stone pillars and a solid stone capstone around the top! That is so…odd. Shivers ran over Hania's arms; he pointed a shaking finger from pen to path. "The pen is like the pathway. It's made of stone that is free of silver."

Dreogan was pacing around and testing the bars, frustration in every movement of his lanky frame. The other three sat in the middle, as if they were defeated.

"Hania! Skelly!" Dreogan howled at the sky.

Chval threw a rock at him. Then lowered his head to his knees.

Other than the leader, the Bloodstone Warriors were scatter about, searching the campsite and around it. How long before our tent is found?

"Come on." Skelly pulled on Hania's arm. "The sooner we get back home the sooner they'll be free."

They wound their way through the maze of tunnels. Making their way to the opening that came out by the dock.

15

"There is something bothering me." Skelly stepped over a narrow fissure. "Why didn't they use the Sleep Spell?"

"I was wondering the same thing. Maybe we're too close to Atwater and it would have tipped off our people that they were nearby."

"Ouch!" Skelly rubbed his head where he hit it on an outcropping of stone hanging from the ceiling.

"That wouldn't happen if you quit shooting up six inches each year." Grinned Hania.

"Yea, but if I didn't, who would protect you from Chval and Company." He checked to see if he was bleeding. Satisfied he was okay, they moved on. Skelly kept an eye on the ceiling as well as the floor.

"You had me band my head. Why?"

"So they couldn't find us," Hania grinned over at him, "or put us to sleep."

"So that is why there is a silver lining inside of all military and law enforcement helmets." Skelly took off his pack and slid sideways through the tunnel's narrow part, dragging the pack behind.

"That is what the maiden that returned to Bainbridge told them to do. Silver stops the Sleep and Find spells." Hania followed without removing his pack.

Skelly shrugged his pack back on; they were almost down to the dock area.

"Shoot, which way!" Hania looked at the two tunnels facing them. They hadn't been in this section for such a long time.

Skelly raised his hand and shut his eyes, trying to feel for air movement.

"Is it to the left or right?" Hania asked. They didn't have time to get lost.

Lighting a second torch, Skelly pushed him to the left. "Whoever gets there first, takes the raft and goes." He shouted as he headed to the right.

Hania raced along the left hand tunnel. He stopped and sniffed the air. Warm, humid, sulfuric. This tunnel did not lead to the outside; it went to the sulfur mud pots. He turned and raced back the way he had come.

He reached where they split up and dashed down the other tunnel. Two more turns and he was running in fresh air. Soon Hania was at the opening by the docks, Skelly's pack leaned against the wall just inside the opening. Skelly was still at the dock. Why hadn't he left?

Panting, he put out the torch and jogged over to the dock. Skelly stared down at what was left of Tesar's hard work. It looked as if a giant had taken a knife and diced it to bits on a chopping board. Must have been done by the Bloodstone Wizard. It was gone.

"Now what?" Skelly nudged at a few bits floating against the dock.

"The only help is across the lake." Hania mumbled to himself.

"Then there is only one thing for it." Skelly stripped down, exposing rippling muscles. "I'll do it. I'm the stronger swimmer."

"You can't make it all the way to Atwater. It's too far! What about the Lise? You could have a seizure and…"

Skelly looked down, pondering; then he grinned at Hania, his dark eyes twinkling. "Nabi's retreat. It's not far and he keeps a couple of one-man skiffs there…for races."

Hania grabbed Skelly's arm. "Anacondas! They hunt in the shallows!"

"I'll stay in deep water." Skelly pulled his arm loose.

Hania had a bad feeling about this. "Let's pray first."

"What?"

"Pray for safety, and success. Please!" Hania felt frantic, he didn't know why. Or did he?

"Don't you trust me?"

"And my safety too. I have to stay on the island and out of sight." Hania threw a glance in the direction of the campsite.

Skelly relented. "I'm not used to saying prayers. That's something that healers do, not fishmongers or historians."

Hania raised an eyebrow; they both knew that Nabi was a prophet as well as an historian, but as Hania finished the prayer some of the anxious feeling left him.

"Let's do it." Skelly tried to sound brave.

"Wait!" Hania sat down on the dock and pulled out the Wilderness Kit.

"They don't have a lot of time." Skelly hissed at him.

Hania opened his flask of Fo-ti juice, pouring half into an empty flask before adding the proper amount of Foxglove. He shook and handed it to Skelly. "Take a drink before you go. I don't want the stress…" They both knew what would happen if the Lise caused Skelly to have a seizure while in the water. The Foxglove in the Fo-ti should stop the seizures, but under stress? They would have to chance it.

"Stay hidden." Skelly swallowed and handed him back the flask.

Hania looked at it and took a swallow himself; there wasn't enough of the Foxglove Potion in it to cause harm. He handed the flask back. "There is more Fo-ti at my house, three I think. Bring them back with you."

He watched as Skelly headed down the dock. Just beyond the end of the dock was a movement in the water, an animal cried out. Then silence. The anaconda, a huge water snake, was done hunting tonight; its territory was now safe to travel. Their stopping to pray had saved Skelly's life.

17

They looked at each other; Skelly was several shades paler than he had been. Skelly shut his eyes, mumbled a prayer, and then entered the water. He waved and then swam for Nabi's island.

Hania watched until he could no longer see Skelly's head bobbing just above the water. He turned and re-entered the caverns.

2

Raghnall smiled as he surveyed the catch, four strong young bucks. Most of them huddled in the slave compound's dusty center; he could almost smell the fear. The one that had yelled now slumped in a corner, glaring at the rock thrower.

Slaves were funny...entertaining really...pitiful lives in the wild or in captivity. *Next raid, I'm going to concentrate on females. I'm still young enough to breed a new batch of Bloodstone Warriors. And the Stone Ceremony is coming up.*

If I could donate some Atwater pairs...it would surpass what High Wizard Qwinn did 20 years ago. He donated the maidens from Bainbridge. Qwinn is getting old and as one of his sons, I have a good change of being chosen as the next High Wizard. But I have to push Murdoc out of the running; I need this and then a successful raid into Atwater itself.

Vritra came to him, saluted, and bowed. "Another tent was found, my lord." He directed Raghnall's sight up a boulder-strewn hillside to where Aja was standing by a tree, pointing behind a large boulder. Now why would a tent be there? Was it a storage tent? He glanced at the slaves. All but one, were looking up the hill. The rock thrower glared at him. Was he their leader?

He climbed the hill and smiled at Aja. "Found another tent?"

"Yes father." The boy blushed with pride. "I used the Find Spell, but I got here too late. They are gone."

Raghnall ducked into the tent and looked around. Two depressions. Two more were here, boys, girls, or adults? Maybe that explained why the tent was separate from the others.

Aja followed him. "I tried the Find Spell again to see which way they had gone. But nothing happened."

"Well, let's just try again." Raghnall smiled at the boy. Aja was Stone Born, a Wizard like himself.

His elite corps of Bloodstone Warriors also consisted of his sons, not Stone Born, just the offspring of his concubines. They didn't have the ability to manipulate the Bloodstones.

Raghnall knelt next to the young Wizard and pulled out his own Bloodstone. Looking around he found a small piece of leather thong lying in a corner. Picking it up, he ran his thumb down the smooth side, holding it with the rough sides against his fingers. It had broken off a longer string; holding it in one hand and his Stone in the other, he beckoned the boy closer.

"When you have something that belongs to them, it works better." He did the spell.

A static shock caused him to drop the thong and shake his hand. His fingers burned.

"What happened?" Aja looked in stunned disbelief from the thong to his father and back.

Raghnall moved to the slit in the tent's back and touched a shinny spot near the top. Silver paint.

"Silver." He growled and pointed it out to Aja. "Let's go question the slaves."

Raghnall stomped down the hill; gravel crunching with every step to the side of the compound. *I'll show Aja another way to capture the two from the tent.* He looked over the slaves and chose the rock thrower.

Using his Bloodstone, he sent a finger of energy out to drag him to one side of the compound. "Your name."

The buck just looked at him. Using the Bloodstone he sent other strands of energy that raised and shook him. "Your name, boy."

"Chval." Chval bit out, shocked to be above the ground.

Raghnall dropped him. "Now we talk, boy." Raising a chair of stones from the dust, he sat and turned his full attention to Chval.

"Who was in the tent on the hill?"

Chval glanced at the hill. "Hania and Skelly."

"I know there were two of them…their names are not important. What were they? What was their function?" Raghnall leaned back; the chair accommodated his movements.

"Ah." This Chval seemed at a loss for words as he glanced at the other boys. "Punching bags?"

Raghnall raised an eyebrow.

"Outcasts…weaklings." Continued Chval, his tone becoming sharp.

Raghnall stood and walked to the compound. He ran his hand down the glassy smoothness of one of the bars; he looked down at Chval. He was a good-looking young man, but a bit of a clotheshorse. Who wears a silk shirt to go camping? Like most inhabitants of the Green Crescent, he had wavy hair...brown. "Are you telling me that a pair of puny weaklings have escaped me? Are running around loose on the island...eluding my men?"

"Well?" Chval shrugged, his brown eyes defiant.

Raghnall thrust a finger at the boy that had earlier rattled the bars. "What's his name?"

"Dreogan." Chval drawled, relieved to have the attention leave him.

Raghnall moved over to the boy. Dreogan glared at him. He was a lanky, not yet full-grown, youngster, a little shorter then Chval. His brown hair was curly like a sheep's fleece. Once he was broken and muscled up a bit, he would make a good asset to his herd.

"You called out their names." Raghnall raised an eyebrow. "Are you in the habit on calling on weaklings for help? Somehow, I doubt that." He raised another chair and sat, eyes locked onto the boy. "What was their function?"

Dreogan didn't answer. Raghnall raised his Bloodstone and snake-like strands of energy left his hand and wound around the boy.

As the bands tightened, another boy shouted out. "One's a potion maker. The other is a...a fishmonger, I think."

Raghnall flicked his hand sending a ball of energy to knock the boy across the compound. "Did I ask you a question? You will not speak until you are spoken to." He dropped Dreogan and turned to the crumpled boy. The stones in the chair moved as smoothly as if they were oiled. This one was short...but well muscled...a laborer; he would bring a good price.

"What is your name, boy?" Raghnall raised and pinned him up against the bars. Behind him, Aja snickered. Raghnall shot him an indulgent smile.

"Tesar." The boy gasped, his brown eyes round with fear.

"You notice, Aja," Raghnall addressed his son. "This one will be no trouble to break. In fact...he is already there."

"Yes, father." Aja, licking his lips, stared at Tesar. "When we get back home can I choose one for my personal slave?"

"Of course." Raghnall chuckled and mused up Aja's soft hair.

Aja broke away and wandered around the outside of the compound, looking over the slaves, trying to decide which one he wanted.

Raghnall tuned his mind back to the two missing boys. One was a potion maker...yes...he would know about silver paint. And it's uses.

He looked at the compound. These boys didn't seem to know much about the Bloodstone Cult. They were not well taught. So, did that mean that the Atwater Clan has become complacent? None of the boys so far, had claimed to be warriors. He looked at the last one. Not much taller then the one called Tesar, but well muscled.

"Name and occupation." He dragged him over and pinned him to the bars.

The boy looked sullen. "Barra. Hunter."

"That one." He pointed at the one called Tesar.

"A carpenter."

"That one?" He pointed at the rock thrower, Chval.

"Hunter."

Hunter? The pampered kind no doubt.

"And him." He pointed at the last one.

"Farmer."

"One boy was a potion maker. What was the other?"

"A scholar, a record keeper, and historian; his father is a fishmonger." His brown eyes glanced over at Chval.

Raghnall dropped the boy. Not a warrior in the bunch…well…that was interesting. He leaned back in the chair. *Rather than hunting for the two missing boys, I aught to head back.*

I'll show Qwinn…that the Atwaters are ripe for the picking…and then lead a campaign against them. Murdoc would have to follow. How delicious.

Yes, they would head back in the morning. He called his men to him.

3

Hania waited until he was far back into the caverns before he lit another torch. After smoldering a bit, it burst into flame. He slumped to the floor, letting time and the cave's coolness remove the fatigue from his limbs. Heat and exertion always made the Hesutu worse. The caves helped to revitalize him. It was the same with Skelly and his personal trial, Lise.

Who would have thought, that the years of hiding out in here would turn out to be so useful. For years they had explored the caverns during the heat of the day. Keeping out of the other boys' sight. The men in the village brought their sons here for camping and hunting trips.

The caverns were old silver mines. Played out, but you could still see a glint of silver here and there. Hania and Skelly knew them pretty well. They didn't need torches, for the most part, to go through them. *But, I do not want to be in the dark right now.*

He picked up a chunk of ore, flipping it over. He stared at the flicker of torchlight as it touched the flecks of silver. Silver, the only thing Bloodstones feared. Did the Bloodstones know they were camping next to an old silver-mine? Would they care?

As soon as the quivering in his legs stopped, Hania hoisted himself off the ground. Tossing the rock into the small stream that ran along the passage's right side, he headed back to the ledge overlooking the camp. *I must keep an eye on them.*

He heard a noise ahead in the passage. Panicking, he stuck the torch in a crack in the side of the passage and backed into a dark offshoot, pulling out his bone-handled hunting knife. It would be useless against a Bloodstone Warrior without any silver. He took out the small bottle of silver paint and clamped it between his knees to open it. Was the sound getting nearer? He smeared some silver paint on the blade of his knife, recapped the bottle, and slipped it back in the kit.

Waiting he peered around the opening. The sound moved closer. His good leg started to shake; he gripped the bone-handled knife's carved grip so hard it hurt.

A raccoon appeared, blinking into the light; a female. It had a silver fish in its mouth. She fishes in the caves instead of the lake. Where's its den?

The raccoon stood, her nose twitching, staring into the passage where Hania crouched. Could it smell him? It trembled as it rocked back and forth in indecision.

Finally, maternal instincts overcame fear. It scampered past the light and darted up a dark fissure. No doubt it opens near the surface. Raccoons liked their nests near the surface and close to water so the young could wash their food.

And speaking of water, Hania reached out a hand to where a spring dribbled cold water down the wall. He splashed the water on his face and took a couple of gulps to steady his nerves. The caverns were full of small springs. In fact, the whole island was covered in numerous springs. Some were hot, some cold and some just right for bathing. That way you were safe, far from the lake, and free of anacondas and caimans.

And thinking of caimans, those nasty, ill tempered, small crocodiles brought his worried thoughts back to Skelly. Was he okay? Three years ago, he had almost drowned. After that, whenever he got over heated or too tired, he would go stiff and gasp for air, just as he had done on that day long ago.

And if that happens while he is in the water. *Why did I let him go? I should have done it…don't say that…you couldn't have made it. Had Skelly made it Nabi's yet?*

You have a job to do and second guessing yourself is not useful. He chided himself as he yanked the torch out of the crack. He headed on up the tunnel. Nearing the opening above the camp, he put the torch out in the stream of a spring and crept to the ledge.

Pulling out the spyglass, he looked down into the camp. The Bloodstones' leader pulled the boys forward one at a time, gesturing towards the hillside where Hania and Skelly had pitched their tent.

They must have found it! He looked down; no one was climbing the cliff. Relief washed over him and he breathed a prayer of thanks.

All the boys were still alive. The leader put two guards on the boys and headed in the direction of the tents. No doubt to sleep the rest of the night.

Things were quieting down in the camp. With the guards around the compound, Hania couldn't get word to them that help was on the way. Part of him was excited over becoming a hero. The other part was worried that something would go wrong.

His thoughts returned to Skelly and the hundreds of things that could go wrong.

4

Skelly, at that moment, was swimming towards Nabi's retreat in water that was cooling even as the night passed. Using smooth strokes, nothing jerky. Not making a sound that might attract predators. He checked for the fourth time to see if his knife was still safe in its sheath.

Gliding over onto his back, he opened the flask of Foxglove laced Fo-ti juice and swallowed. Better safe than sorry. He recapped it and turned around to reorient himself. A small treeless island rose out of the water to the north. He turned west, treading water.

Something bumped him from behind. In a flash, he buried his knife into a log floating on the surface. He hung onto the log, heart pounding, and feeling weak. *What am I doing out here…I'm no hero…how can I succeed?*

His face tight against the wet bark, he floated a while, waiting to recover from the fright. It smelled of fish; everything smelled of fish. Thoughts of caimans attacking in the dark filled his mind. *Stop that!* They are only aggressive hunters during the day when they can see their prey, but not at night. At night, caimans lie in wait. At least that is what his father, the great fish master, had taught him. Anacondas hunt day or night; but they like hunting in the shallows. Pulling the knife out of the log, he re-sheathed it.

He looked at the tiny island. *Maybe I should go there and rest from this fright.* The thought came again…stay in deep water. *I need to rest*, he argued. Something was moving through the water in the island's direction.

Skelly froze. When he realized what it was, he relaxed. A capybara swam towards the island. The huge rodents body making silvery ripples in its wake. The capybara was a favorite food of both caimans and anacondas, and just about every other predator in the Great Swamp or along Grassy Lake. The fact that one was nearby and swimming for the island must mean the island was safe.

He turned to follow it. As the capybara reached the shallows, the water erupted with snapping jaws. The capybara screamed, then fell silent. It had swum into an ambush of caiman.

Clinging once again to the damp log for support, Skelly whispered an urgent prayer for forgiveness. He had been arguing against the Great Spirit's promptings. He also gave thanks for the extra warning. Then he turned back for Nabi's island and stuck to deep water for the rest of the swim.

Climbing onto the ironwood dock, he gave one final prayer of thanks…thanks that he had even made it. *Never thought I would be praying so much.* He looked out over Grassy Lake and shuttered. Taking a deep breath, he headed for the boathouse, his bare feet leaving a wet trail.

Only a single one-man skiff was there and it had a hole in it. *Now what? Swim the rest of the way? Was there any chance I could make it?* He slapped at a nocturnal mosquito.

What about a signal fire? Could it be seen from Atwater?

He turned to Nabi's workshop; maybe he could find something to keep the boat afloat long enough to reach Atwater. Entering he struck a light to the lamp. The other skiff was in here, the smell of restoration fresh. But there was more. Gleaming in neat rows along two of the walls were silvered weapons. These were not the decorative ones from the temple, but well balanced ones from the Forge of Bainbridge. He could see the maker's seal.

On the workbench lay a thick piece of oiled leather. Small flecks of silver imbedded in it. Nabi was doing the yearly maintenance of the weapons from the armory. He checked one. Sharp.

I could write a note, light a signal fire, and take the silvered weapons back to the island. Then we could keep an eye on the Bloodstones until help arrived.

Last time he was here, he left some clothes. He found them in the spare room and pulled them on. No shoes. He grabbed several bags of jerky and dried fruit. *What else would we need?* He chewed on some jerky as he searched. It was late and his mind seemed so foggy.

Hania will have to make some Fo-ti juice, there was none stored here. And no extra clothes for him.

A few water skins will come in handy. He wrote the note and tacked it to the front door. Then went to build the signal fire.

He gathered together a bunch of brush and piled it on the shore facing Atwater. With the flint and steel from the workshop, he got on his knees and prepared to light it.

"Hold, young man!" A voice commanded from behind him.

5

Hania lay on the ledge overlooking the camp, rubbing his eyes. He was getting tired of watching the Bloodstones. Easing into a sitting position, he massaged the aching muscles in his legs. After taking some Willow Bark Potion for the pain, his eyes started to droop. He looked through the wilderness kit again; small bottles and water proofed packets of all sorts of stuff. Finding some Ci Wu Jia potion, he took just enough to help him stay awake. Had to be careful with that stuff. He put the spyglass back to his eye. So quiet…even the animals fear the Bloodstones.

The leader had taken Chval's large, multi-roomed tent; he and the young boy had gone inside. The two men not guarding the Atwaters had crawled into Barra' well used pup tent. Watching the other men prowling the campsite, he noticed that they had tattoos down their arms. Biting his lip, Hania racked his brain, trying to remember if his father or grandfather had ever talked about Bloodstone ranks or tattoos. Nothing came to mind, but he managed to make his lip bleed.

Were the marks normal for all Bloodstones or were these men part of an elite corps? They looked tough. The leader was a tall, handsome man and something about him nagged in the back of Hania's mind. Cognitive difficulties. Another symptom of Hesutu; he did not need it at this time. Why had he been given such a trial?

He shut his eyes, to rest them and to pray for a clear mind. Rolling over after the prayer, he looked at the stars. He needed a break from watching the camp and a chance to ponder his place in the universe.

He lay there, watching the constellations pace off the night, the constellation Capybara fleeing the milky white constellation of the Anaconda. The Anaconda with its two red eyes and long milky body made of so many closely packed stars that you could not count them, showed up in the spring sky. When she showed up it was time to plant. His eyes searched out other constellations as his tongue nursed his sore lip. As his eyes picked out the Warrior plunging his silver sword into the heart of the Bloodstone Wizard with its three red stars it hit him. The leader had a braid. His hair was light brown with gray at the temples, long, and pulled back into a braid, but the braid had been blood red, like the constellation. That made him a Bloodstone Wizard. None of the others had braids. What did that mean? They weren't wizards?

They were tattooed on their arms, but not the Wizard or the boy. Was he too young or was he of another class? Did he have a braid? Hania had been so worried about the men that he had not bothered getting a good look at the boy.

Next time he saw the boy, he would check.

Did it have something to do with rank or class...or was it guild membership? Did that matter? They were the enemy.

Slavers, they were dirty rotten slavers. He clenched his fists. And they had captured Atwaters; it was his duty to stop them. How?

Hearing something, he rolled over and put the spyglass to his eye. The Wizard had come out of his tent and went into the bushes. When he emerged, he changed the guards. After staring at the captives for a while, he returned to the tent.

Hania took the spyglass from his eye and rubbed the bridge of his nose. Now another thought came to him. Verses from the Prophecies of the Spirit Warriors started to wend their way through his tired mind.

Oh no, he told himself. *You're not a Spirit Warrior.* The thought was laughable...he was in poor health and a boy...not a man; surely the Spirit Warriors would have to be men. They had to be strong...seasoned by many years of experience...like the Warrior Constellation.

Another verse popped up. *"Young, untried, though they were: Their hearts were pure."* He shuttered. His grandfather had quoted to him from the prophecies when he had worried aloud about the Bloodstone Warriors' return.

"They will defeat them once and for all." His grandfather had told him.

"Through hard trials, they find the Stone Born Maiden." Yet another line, popped into his mind and as improbable as it was, he found himself eager for the hunt.

Nonsense, he thumped his fist against the ground, *we are not the Spirit Warriors*. The dust he stirred loose flew into his mouth and he had to spit it out.

He wished he hadn't even started thinking about the stupid prophecies, *"Stone Born Maiden,"* he turned to watch the camp again.

6

Onid woke with a start, the echo of her cry fresh in her own ears. Her chest, where the silver-bladed dream knife had stabbed her, hurt. She realized she was not in the dark; a candle in a hurricane lantern glowed from the doorway where her mother was standing.

"I cried out again, didn't I?" She closed her eyes in frustration.

Her mother came over, sat the lantern on the bedside table, and settled on the edge of the bed; she smoothed a strand of hair back from Onid's sweaty face. The peppery smell of the ointment she used at night brought Onid to full wakefulness.

"The dreams are coming more frequent." She sat up. "Should I go and see Kendra?"

"Seven nights in a row." Her mother whispered and turned away, pretending not to hear her.

Her mother should have been beautiful. Her grandfather looked younger than her mother or to be honest, her mother looked older than her grandfather.

Wiping her face on the sleeve of her nightdress she sighed. "I'm a freak, mom. We're both freaks."

"Having gone through many trials does not make you a freak." Her mother smiled. "It makes you tough."

Onid looked into the lined face of her mother. "Trials...what trials? I haven't been through..."

"What do you call these dreams?"

"Agreed...I die every night."

"Were you alone?" Her mother tried too hard to sound casual.

"I'm always alone." Onid chewed her lip; it was salty.

Her mother moved uncomfortably. She was plagued by all the discomforts of old age, of people that were much older. That was why she used the Cayenne Ointment and drank a lot of White Willow Tea; there was a pot constantly brewing over a slow fire; as far back as Onid could remember.

"Mom, what do I do?" She jumped up out of her bed and started to pace around the room, the glazed tile cool to her feet.

"What does the Prophetess say?"

"Maybe Kendra is losing her gift…or she is being evasive." Onid glanced at her mother.

"Perhaps it is time for a fast." Her mother got up.

"Where are you going?"

"To sleep in. We are fasting tomorrow…but first…a prayer."

Her mother left. That was what she always did, fast and pray…maybe that was what was needed. She knelt down by her bed and after some time slipped back into her covers without praying. Try as she might, prayer just didn't come. It hadn't come for a long time. *That does it,* she pulled the goose-down comforter up to her chin, *I'm going to see Kendra and demand some answers.*

7

Hania watched the camp until his eyes hurt. The medicine he had taken to relieve the pain in his leg was still making him sleepy; he didn't want to take anymore Ci Wu Jia potion. He got to his feet and went back into the cave. He paced about to limber up and to combat the sleep that threatened to overtake him.

He stopped. What if the Bloodstones saw the Atwater boats coming? Would they fight...kill the captives...flee over the stone walkway into the Great Swamp? Could the Atwaters follow them through the swamp if they did?

His head ached with the all the thoughts that swam through it. What should he do, what could he do?

As he paced and gnawed at his lip, he prayed. He felt so inadequate to the task; then a story his father had once told him came to mind. It was an old tale of a war campaign. Diversionary tactics. He lit another torch, climbed down though the caverns, and searched through the supplies they had stuffed into Skelly backpack.

A fresh breeze told him that it was raining outside. He strained his ears, no thunder. *Not much of a rain...good. I'll set a bunch of small fires around the island...keep them busy and off guard.* Returning to the ledge, he took one of the fishing spears they had dragged up here with them, why...he didn't know...they were useless against the Bloodstones. Now he would put one of them to good use; he knocked down a few old swallow nests for kindling and tossed them into a net bag.

But what if they become suspicious of the fires and start looking elsewhere? Am I doing the wrong thing? He fell once more to his knees.

A small warm feeling came and he felt he was doing the right thing...that it was a prompting. Encouraged, he rose and headed down another tunnel. This one came out near where the stone pathway led into the swamp.

He stopped. How soon could they arrive? Mentally he added up the time for Skelly to swim to Nabi's, take a boat to Atwater, and then raise the alarm. He paced off the time it would take to load the boats and get back here. Feeling sure it was time to start the diversion, he looked out. The rain had stopped, the air fresh; it had been a short squall.

Gathering dead brush, he piled it on the shore, then knelt in the mud and pulled out a nest. He stuck it under the pile of brush and lit it. As it got going, he rinsed off his bare feet and slipped back into the caves, careful not to leave a trail.

After setting a few fires in strategic areas, he slipped his boots back on and returned to the ledge overlooking the camp. He watched the reaction to the fires. Four of the Bloodstones were pacing around the campsite; the other two returned from investigating the fires. The leader yelled at his men and then at the boys, but Hania was to far away to make out the words. The boys sat huddled in the center of the muddy slave compound. The Bloodstones all turned and stared into the dark.

Are they thinking that the two of us would attempt a rescue all by ourselves? Hania shook his head.

He had been tempted to rush out and set fires and then rush back to the caverns. But now was not the time to break old habits. He and Skelly had kept the caverns a secret from the other Atwater boys for years by never returning to the caves without walking on stones to hide their footprints. And somehow, he felt it was even more important to do the same now. Though he didn't know why. Or did he?

He looked at the sky. The Atwater rescue team should be on their way by now, if Skelly had made it back.

8

Skelly froze at the command to hold. Was an Atwater villager behind him? Or had a Bloodstone Warrior followed him here?

Swallowing hard, he turned around. With relief, he let the air out of his lungs; Nabi, prophet, historian, and mentor stood there with a quizzical look on his wizen face.

"Were you about to set fire to my island?" Nabi nodded at the brush, his gray eyes locked on the band of silver painted around Skelly's head.

"Bloodstones." Skelly did not know what else to say.

"Yes...that is why I was prompted to come here." Nabi confirmed to himself. "This way!" He called, not waiting; Skelly had to run to catch up.

They returned to the workshop where the silvered weapons were hanging. "And where did the bump on your head come from?" Nabi headed for the nearest wall.

"Low hanging rocks in a tunnel of the old silver mine."

"I see." Nabi seemed relieved. "Now...yes, yes," Nabi mumbled to himself. It was as if Skelly was only there to fill an order from someone else.

"Now let's see, 'Sunlight glinted off their spears, morning light.' Um how many?" He looked at Skelly, waiting for an answer.

"Ah...Six?" Skelly shrugged as questions ran through his mind. "How did you know what I was after?"

Nabi chuckled. "You are wearing your old clothes. The ones you left here." He piled six silvered spears into Skelly's arms and moved on down the racks.

"Only one thing will force someone to swim the lake in the middle of the night with silver paint banded around their head." His eyes clouded over with pain. He looked at Skelly, shuddered, and turned back to the weapons. "Young, so young," He mumbled.

Skelly told him what had happened so far. "I don't know if Hania will still be free when I get back.

"Hania has always been a wise and sober child. If anyone can keep his head in a crisis, it is Hania. Guard him well, Skelly." Nabi piled six swords and scabbards into his arms. After six daggers and their sheaths, he paused...rubbing his chin and chanting verses from scripture under his breath.

"Over here." He went to a bin with a bunch of slingshots hung on the wall next to it. "We have only paint balls here. " He turned to Skelly and plopped the slingshots on top of the pile. "You will have to stop in Bainbridge and get some acid balls. Don't forget! Go to The Forge and ask for Gaho." He turned and headed to the other wall.

"What are acid balls?" Skelly asked as he wondered how they were supposed to get to Bainbridge.

"Glass balls filled with acid and silver paint," Nabi grinned. "Bloodstones hate them."

Skelly thought about the glass paint balls the boys used for target practice. What if you added acid? He shuttered. But they're slavers, they deserve it.

Nabi was staring up at the bows, arrows and cross bows hanging on the wall. "Arrows notched,..." he muttered and put six scabbards full on the pile. Then took one off. "No, wait,..." Facing skyward, his eyes closed.

Skelly was getting a bit nervous listening to Nabi muttering scriptures. He had heard them before, but not in this content. He caught a few words, here and there, and they scared him. "Pain and suffering?" Was this about him and the other boys? "Mortal danger?"

"A silvered bolt flew true, a bolt flew true!" Nabi shouted and yanked a crossbow from the wall, plopping it on top of the pile along with a rack of bolts. "You're good with a crossbow, Skelly. I've seen you out hunting with Hania."

Nabi looked over the pile of weapons in Skelly's arms and smiled. "That will do...it's a good start. Don't forget to visit The Forge at Bainbridge." They headed back outside.

"You were reciting scripture just now, what was that about?" Skelly asked as they reached the door and Nabi plopped two jars of silver paint atop the pile.

"Bits and pieces of prophecies concerning the Spirit Warriors." Nabi said almost reverently. "Don't worry, Hania has been taught most of it." He pulled the lightweight skiff off the workbench along with its paddle and carried it to the dock. "At least the parts we have been given...might be more...I don't know...too early...must consult Xavier." They loaded the weapons on board.

Skelly climbed in and looked up. "I don't know what to say…thank you."
"I'll head to Whitewater," Nabi climbed into his own boat. "Warn them that it has started. We'll follow as soon as we can." He reached down into the boat and pulled out his paddle. "The salmon ran early, so most of the villagers are there."

Skelly pushed off from the dock and into the lake. *What have we gotten ourselves into?* He thought, looking down into the boat where the pile of weapons lay, gleaming in the moonlight.

The trip back to the island took a lot less time than the swim. The boat may have been old, but it was well built and floated high in the water, even with all the weapons.

As he neared Manhood Island, he quit paddling. *Where should I land…where was it safe? The dock?*

A fire flared at the island's south end. Skelly turned away from the dock and paddled in the direction of the fire. Did safety or a trap wait by that fire?

Something hit him in the head and fell with a thump into the boat. He reached down and picked it up, a pinecone. As he scanned the shore, another one hit him in the chest. He turned the boat. A torch flared on the shore, waved back and forth twice, and was doused.

Hania, it had to be. He paddled hard towards the shore and grounded the boat along a patch of reeds. He and Hania clasped hands and Hania pulled him ashore.

Hania even had Skelly's clothes and sandals, tied in a bundle.

9

"Skelly, you made it!" Relief poured through Hania as he hugged his big friend. Skelly pulled away.

"It's not good news."

Hania, looking out towards Atwater, started. "What do you mean?"

Skelly grabbed the boat and pulled it up onto a grassy part of the shore. "The salmon ran early, most everyone is at Whitewater. Nabi is heading there now."

Hania couldn't believe what he was hearing. He looked at the small boat with its load of silvered weapons. Was it just Skelly and him? Against trained Bloodstone Warriors…what kind of chance did they have? Then once again the prophecies concerning the Spirit Warriors came chanting into his head.

Groaning he sank to the ground. 'Young and untried…' No! They couldn't be them. He started to shake. Was it from fear or anger? Both. *I do not want to be a Spirit Warrior.* Yes, in daydreams; in daydreams it was safe; in reality, pain was involved. *I have enough pain with this stupid disease and so does Skelly.* They had enough trials with what was already their lot. Why would The Great Spirit add more?

Skelly's hand touched his shoulder. "We're their only hope now."

"I know." Hania took a deep breath. "We better unload the boat." Now he was going over the prophecies looking for clues to help them. If they were the Spirit Warriors, then they had better be careful not to do anything stupid or foolhardy. Every campaign against the Bloodstones would have to be worked out with caution. It was now war.

He never thought that he would be missing Chval, but right now, he did. Chval was good at this kind of thing…not him.

They unloaded the boat, stashing the weapons just inside the cave, and then pushed the boat into the bank of reeds to hide it.

As they rinsed off their muddy feet, Hania looked at where they had slogged through the marsh, their tracks quite visible. A caiman came to investigate the noise. It's mottled reptilian hide, the same color as the brackish swamp water, gleamed wetly in the moonlight.

Skelly looked at Hania, a wicked little grin broke out on his face.

"Skelly…no, it's too dangerous." Hania grabbed his hand.

"I know what I'm doing." Skelly assured him. "Go get a spear and poke him if he gets too close."

Hania slipped his boots back on and scrambled for a fishing spear, not a silvered one; the caiman was not a Bloodstone.

Skelly was out of his mind. Caiman baiting? It would muck things up and hide their tracks, but what if the caiman got Skelly?

When he returned to the shore, Skelly had dressed back in his regular clothes, stuffing his old clothes into his tunic along with one of his sandals; then putting on the other sandal, hung his bare foot out over the area where their tracks took off into the marsh. He splashed it around a little, dragging it back and forth. Tempting the caiman with a delicious Skelly snack.

Hania stationed himself on the rocks above Skelly and took aim at the caiman. *If it gets too close, I'll have to kill it.*

The caiman eyed Skelly and inched forward, jaws open and expectant. It slid its body over the footprints eliminating them.

"Come on." Skelly whispered. "Just a little more."

The caiman stopped and eyed Hania. "I'm going to have to back off some." Hania warned Skelly. "Be prepared to move."

He climbed towards the cave.

Skelly inched back a little, too. The caiman's attention shifted back to him and snapped its jaws in anticipation, moving its head back and forth as if judging the distance.

"Move!" Hissed Hania as the caiman lunged at Skelly. He threw the spear. The caiman saw it coming and twisted out of the way.

The spear stuck quivering in the muck. The caiman stood at the cliff's base and hissed up at Skelly and Hania; then it turned and took its frustration out on the spear. It tore it to pieces and with one last glare at the boys, returned to the water.

"Those are the meanest tempered crocodiles in all the Green Crescent." Hania pulled Skelly into the cave and white faced they slid down the wall and waited for their hearts to quit pounding.

"Why did I do that?" Skelly put on his other sandal. "What got into me?" He stuffed his old clothes into the bottom of his pack.

Hania walked over to where the silver weapons lay and looked down. Was that what courage was? You did what was dangerous because you had no choice?

"We had better go see what the Bloodstones are up to." Hania said strapping on a sword. After grabbing all he could carry, he headed back up the passage.

Skelly gathered up the rest of the stuff and followed. "There wasn't any Fo-ti at Nabi's, so you will have to make more or use…" He held up his flask.

They didn't say anything more until they reached the passageway overlooking the camp. Skelly left to retrieve his pack left inside the dock opening.

"Are we?" Skelly asked as he returned.

"Are we what?" Hania knew what he was asking; it was bothering him, too.

"You know…the Spirit Warriors." He went out on the ledge and peered down at the camp before moving back.

"It…it sure looks that way." Hania was not happy about it and neither, it seemed, was Skelly.

"So what are we suppose to be doing? Nabi said you knew most of our prophecies."

"I've been going over them in my mind. Looking for clues." It seemed that the part having to do with pain and suffering kept popping up the most. Hania was sure that Skelly would not like to hear anything about that.

"And?"

"We watch and wait for a chance to free them." Hania remembered another verse "Patience and pondering gave upper hand."

"Patience." He muttered. "And planning." Once again they stationed themselves on the uneven ledge.

Two of the Bloodstones were moving around the compound. The guards. The flap on the Chval's fancy tent moved, now they would have to be on their toes.

10

Raghnall stretched as he left the tent. Smoothing the few stray hairs dislodged during the night back into place, he visited the shrubs. Then following the sound of a knife being sharpened, he headed over to where Edur was fixing breakfast.

"Greetings Edur!" Licking his lips in anticipation, he breathed in the food's delicious smell. A good cook was always a plus on expeditions like this one. "Wine?"

"Sorry, my Lord Raghnall. We are out." Edur was curled into a position of abject submission; no doubt he expected to be punished.

"It happens on trips like this." Raghnall was feeling generous this morning. "You have some fine wine waiting at the ship?"

"Yes, my Lord." He murmured as he deftly sliced a wing off a roasting Wood Duck, it was the only part that was suitable for eating at the moment. Blowing on it to cool, he handed it to Raghnall and turned back to his cooking.

Raghnall headed over to where the slaves were waking. He sat again in the stone chair and Edur brought him a platter of fresh baked flatbread, more duck wings, cheese, and fruit.

The slaves were still damp and muddy from last nights rain. They looked miserable, but not miserable enough, not yet…not quite.

"Morning boys." He watched as their mouths watered at the sight and smell of a well-cooked meal. Eating it in front of them was twice as satisfying; leaning back, he nibbled on the perfectly seasoned wing.

When they were hungry enough, they would submit…breaking in new slaves was so satisfying. Aja wandered over from behind the tent.

"When are we leaving?" Aja took a platter from Edur and started eating.

"Right after breakfast." The fruit was not up to Raghnall's usual standard, but they were on a raid. *When we bring the ships up against Atwater in a full attack, I'll make sure we are stocked with the finest my vineyards and dairies can produce. There was no reason to suffer with less than the best.*

He stood and tossed the leftovers into the dust. The slaves' eyes were now fastened upon the ground where the food lay. He would let the animals and birds eat it. Later, that was what the slaves would eat, but not yet.

"Father, what about the other two?" Aja tossed his leftovers down like his father.

"With a raid, you come in, grab, and leave." He smiled at the boy. "You do not wait around, that invites retaliation. We are small in number…but, when we return,…" He rubbed his hands together. He and Aja looked towards Atwater.

"When?" The boy whispered. As if spies from Atwater were listening.

"As soon as the next big rain." He could see it in his mind…oh, the glory of it!

His men were finished eating now and Edur was carefully packing up his cooking gear.

Raghnall called over his wrangler, Zigor. "Ready to head back?"

Zigor walked over patting the long bullwhip hanging from his belt. "Yes, my Lord. I am more than ready."

"Istaqa and Vritra, you go in front." Raghnall ordered and walked over to the slave compound's backside. Istaqa joined Vritra, stuffing souvenirs into his pockets.

"This is how it works." He smiled at the slaves. "You follow Istaqa and Vritra. If you try to escape, then Zigor gets involved. You don't want Zigor to get involved. It is very painful…for you." Raghnall paused. "Actually, Zigor likes to get involved."

Zigor grinned and his whip sang through the air. The boys scuttled to the other side of the compound, eyeing both the whip and Zigor.

Raghnall took out his Bloodstone; it was still at full power. Istaqa and Vritra headed for the stone pathway leading into the swamp. Using the Stone he lowered the compounds front and back as Zigor strode into place.

The boys scrambled over each other in the direction of the pathway. Edur picked up his gear and followed. Aja and Raghnall meandered behind.

"Now Aja, watch how Zigor drives the slaves." Raghnall pointed as Zigor's whip sang through the air. The slaves bunched up, jumping out of the way of the snap of the whip. Zigor coiled the whip back up, his attention not leaving the knot of slaves.

In Raghnall's minds eye, he could see shiploads of slaves. The wealth of it made his hands itch. *New lands ruled by my Stone Born sons, with all of Cerebrus at my feet. Honor, coming to my family, with me at the head. And there was Murdoc, having to stand with the rest of the crowd...praising me.*

Raghnall laughed aloud as he followed the procession onto the walkway of stones. He turned and looked with satisfaction back at the island. Then, he followed his men into the swamp.

11

Hania looked down at the floating path of stones. So much for patience and planning, they were out of time.

"They're moving out." Skelly jumped to his feet. "What do we do?"

"Follow them." Hania turned and tossed everything into a jumbled bundle, the swords and spears poked out in every direction. *Hope I'm making the right choice.* He cut off a piece of the rope and tied together the whole lot, stuffing in the strays.

Skelly gathered up his gear as well, jamming what fell out of Hania's bundle into his overfilled backpack. After lighting a torch, they rushed down through the tunnels, not stopping at the occasional clanging or thump of some fallen item. Climbing out of the caverns, they ran to the shore.

Hania held his breath and stepped onto the pathway. It was bumpy like a cobblestone road, but it seemed solid. He put his full weight on it, bouncing a little as he resumed breathing. Shrugging, he started across...Skelly followed.

Hania glanced up. Yes, they were heading south...a marker. He turned back.

"What are you doing?" Skelly grabbed his arm. Hania looked up at him.

"Can you run back and put a marker on the shore so they will know which way we went?"

"If the pathway goes, they couldn't follow us anyway." Skelly turned him back around. "It's just us."

"Has Nabi told you any of the prophecies about the Spirit Warriors?" Goosebumps raced down Hania's back.

"No. Why?"

"Just wondering." It seemed the words 'It's just us' was in the prophecies, but he wasn't sure where. Hania swallowed his panic and they headed into the Great Swamp itself.

The path of stones made little bridges over Mangrove roots and curled itself around large Live Oak trunks as it meandered in a southern course across the swamp's uneven terrain.

"You're right," Hania pushed a dripping curtain of hanging moss out of the way. "If the path disappears, they couldn't have followed at all."

"It doesn't feel stable to me." Skelly bounced on it. "It has a give…feels like a hanging bridge."

"A little less." Hania tested the edge. It sank and then rose, dripping with fetid swamp water, to the level of the rest of the path. "I don't trust it."

"Then why are we here?" Skelly sounded just a little alarmed.

"Because…we might be…the Spirit Warriors." They marched on, ducking under low branches and slipping on the path's uneven wet stones.

Hania felt himself slowing down as they pushed on; his legs began to go numb, starting at the toes and moving up. Both of them started staggering along…the fatigue that plagued the diseases they both had soon caused them to stop and rest, waiting for strength and steadiness to return to their legs.

Hania looked back to where they had come, the path disappeared into the mist that seemed to hang over the swamp. Then he looked ahead, the same thing there. He swallowed the last of the Fo-ti juice, recapped the flask, and stuffed it deep into his pack. His eyes searched around, looking for a certain 6-foot vine with long heart shaped leaves. They needed the Fo-ti vine's root and soon.

"I don't like the feeling in here." Skelly glanced around, draining his own flask, the one laced with foxglove.

Hania knew what he meant; it was too quiet in here. No sound of birds or anything. You would at least expect a snake's slither or scratch of rodent. There was only the sound of water dripping off moss and leaves.

"Do you think the Bloodstones did something? Did something to repel the wildlife away from their path?" Hania rubbed his chin, not that doing so would help, but he had watched old Nabi do that when he was pondering something. He yanked his hand away in frustration.

What worked for another, would not work for him and he felt funny doing it. "Let's go." Hania headed down the path.

After winding through the swamp for most of the morning, pacing their selves so they wouldn't overtire, they came to a stretch of open water, a river judging by the water's movement. They could see some land being obscured by the mist settling along the river. The path made a beeline for the land, swaying with the current.

"Are we on the other side of the swamp?" Hania leaned against a Bald Cypress trunk, once again waiting for his strength to return.

"I don't think so." Skelly's brow was wrinkled. "I think that...that might be one of the stepping stone islands. Salina is the most northern of the named islands. Never thought I would ever see it."

"We better get going while we can still see." Hania did not like the way the fog was thickening.

Nerves on edge, they started over the river. The stone pathway swayed with the current...moving up and down...like a boat on water or a floating pier.

"I don't like this." Skelly splashed along side Hania, the stones under him were sinking more than the ones under Hania.

Out of the corner of his eye, Hania could see movement in the water, the wake pointed like an arrow towards the path.

They looked at each other...it was an unspoken agreement...Skelly grasped Hania's sleeve and they ran, plowing through the water as the pathway sank lower and lower into the river.

12

Chval sat on the ground between Dreogan and Barra. The stiff leather collar on his neck had rubbed a spot raw and he could feel it burn. He wasn't even sure where the collar had come from; they all had them, all tied to a rope strung between two worn stone pillars.

The collars were seamless as well as the tethers that fastened them to the rope. No buckles to undo...no knots to untie.

He remembered the tall slaver, the one with the blood red braid hanging down his back, had touched the back of his neck when they had stopped to eat. Was that when they had put the collars on us? When our minds were on the pitiful cold gruel that we had been given to eat?

A shaft from a broken arrow lay in the dust, the island was covered in dust...it tasted salty; or that may have been from sweat. He picked up the shaft. It wasn't broken, just the head missing. He jabbed it into the dust. *I wish I could stab it into a slaver or two.*

As he drew it through the dirt it snagged on something...*something is just below the surface.* He glanced over to where the slavers were resting. Barra noticed him and raised his eyebrows in a silent question.

"Keep a watch out," Chval hissed without moving his lips.

Barra and Dreogan moved so that Chval was shielded from the slavers while Tesar kept a watch out. Chval dug faster, attacking the ground with the arrow shaft and his hands. It was a knife! The blade was pitted and the tip broken, but maybe the edge could be sharpened enough to cut the binds.

The slavers were busy eating what smelled like a hot meal, laughing and boasting about what they would do to Atwater and the other Green Crescent homelands. They may bring more gruel over later, but they were too busy right now being fools.

Chval lifted the blade to his tether, sawing back and forth. It was too dull. He pulled his leggings tight, stropped the knife, and tested it by cutting a piece of legging off.

He tried again without any effect. Frustrated he stropped it again, this time testing it on the edge of his boot sole.

"Hurry up!" Tesar shifted closer. "They are almost done eating."

Again Chval tried to cut the bonds, to no effect.

Dreogan grabbed the knife and jumped up to try the rope. "They're bewitched," his shoulders shook in anger as he sank back down.

Barra snorted through his nose. " You mean we can't escape? We're doomed...we're now slaves? I can't believe it!"

Tesar yanked hard on his bonds in frustration.

"They're coming." Dreogan slipped the useless knife into his boot.

The Bloodstones followed their leader, 'Lord' Raghnall, over to where the boys sat in the dust. The youngest Bloodstone, a toe-headed youth with his own red braid, had a pot in his hands and with a grin he dumped the contents at their feet. Leftovers. Fit only for dogs.

"Well? What's wrong? Eat up." Raghnall sneered down at them while the boy chuckled and kicked the food at them.

In the silence that followed, Tesar reached a tentative hand towards the food. Chval grabbed his arm and pulled it back.

"We're not dogs." Chval swallowed hard.

"Hump...we'll see." Raghnall patted the young Bloodstone, Aja, on his shoulder. He turned his back on them and headed in the direction of the buildings clustered on the island's high ground.

The boy, Aja smirked and barked like a dog before turning and catching up to the Bloodstone Warriors. They laughed with him...punching each other's shoulders as they went.

Chval sighed and let his head drop.

"Well...do we eat or not?" Barra snapped at him.

"Do what you want." Chval muttered into his knees.

He could feel himself slipping into despair. Why was this happening? Skelly and Hania, those cowards, running off and leaving them, hiding out who knows where.

He raised his head and watched the sun slipping behind a cloud. A tear ran down the side of his nose and he brushed it away.

Are we no more than dogs? No, we are more; we must be more. How am I going to save us...what can I do? His head drooped.

13

Splashing nosily, Hania and Skelly ran as fast as they could; eyes fastened to the path as the fog was getting thicker. Had the Bloodstones done something to keep someone from following them…had they done something to the fog or was this just natural?

Hania started hearing the reawakening sound of normal swamp inhabits as he ran through deeper and deeper water.

"The spell is fading." He gasped out.

"I know." Skelly grabbed his arm and pulled him back just as the path's edge started breaking up. The path was getting narrower, the edges sinking faster than the middle. They pushed on. Screeches of birds and snapping jaws surrounded them.

The rope around the weapons broke. Skelly made a wild grab, but most of them fell, disappearing under the water. They couldn't stop…all but a few of the silvered weapons were gone.

"We're almost there." Hania gasped as they reached a reed bed and slowed down. The fog on the river was behind them, the ground was back under them, and the path of stones hadn't sunk here.

They collapsed onto the bank of sand, breathing hard.

Skelly started to breath in little gasps. Hania sat up and turned; Skelly had gone ridged. Even the muscles of his face pulled tight.

Not now! Hania searched through his pockets. The journey through the swamp had been too much for Skelly. Had he forgotten to take the Foxglove laced Fo-ti juice as often as he should? He reached for Skelly's flask…empty.

It was too late. He stared at the flask. He couldn't take it because it was gone. And as for straight Foxglove potion…he couldn't take it during a seizure. They would just have to wait for it to pass; at least Skelly's seizures were quiet. He could hear laughter and voices. The Bloodstones…they were still on the island.

He glanced around, taking stock; a caiman was looking at them through the reeds. Most of the weapons were gone, he retied the rope; it was frayed, cut through by one of the blades. The sound of laughter coming from the buildings at the high end of the island marked where the Bloodstones were. Somewhere over there were the other Atwaters.

Towards the west were dunes and salt grass; he started to drag Skelly and the bundle of weapons that way.

There was a problem. If he moved away from the damp sand, he came to almost a stand still, his feet sinking deep, without holding, into the hot dry sand. It was like trying to pull a live tree over.

If he moved to the damp sand, it was easier. But the caiman, sliding along the riverbank, eyed them hungrily.

What if I take Skelly to safety and come back for the last of the weapons? But, what if the Bloodstones found them? They would know that someone was here. In the end, Hania stacked the small bundle of weapons on top of Skelly and dragged both, moving back and forth between the dry and damp sand.

The sun burned down on them. His arms and legs began to tingle, a sure sign that he was close to collapsing.

The mist, rising from the swamp curled over the river and back, a breeze played with it, hiding and revealing the caiman. How long before it was brave or hungry enough to rush them?

14

Sitting on the edge of a ledge halfway up the high cliffs that jutted out into the valley dividing The Forge from Bainbridge, Onid pondered. Kendra was off to Pendragon. *Just when I need to see her, she's gone for a meeting with Xavier. I wonder what they are discussing…are they talking about the Spirit Warriors or me?* She pulled one knee up and rested her chin on it. Maybe they are going over the future of this valley.

Her family…her home…her people. *Why do I have such a protective feeling about them?* Her eyes traveled the valley from the gorge to the town nestled between the two falls, then progressed from the temple along the road to linger over the foundry that had been her home from birth.

Her grandfather came out of the mine, removing the cloth that protected his lungs from the dust of coal mining. "Thought you weren't coming today." His deep voice warmed her like stew on a cold day.

Onid picked at a spot of dirt on her leggings. "Mom said to come up here and talk to you."

"Something bothering you?" He sat next to her.

"I keep having these dreams." Onid picked up a stone and threw it out into the gorge, watching it disappear into the foam at the bottom.

Her grandfather looked out into the valley, he cleared his throat. "Every night?" His voice cracked with tension causing her to look up in time to notice his eyes mist up. "How many nights?" He blinked and shook his head.

"Seven." Why was that important?

"Then it is time." He shut his eyes, sighed deeply, and looked at her. "It is time…I hope you are ready."

"Time for what?"

Her grandfather sat down and put his arm around her. "Time for you to leave, to go find the Spirit Warriors." He hugged her closer to him. "I have not looked forward to this day. But we have all done our best to prepare you."

A chill ran though Onid. "Are you afraid for me…do you think I will fail?"

"No, but we love you…we care about you. And being human, we would rather you did not need to do this." Her grandfather sighed and ran his rough hand though her hair. "But you were chosen. And given this task long before this world was even created. The Great Spirit knows you can do it."

"I'm going to see if Kendra's back yet." Onid stood up and brushed the dirt off her backside. "I'll see you tonight." *Am I ready?*

As Onid looked back, she saw her grandfather still sitting there, looking out over the gorge, tears streaking the dust on his face.

Again she had the odd feeling of anticipation, like she was moving towards something. She took the path that led to the temple. Everyone goes to Kendra for a blessing to help them decide what to do. Kendra tells me it's my choice…mother just prays.

She reached Kendra's house, next to the temple. Hearing voices, she moved to the window pushing the guilt of eavesdropping aside. Who was in there?

"I have been dreading this day." Came her mother's voice, "From the time Xavier told me the child I carried was the Stone Born Maiden."

"We have been over this many times," Kendra's voice was calm, "Before this life, you were chosen to bear her, to nurture her, to love her…"

"To prepare her. But is she ready?"

"From her birth, she was schooled in the martial arts. She is a Master Swordsman! One of the finest!" Kendra moved passed the window and Onid ducked down. "She has been trained as a Warrior. She can scale shear cliffs, survive in the wilderness, and she has studied the scrolls extensively. She is ready."

"But am I ready? Am I ready to give her up to what the future may hold?"

"Is it time?"

"She has had the dreams…seven nights in a row."

"She must now go and find the Spirit Warriors. And she must chose wisely, from among them, her protector." Kendra sounded tired.

"I have already given up so much."

"You're not the only one."

"I know…her father."

She could hear footsteps heading for the door. Moving back out of sight, she saw her mother hurry in the direction of The Forge.

She had not heard of this before. My father? Her eyes turned to the place of records. Maybe the answers were in there…Kendra is always telling me that my future was up to me.

51

She had been told many times to study the prophecies concerning the Stone Born Maiden and the Spirit Warriors. And she had been trained, all of her life, as a warrior. Not as a future wife and mother, like the other girls in her village. She moved away from Kendra's modest home and entered the Place of Records.

After checking the index listings, she pulled down every scroll that mentioned the Stone Born Maiden or the Spirit Warriors. She began to read, looking for anything she may have missed. There has to be something about my father. Who was he or is he? Why haven't they ever talked about him? There was no bitterness in mother's voice, no anger over...she let that drop...she didn't even want to think of it.

15

Struggling, Hania pulled Skelly up the sand dune. The caiman hissed and thrashed at the water's edge as Hania dragged Skelly over the dune's top into a hollow, right on top of the remains of a rutted roadway. They were finally away from the river and out of the caiman's sight.

Sweat ran down his face, the salty sand stuck to it and blew into his eyes, making them sting. Even his back and sides were covered with sand and sweat.

It had taken more out of him than he had thought. He sucked in air as he leaned back against the side of the hollow. He looked over at the weapons bundle setting lopsided on top of Skelly's bulky chest. Two water skins dangling out the end flicked about with each gasp. So few weapons left…so few. Closing his eyes, he waited for the nausea to pass; he had pushed himself too far.

When Skelly woke, Hania handed him the Foxglove potion. Shaking, he sat up and took the last of it. Now they were out of both Fo-ti and Foxglove. Need to find and process the plants. This island is too dry, no need to look; they wouldn't grow here.

"How long was I out?" Skelly pushed his dark hair out of his face, leaving four dirty streaks.

Hania was too tired even to smile; he looked up at the blazing sun. "About a hour."

"Where are we?"

"You said Salina…what was the last thing you remember?"

Skelly was quiet for a moment. "The weapons falling."

"That happened just before we reached land." Hania leaned back into what little shade the sand dune cast.

"We need to check and see if any of the old bridges are left. Can't leave the same way we got here." Skelly stared back at the swamp, this time the seizure hadn't taken much of his memory of what was going on.

Hania shook his head. Skelly was right…the path was gone. "Know where the bridges are?"

Skelly twisted around and surveyed the island, taking in the roadway. He smoothed an area of sand and drew a map, dredging it from memory, after finishing he pointed along the ruts to the southwest.

Hania gave him a hand up. They gathered their gear and moved in that direction, keeping low so the Bloodstones' wouldn't see them.

The bridge heading west was gone, fallen from age or on purpose, they didn't know. The one going south was not in much better shape.

Skelly stared at it, nodding his head. "We could use the rope."

"Use the rope for what?"

"To bring down the bridge after we cross it."

"Why?" Hania was confused.

"So the Bloodstone's can't follow us."

"They would use the Bloodstone to rebuild it, or make another path of stones."

"I don't know. The Bloodstones can't be all-powerful, we beat them once before."

Hania didn't know if Skelly's theory was right, but it was all they had. "Alright, you get it ready to come down, and I'll go see if I can rescue them." Hania dug into the weapon bundle, retrieved a dagger, and strapped it on.

"How long to." Skelly snapped.

"What?" Hania was confused.

"How long to rescue them, not if." Skelly gave him a determined look.

"How long to." Hania grinned. Think positive. He turned and headed for the buildings at the high end of the island.

There were two sets of ruts heading that way, splitting around a large brackish lake. Nothing grew next to the lake, not even salt grass. It smelled bad and even from the road he could see salt crystals forming on the underside of rocky overhangs.

He slipped into the decrepit ghost town on the hill at the island's north end. A sound of snoring came from the one structure that still had its roof. Hania edged around it, praying that he wouldn't be caught.

The boys were sitting in the dust of what looked like a town square or work area, the stone buildings all opened out onto it. The weather worn pillars they were tied between may have once held an awning to keep the sun off the workers, though it had been a long time since workman had last done whatever it was they had done here in the past. The sun seared down onto the boys' heads; they were covered with sweat and sand, looking miserable.

Hania hesitated, were they worth it? *Was it worth the chance, that I lose my freedom to free them? What about Skelly's freedom? But…could I live with myself if I turned my back on them?* His heart was pounding so hard that he felt the top of his head was about to come off.

Great Spirit, protect me, he prayed as he pushed away from the building and padded into the square.

"Hey!" Dreogan got out before Tesar clamped a hand over his mouth. It was a tense moment waiting for a reaction from the Bloodstones. When none came, Hania moved closer and pulled out the silver edged dagger.

"That won't work!" Chval hissed at Hania.

Hania just grinned and cut Tesar free. "Head for the south tip of the island." He moved down the line, cutting them all free, leaving the tethers and collars hanging from the line.

Chval grabbed Hania's hand and stared at the dagger before shoving Hania's hand away and headed for the island's south tip. He seemed angry, but why? He had just been freed.

Shaking his head in bewilderment, Hania followed Barra out of the square; they caught up with the rest at the bridge.

Skelly told them to go over the bridge one at a time. Chval pushed Skelly aside and went first.

"What's wrong with him?" Skelly asked as he sent the others over.

"Have no idea…but he seems angry with us for some reason."

Hania went next to find Chval pacing and glaring at him. Skelly arrived and picked up the end of the rope.

"We need to pull hard on these." He handed the ends to Dreogan and Barra, then turned and guided them with hand signals until the bridge tumbled into the swamp and sank.

As Skelly gathered the rope into a bundle, Chval rounded on them.

"Blasphemy," Chval glared at them, "You have taken the sacred weapons…from the temple." He turned to the other boys. "We are doomed if we stay with them."

"We didn't get these from the temple…" Skelly tried to explain.

"Shut up!" Chval turned and jogged off down the road, the other three boys turned and followed, leaving Skelly and Hania.

"Well that's gratitude for you." Skelly finished gathering up the rope and turned. "What?'

Hania just stared at him. "You did get the weapons from Nabi, didn't you?"

"Of course! I only went as far as Nabi's Island, and when he gave me these and only these, I knew they were for fighting the Bloodstones. Only for Bloodstones." He shrugged his shoulders. "But I never thought that Chval would think we had taken them from the temple."

"They are still in danger, we better go." Hania felt like a mother hen. *Always pulling them back from danger, or am I pushing them into danger.*

"How are we supposed to catch up with them?" Skelly walked along side Hania. "They're way ahead of us by now. So much for learning how to work together."

"Don't worry," Hania knew the powers that had been used on the Atwaters in the past. "They have not banded their heads. I wouldn't be surprised that we will find them all passed out on the ground."

"The Sleep Spell?" Skelly waited in the silence.

"They may use it, now that we are far enough away from Atwater."

Skelly glared back at Salina.

""It would take days to tell you everything I know, just as it would take days for you to tell me everything you know." Hania turned and looked back. "And we don't have days."

They pushed onward. When they did catch up to the other boys, they were not passed out on the ground. They were at a freshwater spring on a thick wooded island, drinking their fill.

They backed away as Hania and Skelly arrived at the spring. Chval swaggered up to Hania and nodded his head towards the other boys.

"Some of the boys," He shot a glance over at them. "Think that you got those weapons from the armory."

"I got them from Nabi. He took them from the armory, not the temple." Skelly shrugged.

"But if that was so, then why didn't you let us kill the Bloodstones." Chval folded his arms waiting for the answer.

"You weren't banded." Hania explained. "Without a band like this," Hania indicated his and Skelly's silver paint bands. "They would have felt you coming, you wouldn't have gotten anywhere near them."

"Well, why didn't you band us then." Chval pointed at his head.

"We lost the paint when the stone pathway started to fail." Hania shot back.

"Oh? What is that?" Chval pointed at Skelly's belt where a pot of silver paint hung. With a snort, he turned and they all left.

Hania stared open mouthed at Skelly.

"I found it under the bridge when I was roping it up to pull it down. Didn't know it had that use." Skelly shook his head. "Sorry."

They took their turn at the spring. Even splashing cool water over themselves; washing off the sweat and sand.

"I wish I could somehow figure out how to get them to trust me. They won't be safe until they start listening."

"And then they'll be safe?" Skelly filled the two water-skins that were stashed with the remains of the weapons bundle.

"Well, they would be safer."

16

"I can't believe it!" Chval growled at Dreogan as they stomped along. "Of all the stupid things to say."

Dreogan grunted.

"Put a band of silver paint around your head and you will be unbeatable…what a fairy tale! What does he think we are? Children? It is cold, clear thought that will get us home…not a silver band."

Dreogan looked back the way they had come. "Do you think the Bloodstones are following us?"

"If they are, capturing Hania and Skelly will slow them down." He slapped at a mosquito. "Gads, I wish we had something to keep these bugs away.'

Dreogan dropped behind and Barra moved up by him. "What were you saying to Dreogan?"

"Just venting about Hania and Skelly." Chval slapped at another insect.

Barra cocked an eyebrow. "Want me to bag some Wood Ducks for supper?"

Chval laughed. "Oh yes. Anything to get the taste of that gruel out of my mouth."

Barra nodded and loped out of sight; Chval's stomach growled. *Well, he's a good hunter…I hope he bags some fat ones…I have never been so hungry.*

Tesar jogged up, matching his stride to Chval's. "What are our plans for getting home?"

"This is part of the road of the ancients. So if we follow it, we will get to one of the Green Crescent clans…from there…take the ferry home."

Tesar clapped him on the shoulder. "That's was makes you a leader, you know how to get things done."

"Well, I don't place all my bets on fairy tales," he smiled at Tesar, "or old prophesies."

What bothered him was Dreogan's silence. He was falling farther behind…was he waiting for those two losers to catch up?

He glared back at Dreogan, but a little trickle of guilt washed down the back of his neck. *Skelly and Hania did rescue us…they were willing to risk their own freedom. Am I made of the same cloth?* He pushed the nagging fear, the guilt, away to the back of his mind, *got to keep my mind on getting us home…all of us.*

17

Filling up the last water skin, Skelly turned to Hania. "Why are they always blaming us? We come after them, rescue them, and they…"

"They're afraid and want to blame someone," Hania glanced back the way they came, "and they do have a lot to fear." He pulled his thoughts away from the Bloodstones.

I need to get my mind back on what we need now. Looking around, his eyes searched for a certain vine. Was that one? He pushed through the damp undergrowth of ferns and Evening Primrose.

"Skelly!" He dropped to his knees, a Fo-ti vine was growing next to a Bald Cypress…those long heart shaped leaves of the Fo-ti never looked so good, hope it's old enough to harvest. Pulling out his old knife, he used it to dig up the root. His hands shook as he stuffed it in the net bag; Skelly helped him struggle to his feet.

Skelly grinned, "It's a good thing you are not that aggressive when we eat." He frowned, "Now all we need is some Foxglove. We need to keep our supply up."

"Keep it up? We're out." Hania sighed, "I feel that the stress level of this Manhood Trip is higher than the usual."

Skelly snorted. "Almost forgot…a survival trip to see if we are ready to be adults."

"I think we passed that a few squares back," they returned to the spring.

After washing the root, Hania sliced off pieces to chew raw. That would have to do until they could process it correctly.

They repacked their supplies and chewing the fibrous Fo-ti, searched the island for Foxglove, not one fuzzy leaf to be found, maybe the next island. As they crossed the next bridge, it started to sway, collapsing as they reached the end. It was as if an unseen hand pushed them towards a prearranged destiny. And if it was…was the hand friendly, or not?

"What shape is that silver paint in?" Hania asked.

Skelly ran his finger around the jar's top. "The seal is unbroken...it is undefiled."

A chill ran up Hania's spine. 'Silver undefiled, anoint their heads,' wasn't that in the prophecies? He wasn't sure...but it seemed very familiar.

18

Raghnall stepped out of the building, yawning and stretching. He scratched the spot where a mosquito had bit him; a result of not getting the insect barrier up fast enough. He turned. Let's see if sitting out in the sun for a few hours has made the slaves a little more receptive to their fate.

He blinked his eyes. The scene did not change; they were gone, the empty tethers and collars were swinging in the slight breeze coming off the river. Swearing, he called the other Bloodstones to gather around.

"How is this possible?" Vritra stomped over and yanked on the line.

"Where are they now?" Aja scratched his head.

Raghnall picked up an arrow shaft sitting next to a hole dug in the dirt. "They must have dug a silvered knife out of the dirt." Snapping the shaft in half, he tossed it onto the salty dust.

"A left over from the great war?" Edur spat on a wet-stone and drew a blade across it.

"Very likely." The fact that we are still alive rules out a rescue by someone that understands the relationship of silver to the Bloodstones.

Raghnall pulled out his Bloodstone and taking one of the empty collars in his other hand, did a Find incantation. A band of energy pointed southeast.

"They are following the old road." He walked to where he could see the bridges. Even from here he could see that the one pointing towards the southeast had fallen within a days time. Cursing again for wasting precious energy from the Bloodstone, he walked around the island trying to see if he could tell what the captives did before they left.

The wind swirled dust devils around so it was impossible to tell. *I could ask the Bloodstone to reveal the information, but that would be a waste of precious energy.*

The Bloodstone was not dark enough to be frivolous; maybe he should have sacrificed one of the slaves to it. On the other hand, the Bloodstone society was getting too complacent, they relied on the Bloodstones too much. He shrugged. *The fact that certain skills have been lost is something I'm taking up with my father, the High Wizard Qwinn, as soon as I return.*

On these deep forays to test the Green Crescent, it was not wise to waste the Bloodstone's power. No need to make them do such menial tasks; things that they could do themselves.

"Pack up, we're heading out!" Raghnall shouted over his shoulder.

"What about the new slaves?" Aja asked.

"Don't worry, they are following the old road. It makes land fall just this side of the pass north of Egil. We will set a trap for them."

"What if they get there first?"

"Now, Aja, that is a good question. How do we slow them down?" Raghnall waited.

The boy squinted up his eyes the way some of the older warriors did while stalling before answering.

"The same way we slow down escapees?" Aja grinned up at him.

"Correct!" Raghnall smiled at the boy with pride, already one of the brightest of his Stone Born Sons, even at eight years. He turned and pointed the Bloodstone southeast. This is the kind of thing the Bloodstones were meant to do. Because the Find Spell had worked, he knew they hadn't banded their heads. He sent a Sleep Spell off to do the job.

19

Hania and Skelly trudged along the Road of the Ancients, stopping to search each island for Foxglove, slicing off pieces of Fo-ti as needed. The sun beat down on them.

"I can see why these were called the stepping stone islands." Hania paused at the next bridge and motioned Skelly to go first.

"You're smaller, you go first." Skelly said. "Let's not take anymore chances with another bridge collapsing."

Hania crossed and found he was standing on a large bare rock and looking at another bridge. No Foxglove here.

Skelly joined him and grinned. "Now you see what that really means."

"How many bridges are there?"

Skelly shrugged. "It goes on like this until the end of the swamp…bridges linking rocks and islands together like a necklace of unmatched stones." He nudged Hania towards the next bridge.

"Tell me all you know about the Great War." Hania asked as Skelly caught up with him again.

"All the Green Crescent clans joined together against the great and evil empire of Cerebrus. But until now I didn't really understand how evil they were. Before it was just stories in scrolls."

"How long did they fight?" They started to search the next island.

"Years…until half the population was gone…but there was more dead on their side than ours." Skelly reached down and fished a pebble out of his sandal.

"War is not a good thing." Hania said. "But…"

"But what?"

"I am afraid…another war is coming."

Skelly grabbed his arm, "How sure are you?"

"It is not for sure," Looking behind a promising rock, he cut off another piece of Fo-ti. "I think it depends on us."

They finished searching the island, no Foxglove. "Do we start the war?" Skelly asked after they crossed the next bridge.

"I'm not sure."

"How can I live with myself if that is what we're doing."

"If we give in, it'll go back to the way it was. The way it was before the Great War." Hania sat and dumped sand out of his boot, frowning at the hole he found. "If it is a war, this will be the first battle of the last war between Cerebrus and the Clans of the Green Crescent."

They crossed over two more bridges; again searching each scruffy island, no Foxglove, and the sun was going down. Hania stopped. Had they crossed over to the other side of the swamp? He looked around at all the trees. Mature trees were everywhere. Along with Bald Cypress there was Red Maple, Black Gum, and even the small bronzed hued Wax Myrtle.

Skelly joined him. "Tale," he said, nodding towards the trees.

"Tell what?"

"No, Tale is the name of this island, it's a ghost town now. This is where the first Bloodstone attack came…or I should say ended. They took the small fishing village of Egil, and then they came here. Those that escaped went north…as far away from the ships of Cerebrus as possible." Skelly shook his head. "They never returned."

"Well, what was the name of that island where we filled up our water skins?" Hania asked.

"Not all the islands were named. Just the ones with settlements." Skelly was looking around with his eyes round from wonder. "I have read of these places, but I never thought I would ever see them."

"So, on Salina," Hania prompted.

"They mined salt. There's still a lot of salt there, but when closer deposits were found, it was abandoned." They moved into the shade of the forest, eyes still looking for Foxglove as they went. "Well, it is quite out of the way."

"And this one is Tale?" Hania felt much better now that it was cooling down, he hated the heat. "And what did they do here?"

Skelly scrunched up his forehead trying to remember. "They weren't warriors…academy?" He bowed his head. "I should have paid more attention to Nabi."

"This isn't a pathway." Hania said looking down. "In fact it's been a stone roadway ever since we crossed that last bridge."

They came around a bend and stopped short at the foot of a low wide hill. "Look at that building!" Hania scratched his head. "Skelly, what is that thing?"

Skelly climbed up to it, looked in one of the doors, and peered around. He staggered back as he paled. "Tale…was the school,…" He gasped out.

"A school?"

"During the great war, 50% of the clans' people were killed or captured."

"Everyone knows that." Hania shrugged.

"Just before those days, many of the older youth often went away to a boarding school. This school." Skelly looked around. "Much knowledge was lost when this place was destroyed."

Hania grabbed his arm and pulled him around. "You said that all the clans sent their children here?" He walked into the building. "This was a…"

"Library. Judging by the selves and large windows."

The glass was gone. In the center of the floor sat the burned remains of a desk. Skelly examined the ashes. "I think they burned the scrolls, too."

Hania ran out of the building. Following a stone path up a small rise, he found a row of dormitories. He counted the beds in the first one and then after counting over 60 buildings poking their roofs up through the vegetation, he sat in shock.

"They would have wanted the young. They make better slaves." He picked up a rock and sent it into a calm pond that reflected a very tall hill, stairs, and front of a stately building, an observatory judging by its shape.

Skelly sat down next to him. "Now that I know that the men of Cerebrus' and the Bloodstone's are one and the same…"

"The more…evil they seem."

"They may be following us." Skelly stood and pulled Hania to his feet. "Better get back on the road."

They went back down the hill, turned and followed the road around another rise and stopped short. Several of the trees had been cut down. The sawdust was recent…age had not turned it dark.

"Hardwood." Hania said, smelling the shavings. "Maple."

Skelly grinned.

"What?"

"We won't have to worry about the rest of the bridges."

"You're right!" The woodcutters would make sure the bridges were well maintained, so they would be able to make it to the other side of the swamp. With a whoop, they headed down the road.

As darkness fell, they caught up with the other boys. They were asleep, sprawled out on the pathway as if they had fallen as they walked.

"What's wrong with them?" Skelly walked over and lifted Barra's arm. It flopped back onto the ground…not even a quiver.

"Sleep Spell." Hania yawned as he shrugged out of his pack.

"Well, can't something be done?" There was an edge of panic in his voice.

"Sure, but do you want to face Chval's tongue this late at night?" Hania grinned over at Skelly.

Skelly pondered that for a moment. "Nope. But, can they track them?" He unrolled his bedding.

"Help me." Hania said as he opened up the jar of silver paint. "Roll them over so they are facing down." He refilled the small bottle and put it back into the kit. *Always keep your supply up.*

Then he went over to a tree and broke off a few twigs. As he chewed the end of one to make a brush, he handed Skelly a twig to do the same.

"They are going to have some interesting bedsores by morning." Skelly pulled a face as he spat out the taste of sap.

"Aye." Hania agreed as he leaned over and put a band around most of Dreogan's head and rolled him over.

Skelly did the same on Barra. "What do you think they are going to say in the morning?"

"At this point, I don't care." They finished rolling them over.

"Now what?" Skelly asked.

"We close the loop." Hania said as he leaned over Dreogan.

"Good thing they were so tired." The boys had drifted from the Sleep Spell into real sleep without missing a snore.

Hania looked longingly at his own bedding. But before he could sleep, he had to get the Fo-ti simmering.

He and Skelly searched and found a kitchen with pans and gathered wood. It was late when they finally brought in their bedding and spread it out before the fire.

As Hania got up to add bits of wood to the low fire, his worried mind found it hard to get back to sleep, instead he wondered where the Bloodstones were now. And where was this Stone Born Maiden?

20

Onid's eyes burned and she rubbed them. What exactly was Stone Born? She had been called the Stone Born Maiden all her life and the prophecies spoke often about it in conjunction with the Spirit Warriors and even a few mentioned a Spirit Maiden and a Valor Maiden. Were the Stone Born Maiden, the Spirit Maiden, and the Valor Maiden the same or three different people? The lamps threw flickering shadows over the table and into the corners. She grabbed a lamp and turned towards the index; Kendra was standing by the door.

"How long have you been here?" Burst out of her mouth as she stepped back in surprise; clutching the lamp tight.

Kendra's dark eyes flashed with humor. "I have never seen you so studious, especially this late." She came over and sat on a bench, her back to the table strewn with scrolls and patted the seat next to her.

Onid walked over and sat next to her; her back arrow straight, throat dry.

"Relax, I don't bite."

Onid sighed. "What makes me this Stone Born Maiden?"

Kendra leaned back, her face to the ceiling above her head, closing her eyes.

Knowing what that meant, Onid settled back to wait.

But Kendra spoke at once. "You are Stone Born."

"What does that mean? Was I born after mother was hit with a rock?" Onid asked. "Was I born the night a meteor hit the ground...or inside a mine?"

"Have you ever wondered why you didn't have a father?"

Onid turned away from Kendra; it was a mystery she wasn't sure she wanted to explore.

Kendra put her hand on Onid's shoulder. "Onid."

Onid shuddered. "My mother is a honorable woman." Onid declared, defending her and her mother against what she had always feared. Her mother wasn't a whore; it was unthinkable.

"Yes, she is a very honorable woman," Kendra stated, "She has always been so."

Onid looked up. "Mom was married, and he died?" But then why hadn't he ever been mentioned before?

"Kendra!" It was her mother's panicked voice, "I can't find..." She had reached the door, "Oh!"

Kendra gestured her in and she came and sat next to Onid, taking her hand.

"Your mother was about your age...no she was much younger, about four years younger." Kendra leaned back again. "She and her cousins, including my daughter, were at the hot springs."

It got quiet as Kendra wiped away a tear.

Onid sat still; *I didn't even know that Kendra had a daughter...I didn't know she had ever had any children.*

"Yedda, was so beautiful...and could she ever sing." Kendra laughed at the memory.

Onid had heard her mother sing. Her voice was so clear and beautiful; not at all like her body.

"Yedda was mother's younger cousin?"

"No, she was four years older than your mother. She was betrothed to Wulfhere." Kendra walked over, pulled a scroll out of its niche, and showed it to Onid. "See, this is the official account of the betrothal."

Onid looked at it; then with shock, she sat up. The Wulfhere on the document was Wulfhere the younger. "But Yedda was," she read on, her eyes darting over the paper. "Mother, can't be..."

"Only 16 years older than you." Kendra nodded as she rolled up the scroll and put it back in the niche.

"So that's why my grandfather looks so young. I knew my mother looked older than she was, but I didn't know she was this young." She turned to Gaho, "Why the deception?"

"All the Elders got together and decided it would be easier on you if you did not know everything about your birth." Gaho smiled.

"What happened to you?" Onid felt a chill and rubbed her arms. "You are only 32 years old?"

"That is what the Stones did to her." Kendra nodded towards Gaho.

Onid stared into Kendra's eyes, "Tell me what happened."

"It was the day before Yedda was to be wed. She and her bridesmaids, including your mother, went to the hot springs to bathe. They didn't come back."

"What happened?"

"Do you know why we insist that all wear a circlet of silver around your heads?"

"It stops us from being controlled by the Bloodstone Warriors." Onid shrugged her shoulders; it was common knowledge.

"Back then, we didn't know about the Sleep Spell or the Find Spell, we wore silver in honor of those who fought in the Great War. They had circlets of silver, we found...we found them laced with wildflowers."

Onid shivered. Her mother, what had she gone through?

"We followed the trail to the sea and found where they had come ashore. It was at the ruins of the fishing village they had once turned into a slave port, Egil; there was no doubt what had happened."

"Then what?" Onid was confused. "Didn't you follow them?"

"No one knew where their homeland was at that time," Kendra shook her head, "We grieved...we went on with our lives."

"But, mother...did someone rescue her?"

"Yes...and no." Kendra looked over at Gaho. "She was not chosen for the Stone Ceremony...she was not old enough. She was not with child."

"What is the Stone Ceremony?" Onid asked.

"To be able to manipulate the Bloodstones, you must grow alongside the Bloodstones. You must be Stone Born." Gaho stood up, walked over to the window, and glanced outside as Kendra continued.

"Every year they have the Stone Ceremony, where slaves, both male and female are taken to the Temple of the Stone. They are told they have been chosen to serve at the Temple."

"And the ones that were captured with my mother?"

"According to Gaho, they were among the chosen."

"The Mother Stone gives off seeds or eggs, they are small. They are sprinkled over and stirred into the feast that is served. The seeds do not harm the Stone Born, they leave with the natural waste."

Onid did not understand. Seeds go in, seeds go out?

"The seeds are like parasites, living off the host until they are full grown. Then they attack...drain all the blood...killing the host."

"The Stones kill them?"

Kendra nodded. "Then the Bloodstones are harvested and used by the Cult."

"So how does a child become Stone Born?"

"The Stones can detect if a women is with child...they wait until the child is born...then they kill the mother."

"Sometimes, the Stones are not full grown when the child is delivered." Gaho broke in, tears flowing down her face. "The mother gets to care for it...but not for long."

"I climbed into a forbidden passage and watched my cousins die," Tears ran down Gaho's cheeks as Kendra walked over and put her arm around her shoulders. "It was a long time ago, but I have never forgotten, they were in such pain."

"Then there has to be other Stone Born Maidens, they cannot have had only males."

Kendra shivered. "If the child is a female, they take a silvered dagger, kill her and fed her to the Mother Stone. They know it will be a Stone Born Maiden that will destroy them, so they kill all the maidens."

"How did I become Stone Born if you were not chosen for the ceremony?" She turned to her mother.

"I was given to a Bloodstone Wizard...slaves that were believers in the Great Spirit had raised him. We fell in love and were secretly married."

"My father is a Bloodstone Wizard?" Onid started to hyperventilate. "No, it can't be," with shock she slid to the floor. "I am a child of evil...my soul is damned!" *No wonder I can't pray,* she buried her face in the library's corner.

"Onid, he bought slaves to free them. We all lived together on islands as far away from Cerebrus as we could get. They are the hidden believers in the midst of the Bloodstones."

"But how did I become Stone Born?"

"Your father had purchased a beautiful slave named Satinka and her husband. His brother, Raghnall, wanted her for a concubine. Your father refused to sell her back into slavery."

Gaho took her by both hands and looked deep in her eyes. "I was with child, you."

"What happened?" Onid shivered.

"Raghnall went to the temple and got some of the Stone seeds they use in the Stone Ceremony. He wanted to punish your father by killing me, little by little, right before his eyes." Gaho put her arm around Onid. Kendra went to the door to make sure no one was around.

"How?" Onid looked at her mother, the lines around her eyes deepened.

"He came and ate with us, slipping the seeds into the food." She couldn't go on.

Kendra took over the story. "When your father found out, he took your mother out to meet the ship that he was sending Satinka and her husband away

71

on. Xavier and I were on that ship. Xavier called your father to be the Prophet of Cerebrus, he returned to danger and I brought Gaho home."

"It is up to your mother to tell you about her life at Cerebrus; about your father. But for now, I will tell you this; you child, are the Blessed one. You will destroy the Bloodstones and remove their wicked society once and for all."

"Blessed?" Her voice cracked in disbelief.

"Study the scrolls…pray and pay attention to the Great Spirit." Kendra turned to leave. "Your father is a good man, a brave man; and he loves you both, more than life."

And with that, Kendra left the House of Records. Onid looked at her mother. She loved a Bloodstone Wizard! But he was also…a prophet?

"I have a father," Onid bit her lip. "He sent you away because they would have killed me." She looked down and let the tears fall as her mother held her and let her cry.

21

It was so peaceful here on the Island of Tale. The morning birds were singing as Hania rolled over and poked Skelly awake.

"What?" Sitting up, Skelly stretched.

"Breakfast." Hania went outside to take care of nature's call.

Pointing, Skelly laughed. "Hey, they have outhouses."

Hania grinned and made a beeline for relief, Skelly racing behind. There was something odd about the outhouses. They were made of stone and down below you could hear the sound of water as it ran beneath them, carrying away the waste and smell.

"When do you want to wake them?" Skelly asked later as they headed back to pack up their bedrolls.

"Start another fire and I'll wake Barra." Going to where the boys still slept, Hania rolled Barra over; stones had left a nice pattern of marks on the side of his head.

Hania had put a few decorative swirls into his work, something you might find on a girls fancy headband.

With a snort, Barra sat up. "What...who?" He looked at Hania, scrambled to his feet, and looked at the other boys. "What's wrong with them?"

"Leftover traces of the Sleep Spell."

A light flashed on in Barra's eyes as he grinned and cocked his head. "Let the games begin."

"It's not a game."

Barra just grinned and shrugged.

Returning, Skelly pointed to where a curl of smoke rose into the air. "The kitchen is over there, fire's already started."

"Where are we?" Barra tripped over Dreogan and fell back on his rump.

"Barra, would you get up? We need more than tree bark to eat." Reaching down Skelly pulled Barra to his feet.

"What have you found?" Barra let Skelly drag him off in the direction of some stone chicken hutches. The hutches may have attracted new tenets or the descendents were still around.

Hania looked around at who was left. *Who should I wake next?* He shook Dreogan and he awoke with a start. Painted into his band of silver were a bunch of cooking pots and other kitchen stuff.

Hania smiled at his artwork and directed him towards the kitchen. "I'm sure you can find enough pots, there's a well around back."

They had found only the one well so far; it was made of stone like everything else on the island. Maybe all the other wells had been made wood and had rotted and fallen in.

"Ah...Okay..." Dreogan backed away from Hania his face devoid of thought, jumping as Skelly put a hand on his shoulder.

"We found some ducks...Barra is plucking them now." Turning Dreogan around he pointed. "See that smoke?"

"Uh...yes." Dreogan nodded.

"Behind that building." Skelly pushed him towards the kitchen. Dreogan took off like a sprinter at the beginning of a race.

Hania sighed. "You know Skelly, it wouldn't hurt for them to once say 'Thanks Hania and Skelly for pulling our fat out of the fire'."

"We're still the outsiders." Skelly rolled Tesar over. "They're going to want answers." Tesar opened his eyes and blinked up at Hania.

"Caught up have you?" He grinned and sat up. Skelly had put a plain band on him.

They looked down at Chval where Skelly had painted a design of donkeys across Chval's forehead.

Seeing Skelly's artwork on Chval, Tesar fell back giggling, rolling over he got to his knees.

"Glad you two are here, but don't tell him I said so," he nodded towards Chval, and then sniffed at the air.

Hania directed him to the kitchen and then turned back to where Skelly was touching up a few additions to Chval's band, gently so he wouldn't waken.

"Skelly." Hania jerked his head towards the kitchen. "Let him find his own way over, let's go."

Skelly grinned at his artwork and then breathed in deeply. "Yup, he should be able follow his nose. Dreogan and Barra sure know how to cook."

"We need to work on the Fo-ti." Hania nudged Skelly again.

74

Hania gathered moss while Skelly searched the kitchen for something they could use to make a filter. Skelly found some old gourd funnels and after packing them with moss, they poured the Fo-ti potion in and left it to strain as they got ready to eat.

Hania and Skelly joined the other boys just as they were dishing up the food. Tesar, Dreogan, and Barra had gleaned what they could from the wild descendents of the original plants in the garden plots next to the kitchen, mostly onions and potatoes. It mixed well with cut up duck. After a quick mumbled blessing on the food, they wolfed it down. All the best parts were gone by the time Chval wandered in.

The boys burst out laughing at the donkey's tail portrayed down Chval's nose. The rest of the donkey's backside was sketched around his eyes and down to his chin.

"What?" He looked at them, then picked up a pan, polished it with his arm, and looked. "Very funny," he glared at Hania and Skelly.

He grabbed what food was left and gobbled it down while shooting angry looks at the lot of them.

Hania explained about the Sleep Spell the Bloodstone Warriors used. And why they needed the band of silver to protect them.

Chval snorted. "Not true...not true." He shook his head. "We were tired from running all day."

"And you all fell asleep at the same time, falling flat on your faces?" Skelly raised his eyebrows.

"I can prove it!" Chval jumped to his feet. "Got some solvent, Hania?"

Hania nodded and handed it over along with a rag, avoiding looking at him so he wouldn't laugh.

"Watch this!" Chval poured solvent on the cloth and removed the donkey tail down the front of his face. He stood there, triumph on his face. "See?" He spread his arms out, the rag dripping with solvent and paint.

The other boys looked over to Skelly and Hania; the first cracks of doubt showing in their eyes.

Then Chval topped over, out cold.

"Maybe the solvent has something in it." Barra sniffed the solvent, then grabbed the rag, and rubbed it over his face without touching his silver paint band.

They waited in silence while Chval continued to snore on the kitchen's dusty stone floor. Nothing happened.

Hania went out and got the silver paint. *Why in the world is Chval fighting me so hard? Chval has always been the ringleader when it came to tormenting Skelly and me; but it is more than that now, I feel like this is a war over who rules the kingdom and my team consisted of just Skelly and me.*

When he came inside, Barra was sitting at the scrubbed wooden table a glum look on his face. Barra handed the cloth to Dreogan who lifted it to the side of his head and swiped down through his silver band.

The tension in the room was at the breaking point as they waited. Dreogan slumped over.

"Well?" Skelly shrugged.

Dreogan jumped back up, "Just kidding." Then he toppled over for real.

Shaking his head Hania pulled the rag from Dreogan's hand. "The Bloodstones' magic is real," Hania opened the paint jar, dipped the rag's corner in and repaired Dreogan's band. "It is pure evil."

"Then it's time for us to know what we are fighting." Barra clenched his fists.

"You all know part of it," Skelly said, "The Great War."

"A lot of people died back then. Warriors." Tesar jumped up and started pacing the floor; he turned to Hania. "We're just kids!"

I never thought I would hear that from these four, it only shows how scared they are.

"We might be more." Skelly whispered to Hania.

"Don't tell them about that." Hania hissed back.

"Well?" Barra slammed his fist on the table.

Hania told them all he and Skelly knew out about the Bloodstone Warriors and the power of the silvered weapons.

"So the weapons you brought were made to fight the Bloodstones, if they ever returned. Should have paid more attention in school." Tesar sank into the nearest straight-backed chair; he ran a hand through his hair and fingered the band around his own head. His shoulders slumped.

"We're doomed," Dreogan gestured around them, "as doomed as the students, that once were here."

"What here?" Barra asked.

"Don't you know where we are?" Dreogan picked up the rag and paint pot and gave Chval a plain band as Hania returned the solvent to his wilderness kit.

"Where are we?" Tesar walked over to the door, running a hand over the smooth seamless stone.

"Tale," Skelly said, "We're on Tale."

Tesar blanched…he jerked around as if they were surrounded by Bloodstones.

Chval sat up and glared at Hania. "What did you give me?"

"Just solvent," Barra grumped. "We tested it."

Skelly and Hania went outside, leaving the boys arguing and explaining. "I think we made a mistake waking them up." Skelly said.

Hania glanced back. "It's not going to be an easy job keeping them on task." Looking at Skelly's bundle, he swallowed. "We're in trouble."

"What?" Skelly came over to where he was.

"We lost most of the silver weapons."

"Yea, I know, I remember most of them falling when we were running to Salina." Skelly said. "I wasn't ready to dive in after them…I think there was an anaconda coming for us at that point."

Hania looked at the pitiful amount of weaponry. "We can't beat them with this. What are we going to do?"

"There might be weapons scattered on these islands; leftovers from the war." Dumping out what was left, Skelly looked down; a crossbow and bolts, two long bows, five arrows, and a spear.

Stomping out of the kitchen, Chval sneered. "So…you didn't tell us about the Bloodstones. You hid your knowledge so as to keep us in need of you…trying to be our leader?" He shoved Hania hard enough for him to fall on the ground, "A weakling like you?"

Chval walked over to the weapons and grabbed up a longbow and four of the arrows. "We'll see about that!"

As Chval stomped off towards the next bridge, Skelly picked Hania off the ground.

"What is wrong with him?" Skelly helped the others arm themselves as best they could with what was left.

"He has always been our leader." Barra took the last bow and arrow.

"I think it will do him good to have to rely on someone else for a change." Grinning, Dreogan handed the spear to Tesar.

"What about you?" Tesar asked Dreogan; smiling, Dreogan showed him the knife from Salina.

"We need to find all the weapons we can, save the silvered ones as a last resort." Skelly repacked his gear, "Or if we meet more Bloodstones."

"What's the next island?" Hania gathered up his stuff.

"There are a lot of small unnamed islands," Skelly shook his head. "I'm trying to remember…maybe it will come to me as we reach them." Grimacing, Skelly slipped his pack onto his back.

Crossing the bridge they found Dreogan talking to Chval. Chval turned and yelled, ordering the boys to spread out and hunt for weapons.

Chval walked up to Skelly and Hania. "I know how hard it is for you to work in the sun." Giving a small bow, he waved his hand around the small island; it consisted of a large sand dune pushed up against a tangle of Mangrove trees to the north. "So, that's your area," he pointed at the Mangroves.

Sand had blown across the stone roadway into small dunes; no weapons would have lain on the road. The boys were using broken branches to probe beneath the surface along the edges and away from the road.

"Let's go," Hania headed towards the tangle of trees.

"I think he just wants to get rid of us." After peering into the gloom under the trees, Skelly slipped into the grove.

"I know," Hania wrinkled his nose at the smell of decay. "Yuck, these roots are slimy!" He lifted a hand and watched as a greenish brown sludge slid off, a maroon and green Tiger Beetle, escaping the drip, took off through the gloom. Wet moss and spider webs hung down between the trees.

"Watch out for tarantulas." Skelly pushed a web aside with a stick he had yanked off a deadfall.

"I'm more concerned with running into a Gahiji lizard." Hania climbed over a fallen tree, eyeing a pool of water. What was under the surface? It looked peaceful.

"Gahiji's only bite when provoked," Skelly called from his own perch, "Come up here, you're not going to believe this." He pulled Hania up with him.

Now he saw what caught Skelly's interest, it looked like a road built of planks, no rope. It was a construction he was unfamiliar with. Something like furniture construction, but on such a large scale!

"Hardwood, red cedar I think," Skelly thumped on it with the stick he was using; it looked, sounded, and smelled like red cedar.

"Why would they do this?" Hania looked down what looked like a dark tunnel, with green foliage above, below and all around the long suspension bridge. "Dowels with tongue and grove."

"You should see the support system!" Came Skelly's muffled voice as he leaned over to look underneath.

"We're pretty high up."

"We're close to the coast and low enough to be part of the tide zone." Skelly breathed.

Hania nodded remembering the houses on stilts near Stillwater.

"Let's find out where it leads." Skelly grinned and started down the tunnel walking carefully.

Hania followed. Skelly was wise in not trusting something that had to be old and sitting in the Great Swamp for years; the tunnel's workmanship was equal to the stonework of the school buildings on Tale.

Skelly stopped and stooped down on what looked like the tunnel's end. "Look at that," he pointed.

Hania stared; a shrine was built onto a small island up against a very tall, steep hill. "What the?"

Skelly jumped down and walked over to the shrine's door. "This Shrine was built to honor the Spirit Warriors that will someday come here in search of silvered weapons," He read off the inscription over the door.

Hania's legs gave way and he sat down hard. Skelly looked over at him. "Well, maybe it's just a coincidence."

What was it his grandfather was always saying? There is no such thing as coincidence? Hania hung his head...somehow he knew. They were the chosen ones. Now what?

Skelly was looking at the Shrine. "You know...if the people who built this thought that the Spirit Warriors would come here looking for silvered weapons," he looked at Hania.

Hania got up. "Think they may have stored some here?"

"Well?" Skelly stepped into the Shrine, "There's a coffer in here along with the usual alter and benches."

Hania shivered as he walked into the Shrine. Skelly had pried up the coffer's lid, grinning he pulled out a quiver of silvered arrows.

There were bows, arrows, spears, knives, swords, slings, and acid balls. "Guess we won't need to go to Bainbridge," Hania said as he helped Skelly load up all they could carry; they soon emptied out the coffer.

"Nabi said you knew about the Spirit Warriors...our prophecies that mention them, that is," Skelly looked at him. "You said you didn't know if we were..."

Looking at Skelly, Hania bit his lip. "I have bad news..."

"We're not them, are we?" Skelly grumped.

Hania put his hand on Skelly's arm. "No, I think we are the Spirit Warriors. At least, some of us are." Shivering, he stared at the shrine. "I think you...we...just fulfilled one of the prophecies."

"Why isn't that good news?"

"Not all the Warriors...make it." Hania walked away from the Shrine Island to where they would meet up with the others.

"Maybe, we should keep that part…from them." Skelly's voice was shaky, "I…never thought that we could…this is real, isn't it?"

Hania nodded, please Great Spirit…he wiped away the tears that were threatening to come. What was it his father always said when he prayed? Thy will be done?

"Which one of us…" Skelly shrugged at him.

"The prophecies are clear in parts and unclear in others…and there are so many of them." Hania stopped; they had come to the tunnel's end. "I don't know who lives and who dies…I'm not even sure when the deaths occur. During the second battle or the third, I think, not the first."

"Deaths? More than one?"

"There will be many who will die during the second and third battles. But the good news is that the third battle will end with the destruction of Cerebrus and the end of the Bloodstone cult."

Skelly climbed down and Hania handed him the weapons.

"We live in times worthy of note." Skelly helped Hania climb down.

"Well, let's go and present the rest of the Warriors with their birthright."

22

Shimmering heat waves danced over the island's sandy area. Hesitating, Hania looked around before they left the shade of the Mangrove trees. No one was in sight. Did the other boys go onto the next island without us? Or had the Bloodstones caught up with them?

"Go and check the footprints at the next bridge, I'll check back at the other." Skelly said and headed to the bridge they had crossed to get here.

Hania strode to the next bridge. Along the way, he saw signs that the others had dug up some weapons. Holes pockmarked the smooth sand with the sand from the holes dark against paler surface sand.

Skelly caught up with him. "No footprints heading back where we came from."

"No sign of struggle this way." Hania said as they reached the other bridge. Four sets of footprints marked the sand that had blown onto the bridge's stone surface. Everything in the Great Swamp was constructed of stone, everything except that hidden bridge to the Shrine.

One set of footprints looked like its owner had turned back before crossing over. "Well," Skelly scuffed his foot across one of the prints, "Someone is having second thoughts about blindly following Chval."

"Or Chval was checking to see if we were back before leaving." Hania stooped down. "It was someone with a cut in the side of his shoe."

Straightening, Hania and Skelly crossed the bridge to the next island. It was wooded and much larger than the last one; the trees were younger, smaller than the ones cut down on Tale. "Would this island have been inhabited?"

"Hard to tell." Skelly sighed with relief as they reached the shade. Once again they were walking on a well-built stone roadway, it was so well built that the brush was having a hard time trying to reclaim it. The paving blocks were as tight as the redwood bridge on the last island. The road snaked into the trees, the shade making it much easier for them to travel along at a reasonable rate.

The road led into a clearing with what looked like a small inn sitting off to one side and a barn with a paddock next to it. Both built of stone. Barra was standing in the inn's open doorway. "They're here," he called into the darkness behind him.

Hania and Skelly entered the building with their load to the cheers of all but Chval, the boys rushed forward to sort out the weapons based on what they were best at.

Glaring at Hania, Chval stood at a wall with a stub of candle lit. The walls had been papered with what looked like pieces of old scrolls.

Barra clapped Skelly's back. "Where did you find these? Are there more?" He picked out a quiver of arrows and traded his bow for one Skelly had found.

Skelly explained what they found. "Wish we had a Shrine Key, may have been more weapons hidden inside."

"All we found were a few knifes," Dreogan picked out another bow for himself, "And arrows. Lots of arrows, but most of them had lost their fletching. Barra shot some wood ducks and Tesar is cooking them now."

"Thought I could smell something good cooking." Skelly's stomach growled.

"Use the feathers to replace the fletching…save the silvered ones in case we run into the Bloodstones." Hania followed his nose to where the smell of roasting duck floated in with the smoke, Chval pursuing him.

"Hania, we have food!" Grinning, Tesar gestured at the ducks.

Hania walked over. "We found weapons. Go in, I'll take over cooking." Tesar slipped inside.

"You'll take over," Chval snarled, "You'll take over cooking, and what else?" His eyes glinted, "You just happened to release us? You just happened to find weapons? You just forgot to tell us what the prophecies say about the Spirit Warriors?" His shaking hand pointed back inside.

Hania looked past him, at the wall covering consisting of worn scroll fragments. So among them were the prophecies about the Spirit Warriors? "What are you talking about?"

"You, trying to take over…you, trying to turn us into the Spirit Warriors." Chval was standing over him.

"Chval!" Called out Skelly's warning voice.

"Your trained guard dog." Chval backed off. "One day, he won't be there to save you."

"Knock it off, Chval." Barra had come to the door.

"They got us into this!" Chval yelled back, spit flying. "We wouldn't be here if it wasn't for them."

"No, we would be the guests of honor at a slave market," Barra leaned against the door jam, "I prefer being here, thank you."

The other boys came to the door. "Let me tell you about the Spirit Warriors." Chval pushed past them, picked up the candle, and read aloud from the bits on the wall that told of the Spirit Warriors.

There was just a part here and a part there, it seemed like it was about how they started up to where they escaped from the Bloodstones.

"It says the healer knows many of the prophecies," Chval said. "So are you trying to turn us into the Spirit Warriors? Trying to be our leader?"

"I'm a potion maker, not a healer," Hania said, "and I don't want to be a leader." What was with Chval? Why was he acting like this?

"So what happens next?" Chval walked over to where the other boys were, they all looked over at Hania as if expecting him to be able to tell the future.

"I don't know," Hania swallowed. "I'm not a soothsayer and none of the prophecies I know map out what we are suppose to do."

"So, you think we are the Spirit Warriors." Chval pointed an accusing finger at him.

"It makes no difference what I think, either we are or we're not. Period." Hania turned and looked out at the fire, "I think the ducks are done."

They ate overcooked duck in silence with Chval glaring at them all through the meal. Skelly sat protectively next to Hania. The other boys took turns rereading the scroll fragments, trying to figure out what to do next.

Dreogan threw up his hands. "What are we suppose to do?"

"Ask the potion maker." Chval said as he made a mock bow in Hania's direction.

"I told you," Hania said through gritted teeth, "I don't know."

"Well…what about the prophecies you do know? Can you tell us what they say?" Barra looked at Hania.

With a deep sigh, Hania started to recite what prophecies he remembered concerning the Spirit Warriors. "After a long time of peace and wealth, the Bloodstone Warriors shall come again, come again…"

23

Chval glared over at Hania. What kind of game is he playing...does he think he can take over my role...Hania as a leader? Barra was asking Skelly something; they had their heads together. That was just wrong.

"That's enough," Chval came to his feet, wiping the duck grease from his fingers. "We should keep moving."

"Why?" Dreogan asked.

It was the first time in years that Chval had been asked to explain any of his decisions. "We know that the Bloodstones can make stone bridges and they may," he shot a look at Hania, "have put us to sleep so they could recapture us."

Dreogan looked at Hania. "What if going this way is wrong?"

Chval felt his authority slipping; this is ridiculous. "Hania and Skelly started this way; they must have had a reason." *What if Hania is keeping more parts of the Prophecies a secret? Am I falling for Hania's trick to take away my role as leader?*

"Move out." He headed for the next island, the others followed, Hania and Skelly at the tail end, another stinking island, another smooth stone road. *Weaklings as leaders...not a chance! My family has been in charge of the Atwater Clan for generations, I'm slated to be the Chief after my father.*

A dull ache was forming in the muscles in the back of his neck and he reached up to rub it away. Why were things changing? Things should go back to the way they had always been.

Although, the Spirit Warriors...I like the sound of that...I could become the Leader of the Spirit Warriors. Be a hero of Atwater and all the clans of the Green Crescent, just as my Great Grandfather had done in his day. But Hania is trying to usurp my role. I will not let a weakling become the leader of the Spirit Warriors. He ground his fist in his other hand.

"Hania!" He had to wait for him to catch up; Hania was showing every

84

sign of exhaustion. "When I ask a question, you will give a complete and honest answer."

"Sure," Hania shrugged. Skelly stopped and took the stance of a bodyguard.

"Someone needs to be the decision maker, or we won't make it back home," Chval said. Hania looked relieved. That was odd.

"If you have two leaders, when they don't agree, you have a split." Chval continued. "You two are defective…you can't and shouldn't try and be the leaders."

Skelly looked like he was about to clobber him. Hania put his hand on Skelly's arm.

"I don't want to be the leader of the Spirit Warriors." Hania said.

"So, you think we are the Spirit Warriors, then." Chval said.

Hania looked at the ground. "It seems that way."

Hania is keeping something back; I feel it. "I'm the leader here," His voice ground out, "by birth and by skill."

Leaving Hania and Skelly, he turned and stalked past the other boys. He turned. "Let's go. We have a lot of miles to cover."

Barra came up to him. "What about food?"

Chval smiled. "Why don't you and Dreogan move ahead of us? We can then make enough noise the scare the game towards you.

Barra and Dreogan raced ahead. As soon as they were out of sight, Chval started singing loudly, the others joined in. *Yes, it was good to be in charge again…and I'm not going to lose that again…not to Skelly and Hania.*

24

"Can you believe him?" Skelly looked down the road. "I mean, how often do we have to drag them out of the flames before they can say thank you?"

"Chval is missing something in his soul." Hania said, "And until he develops that trait, he will never become a good leader, much less, the Leader of the Spirit Warriors."

"What's that?" Skelly took a swig from a fresh filled flask of Fo-ti juice and handed it to Hania.

"The ability to listen to the Spirit." Hania swallowed and recapped the flask, "Hence the name, Spirit Warriors."

"He does have a problem with listening to anyone but Chval," Skelly readjusted his backpack, "Rested enough? Shall we try catching up with them again?"

"Yea, let's go." Hania pushed away from the tree trunk of a tall White Fir he was resting against. *I hope we'll continue to have lots of shade to travel through; it always helps.*

Once again, he started to go through everything he could remember from the Prophecies; it seemed they would be recaptured soon after the first escape, so his nerves were tight. He knew it was coming, unless…unless they weren't the Spirit Warriors.

He stopped. Why not ask? He closed his eyes and reached towards Heaven with his feelings. The answer surprised him, *quit asking…you already know*, the words came to his mind as though spoken. His knees buckled and he grabbed a tree trunk to keep from hitting the ground.

"What happened?" Skelly was at his side.

"Nothing." Hania didn't want to worry Skelly about what was going to happen.

"Another attack?" Skelly wasn't letting it go.

Hania shook his head as he looked up at his best friend.

"I can tell when something isn't right." Skelly pulled him up to his feet.

"Skelly, before this day is over, we will be recaptured by the Bloodstones." He had let it out. Saying it aloud made it sound even worse than it was.

Skelly's face paled. "Are you sure?" He looked down the road, "I thought we were escaping from the Bloodstones, not rushing towards them."

"Skelly…" *Why didn't I keep quiet,* "There are some things we have to go through…if we are the Spirit Warriors." He was still hoping they were not the Spirit Warriors.

"A refiners fire?" Skelly looked skyward and shivered.

"Let's go." Hania started down the road.

They didn't go much farther before they caught up with the others; Barra had shot a deer. It would be venison for supper tonight.

"Why don't the two of you go on ahead?" Chval said, "We'll catch up after we gut and skin this," He jerked his thumb at the deer they had hanging in a Live Oak tree.

Barra nodded. "It won't take long…look for a clearing with water and wood."

Chval gave them a shove; Hania stumbled, still weak from his spiritual experience. Skelly caught him.

"Let's go." Skelly pulled him along.

"He's worried," Hania shook his head, "afraid that someone else may become the leader."

"You have watched the Elders of our clan," Skelly said. "Is that how they lead?"

"Of course not." Hania kicked at a fallen birds nest.

"Nabi told me how the council works. The Chief asks everyone how they would solve a problem, then they pray about it."

"Can you see Chval asking anyone how they would solve a problem?" They snorted at that. Chval had too much pride, not a good trait in a leader.

A large arching bridge loomed out of the mist that was forming ahead, crossing over the third and last navigable branch of the river.

This bridge, like the others, was made of stone, but this one had high sidewalls and a roof. It disappeared into the mist like a long tunnel.

"Well, what do you think?" Skelly looked into the opening.

Hania looked at it. It felt like a trap…but was it a trap they were supposed to enter? He walked down to the water's edge to see if he could see the far bank.

Is this anxiety just my imagination…did I hear those words or was it the fear speaking? He looked up at the bridge. There were windows in the side every so often; they could always escape that way. *Why am I thinking of escape?*

The other boys caught up with them.

"What are you doing?" Chval asked as Hania climbed up from the river's edge.

"Wanted to see how long this bridge is," Hania breathed in the air. There was a touch of salt in it…were they near the ruins of the old Bloodstone slave port?

"Skelly, how near are we to Egil?" Hania scraped sandy mud off his boots. Where would the Bloodstones have gone…were they behind us or ahead?

"The road exits the swamp between Egil and Bainbridge." Skelly sniffed the air. "A lot closer to Egil than Bainbridge, if the old maps were correct."

"And if we can trust a weakling's memory." Chval crossed his arms and stared down his nose at Skelly; it was quite a feat as Skelly was a head taller than Chval.

Barra and Dreogan coughed and shuffled their feet. Chval was getting more irrational, so much so, that it looked like he was even making them feel a bit uncomfortable.

"The map in his head is all we have." Hania said as he walked over to the bridge's opening, a trickle of sweat sliding down his back. *Chval is becoming more a drain on my energy than the heat.*

How soon would the Bloodstones recapture us? What if we're not the Spirit Warriors? I could be leading all of us into a lifetime of slavery or the Bloodstones could be nowhere near.

As he stood at the bridge's mouth in indecision, he found himself pleading in his heart and mind with The Great Spirit. *Do I want to do this? What if I am wrong?*

Father, I need your wisdom and courage. Is this the path we should be following? No warmth filled him, only calm and he smiled through his tears as he nodded at Skelly, who grinned back.

"Let's go." There was eagerness on Skelly's face that was missing on the others.

Hania shivered and started into the covered bridge with Skelly at his side. Only he and Skelly had any idea what was in store for them; the others followed.

Chval is going to be angry soon…very soon…if I'm right. Hania started a warrior's chant, the others joined in. It was one that had been sung by all Green Crescent Warriors before going into battle and now on parade days celebrating the Evil Empire's defeat.

He could see the fog swirl at the far end of the bridge. The windows in the walls were smaller then he had thought, he could squeeze through…but not the others. The roof had recently caved in at this end and they climbed over the debris. Hania looked up and saw the stars though the swirling mist.

It should be any time now. He was so tense that he jumped with the others when it happened. The earth shook and walls of smooth stone pushed up on all sides, enclosing them in a slave pen like the one on Manhood Island.

Skelly looked at him, biting his lip. Hania gestured that he should calm down.

Chval was anything but calm as he turned on Hania, "Betrayer!" He spat out and fit an arrow into his bow.

He aimed at Hania. At this range, he could not miss, yet Hania only felt calm.

A rope of red energy hit Chval, throwing him back against the wall. His shot went wild over the wall and was met with laughter from the other side.

"Boys, boys. I can't let you harm one another, that can wait…until later." It was the voice of the Bloodstone Wizard, Raghnall.

"Come and get us, Slavers." Chval jumped to his feet, fitting another arrow into his bow. The others armed themselves as well.

This was met with a lot of chuckling from behind the walls. Once in a while a head would pop up in an opening and Chval or one of the others would shoot. The arrow would miss and sadistic laughter would echo from the Bloodstones.

Hania shook his head; they were not trained warriors. The boys had lost rational thought, fear causing them to shoot blindly. He watched as they fired most of the arrows and threw all but one spear. The only success they had was with the glass balls of silvered acid.

When a shriek of pain came from the Bloodstone side, Chval gathered the boy's together. They were down to three arrows, a spear, and Skelly's crossbow bolts.

"Acid balls first, then shoot high," Chval hissed. That worked, but soon they were out of all arrows, spears, and bolts. All that was left were knives and swords…they were defenseless.

The head of Raghnall rose above the top of the wall, he peered down. "My, my. Done with your temper tantrum?" With no more than a wave of his hand, part of the wall raised up, leaving a gap. "Put the rest of your toys through here."

Hania felt like a failure. The others threw down their bows and slings and kicked them through the opening.

"Your knifes and blades as well." Raghnall said.

They tossed all the knives and swords down. The silver gleamed in the starlight as they kicked them through the opening. One didn't go all the way and one of the Bloodstones reached for it.

Dreogan had reached the breaking point…he lunged at the hand with the rusty broken blade from Salina, plunging it in. A howl of pain shrieked into the night, a high voice…a boy's voice. The one called Aja.

With a snarl Raghnall used a red finger of energy from the Bloodstone to pick Dreogan up, tossing him out of the pen. "Zigor! Your whip!"

"The wounded. They…"

"Send for a healer!" Raghnall's voice screamed into the night, "and some decent wine!"

Someone left, the racing footsteps fading towards Egil.

"Now boys, you will see how we take care of animals that attack." Raghnall turned his attention back to the boys. He changed a section of wall to bars so the boys could see Dreogan tied to a stake, his shirt gone.

Zigor unraveled his whip…with a flick of his hand the end snapped across Dreogan's body, leaving a bloody streak. Dreogan arched his back, but refused to cry out.

The whip sang and snapped, without rest.

"They're going to beat him to death." Skelly was shaking.

"No," Hania said, "We are too valuable to him."

"Another part of the Prophecy?" Skelly asked.

"Just a feeling."

Over and over Zigor applied the whip. Chval glared at both Raghnall and Hania, searching for someone to blame.

Soon Dreogan was hanging unconscious. Raghnall walked over and lifted his head, and looking at him cocked his own head. "Not quite up to travel now. We can't have that." He let Dreogan's head drop.

He took out his Bloodstone and a thin red rod grew at the end. He applied it over Dreogan's back; slender red scars replaced the open wounds.

"Father, I mean Lord Raghnall, why do you heal him?" Aja asked.

"Scars can be very useful." Raghnall released Dreogan and flung him over the barrier.

Hania rushed to Dreogan's side. "How severe are your injuries?"

"Leave me alone." Dreogan shoved him away, stood up, and went into a corner to sulk. The only movement was the glare he sent over at Hania, as if he was at fault.

Hania took stock of what they had left. They had less then a pot of silver paint, four flasks of Fo-ti juice, an empty flask, two water skins, and the wilderness kit. How was that going to help? And, oh yes, they had a hank of rope and a couple of bedrolls. He sat, his back against a wall and looked up.

Great Spirit, have I been guilty of wanting to be a Spirit Warrior...am I being punished? If so, punish me not them. He wiped away a tear that had escaped and bent his head down onto his knees.

He could see the Bloodstones through the bars, celebrating.

He could hear Raghnall laughing; see the deer Barra had shot on a spit over a wood fire. The smell of venison cooking only reminded him of how long it had been since they had last eaten.

They would be lucky if they got the bones to gnaw on after the Bloodstones were through.

If only I get a chance. If I could get out and...doctor the wine...the wilderness kit...I still have it...they hadn't taken it...it has powdered Mandrake...if the wine gets here in time. He raised his head and looked towards Egil, a plan forming in his mind as he reached into the kit, slipping the packet of Mandrake into his tunic.

25

Raghnall sat in the fire's glow; the flames danced off the faces of his personal band of Bloodstone Warriors, his Warrior sons. The smell of deer roasting filled the air. Life couldn't be better. This was a beautiful clearing, with an ice-cold spring, grassy meadow, and plenty of wood. A more perfect campsite could not be found, including the entertainment of the new slaves.

Zigor was teaching Aja how to use a whip, so far he had wrapped the end of the whip around three trees, two rocks and Vritra, all to the laughter of the whole troop. He looked up. Yes, we are the masters of our world. Edur should be returning soon from Egil with the good wine and a healer.

Some of his warriors were hurt, but the healer could take care of them. At least they weren't any of his sons, his elite corps.

The slave's knife that stabbed Aja's hand was not silvered; he was unharmed by it. Aja's Stone repaired any damage. His outcry had been from surprise, not pain. He would be more cautious around wild slaves from now on.

He looked over at the slave pen, speculating, his Bloodstone was looking a bit pale. *It was time to recharge it, should I give it a full charge or a half charge?*

Three of the boys were in a corner, the cur that Zigor had whipped and two others, they look scared. The rock thrower, Chval, was leaning against a wall; he looked angry and scared. He needs a little more work.

The other two sat leaning against a wall, the weaklings as Chval called them, only they didn't appear weak to him. Okay, maybe the smaller of the two, the potion maker. But the other one…he was over a head taller then Chval and he was muscular, like he had worked hard in the outdoors his whole life. He could get a good price out of this one.

Usually such specimens were dull minded, but he saw no dullness in the boy's dark eyes. Not even fear or worry, just a little nervous. It bothered that the boy was so calm and watchful.

The smallest one, Hania, watched him like an opponent or an adversary. There was a great deal of intelligence behind those eyes…a potion maker, apprentice healer no doubt. He felt a prickle of fear run up the back of his neck.

Nonsense, he turned away. We are the masters here; the Bloodstones have no equals.

He looked at the Bloodstone in his hand, why did that boy who threw the rock call them weaklings? This Chval was not telling the truth about these two. The smaller one…the one that made his hair rise. *I'll make him serve the wine…put him in his place…then use him to recharge the Stone.* He tossed the Stone in the air, caught it, and put it in his pouch.

Edur returned with the wine and a healer.

The healer checked the injured. "It's been years since anyone has had these kinds of wounds."

"What can you do for them?" Raghnall sent dark looks over at the slaves.

"Wash their cuts and burns in the old manner and wait. They have washed them with river water," The healer shook his head, "No telling what kinds of infections they may have picked up." He supervised the loading of the wounded onto stretchers for the return to Egil.

Raghnall turned back to the slave pen; that smaller boy was still staring at him.

"Is the food ready yet?" He barked at Istaqa.

"Yea, Lord Raghnall," Istaqa bowed, "And Edur brought the fine wine for your celebration."

"Good," Raghnall walked over to the pen, "You, boy, will serve the wine." Hania got to his feet with a slowness that showed his apprehension.

"And then you will serve another wine to the Stone." The boy's face blanched, he knew what that meant.

26

Conflicting emotions twisted inside Hania. There was excitement over the chance to spike the wine, allowing them to escape, and knowing his fate if he failed. He would be killed to feed the Bloodstone.

On shaking legs, he walked out of the slave pen, the wall slid up behind him. Glancing back he saw the white face of Skelly peering through the bars; he nodded at him in an encouraging way.

"This is the wine pitcher, over there are the urns of wine." Edur pointed to the spring with the point of a sharp carving knife and shoved him towards it.

Hania knelt at the spring's edge, it was cold, and the gravel bank shifted a little. Reaching out, he dragged the first urn over to him. He pulled the lid off; the sweet-sour smell of pungent wine filled the air. He poured half the mandrake powder into the urn, keeping an eye on the Bloodstones.

Would it work?

If I fail now, I will die, and the others will be slaves for the rest of their lives. Shaking, he poured the wine from the urn to the pitcher and back again to mix in the mandrake.

"What's taking you so long?" Raghnall shouted from a polished stone table. Like the slave pen, he had pulled it out of the ground. Hania jumped and almost dropped the pitcher, he filled it one last time and walked over to the table and began to fill their goblets.

He prayed that the Bloodstones would attribute his shaking to fear of them and not think anything was amiss.

The Bloodstones ate and drank until the first urn was gone. "More wine, boy," Raghnall slurred at him, the mandrake was starting to work. How much more would they need before they fell asleep?

Hania pulled the other urn from the spring and dumped the other half of the mandrake powder in and mixed it as before. What if we need mandrake? He filled an empty flask with the doctored wine before returning to the table, filling the goblets again.

"Wait, boy," Raghnall stopped him, "Taste the wine," He held out the goblet. Hania obeyed. Could he taste mandrake in the wine? As a believer, he did not partake of fermented wine; he wasn't sure what it usually tasted like, but he knew he would not be affected by the amount of mandrake that was in the sip of wine. Not by such a small amount, he hoped. He found he didn't care for fermented wine. To him, it tasted spoiled. How could people like it? He found it hard not to gag.

"Get back to work." Raghnall growled and joined in song with the rest of the Bloodstones.

Returning to the urn, he filled the pitcher and turned to the table. How much longer?

27

Onid was fulfilling her role; Kendra said it was time for her to go in search of the Spirit Warriors. So here she was. The first was to be a prophet, a young prophet…and then the core from Atwater…whatever that meant. She had prayed at the Shrine in Bainbridge and felt that Dennet was the place to start; also it was the closest.

Standing on the top of the pass, Onid looked down into the valley of Dennet; it appeared prosperous. The main town, small hamlets, farms, canals, and bridges were all neat and well laid out, it looked like what Kendra said all the land had been before the Great War. Although some of the country houses were rather large.

The road she was on, forked into two different paths; one way was well cared for and the other looked like it had been abandoned. Grass and saplings grew in the cracks of the paving blocks, where was the Shrine?

Kendra told her that the Ancient ones had built Shrines every one days walk to provide safe haven to pilgrims traveling to and from the holy sites. Onid put her hand in her pocket. Her fingers closed over the key Kendra had given her, a Shrine key.

One or more rooms were hidden at each site; believers near each site took care of the rooms. Kendra was the one for the site at Bainbridge and had shown Onid how to open the door to the safe haven. Was the quest that dangerous?

She glanced down the abandoned road as she drew level; she stopped and stared. Was that the Shrine? She turned and pushed her way through a tangle of Netted Chain Fern. It was a huge edifice; she stepped into what had once been a courtyard. Stepping over chunks of broken masonry, she worked her way in the direction of what looked like the Shrine near Bainbridge.

"You came." The voice made her jump; a skinny boy was sitting in the shadows.

They stared at each other, Onid swallowed, "What do you mean? Who were you expecting?"

"Do you want to open the chamber or do I?" The boy pulled out a key that was a match for Onid's; at her silence, he shrugged and stuck the key into the hole, a door in the wall behind him opened. He gestured for her to go first.

Entering the chamber, Onid could see it was larger than the one by Bainbridge. The boy, who she could now see had wavy sandy brown hair and gray eyes, sat down at a scrubbed wooden table, "I'm the caretaker here."

"How old are you?" Onid asked. That was dumb, his family must be the caretakers. "I mean," his smile just stayed there, "What's your name, and how long has your family been taking care of the Shrine?"

Why was it in such disrepair?

"I don't have a family." The boy reached into a bag and put some bread, hard cheese, and fruit on the table. "The caretakers had to leave or be killed. They," he looked down, "knew of my gifts…knew I wouldn't be caught." He grinned up at her, he was very pale…must not spend much time outdoors.

"Fill me in," She joined him at the table; he looked about eleven or twelve at the most. "You're an orphan?"

Nodding, he gave a quick prayer and began to nibble at his food, "My name is Farid. I had to sell myself into bondage or starve. I belong, until I make enough to buy my freedom, to the innkeeper that runs the Xavier Inn."

"What happened to the people that were the caretakers here?" She bit into the cheese, "Why didn't you sell yourself to them?"

The boy looked at the floor. "I had been with them from the time my mother died, but my gift showed me that I was to stay until you came."

At that Onid dropped the apple she was about to cut up. "You knew I was coming?"

The boy nodded. "I have seen you many times in my dreams, I was to stay here and warn you about the people of Dennet."

"What's wrong with them?"

"They have gone apostate. They told the believers to leave or join them, the caretakers refused to join."

"Why didn't you just leave?"

"I felt I had to stay."

"I feel…I have to go there," Onid whispered as a chill ran over her skin. She knew what he meant.

"You cannot be seen coming from the direction of the Shrine," Farid's soft-featured face hardened, "If they even think you are a believer, you can be captured and sold as a slave. Or worse."

"Slavery was abolished at the end of the Great War," Onid shook her head, and what was worse? That had sounded ominous.

"Oh, they don't call it slavery, they call it indentured servant or serf so as to skirt the law. They are very careful about following the letter of the law." Farid stood up and brushed the crumbs off his lap. "Leave everything here except the key and a small amount of gold, not much, just enough for a meal and to buy my freedom." He grinned, "No silver…silver is outlawed here."

"Outlawed?" Onid asked.

"It interferes with the Stones."

"Stones? They are using the Bloodstones?"

He nodded.

What excuse could I use to be traveling alone…and why would I need to buy a slave? She dumped her pack out on the table to see if that would give her any ideas.

"What are you doing?"

"I need a reason to be going into Dennet and buying a slave, or like you said, I could end up a slave myself." She sorted through the pile. Her survival gear was well used; all her weapons were silvered and would not be allowed.

"What are you good at?"

"I'm a Sword Master, I've been trained to be a warrior; I don't know how to make cloth or cook, I've worked my whole life in a Forge."

Farid looked at the pile of silvered weapons and grinned, "Are you an arms dealer?"

They both looked down at what Onid had dumped out, it did look like what a dealer would carry.

"But everything here is silvered," She bit her lip, "They won't like that."

Farid raised a calloused hand, "You are about to be let in on one of the most closely guarded secrets of the Green Crescent; in fact, only Xavier, Kendra, and I know of it." He moved over to a stone and pushed it aside revealing a hole, reaching inside he pulled up on a leaver.

With a grinding sound, part of the wall opened and Farid disappeared inside.

Onid followed and found herself in a narrow cave. Handholds carved in the wall led up to where the dim light of the fading sunset showed high above.

"It looks out over the valley," Farid said, "But that's not the secret." Another grinding noise came from behind her, "This is," he pulled her into the dark and she felt a door grind closed behind her.

Farid lit a torch and waved at the maze of tunnels leading away from them,

"Welcome to Prophet's Keep."

"What?"

"After the Green Crescent discovered the Bloodstones' weakness and drove them out, they came back one last time. They had with them a cadre of slaves that had been told if they defeated the Green Crescent rebels, they would be given their freedom." Farid headed down a tunnel, "The armory is over here."

"The slaves were promised freedom? That would be quite an incentive."

"A small garrison was stationed here, their leader was a prophet. They would sneak out at night, capture soldiers and bring them back here, give them their freedom early, arm them with silvered weapons and they would soon be fighting on our side."

"But not all of them would want to fight on our side," they reached a heavy wooden door and Farid opened it, leading her inside.

"That is where the prophet came in, he could tell if they were honest or not; the ones that were spies would wake up just where they had been, but without weapons." He grinned, "The others would wake up in one of our camps…only the garrison stationed here knew of this place." Farid stuck the torch in a holder on the wall.

Onid turned to see a wealth of weapons, thousands of swords, daggers, lances, you name it, and it was here. None silvered.

"Well…take your pick, the finest the Bloodstones ever made," Farid sat back with a twinkle in his gray eyes.

She had never seen some of these types of weapons before, but it didn't take long to pick out enough to make a good peddlers pack. She even took one very ornate long handled sword inset with gold and garnets; might make a good wall decoration.

They returned to the room behind the Shrine and Farid pulled a small sack of coins from under a sleeping cot, dumping out the contents.

Giving him a glance, she counted up the coins, "That doesn't seem very much."

"I have pretended to be mute and clumsy, the innkeeper said if I dropped one more tray of food they would sell me." That contagious grin was back.

"I hope you know what you are doing."

"The caretakers said I was given my gifts and a charge to never use them for any purpose other than to fight evil."

Onid put her foot up on a chair and pulled a silvered knife out of the hidden sheaf. Was he the boy prophet? It sure looked like it.

He handed her a plain dagger, "You may need this."

She slid it in. "What else will I need?"

"You're an arms dealer," Farid put the final touches on the arms display, "That should do it."

Nodding, she found herself obeying a child's words without fear; he must be the one. Setting aside her own sword, she tried out the balance of several blades before sliding one into the scabbard at her waist.

They dropped to their knees and said a quick prayer before leaving.

Farid led her around to a road that would take her into the main village, and then he disappeared back into the trees.

The Xavier Inn was large and well built; she walked in and ordered a meal. The innkeeper was a lady whose tongue ran as fast as her feet, she scampered around taking care of her clients. Her tongue jumping from table to table, from conversation to gossip, how did she keep all of them straight?

"Where are you from dear?" She placed the eating utensils in front of Onid.

"Here and there." Onid said.

"Farid!" The Innkeeper shouted, then leaned over and whispered, "I'm sorry dear…he is a bit slow…he's a believer in the old ways."

Old ways? What than were the new ways?

Soon the Innkeeper brought out a Bloodstone; all the people, one at a time, touched the Stone and thanked it for the food. They more than used the Stones; they worshiped them!

The Innkeeper held the Stone out in front of Onid, she took it and the Innkeeper beamed. Onid could see that it was from a Bloodstone Warrior's armor…flat on one side, faceted on the other. Closing her eyes and nodding, she gave it back. In her mind, she thanked the Great Spirit for the food, not the Stone.

Farid dropped a tray of food.

"That does it!" The Innkeeper shrieked, "Who wants this boy…this believer."

"How much?" Onid asked.

"You want him?" She asked.

"I get tired carrying the pack," Onid gestured at the pack by her chair.

"You're a merchant, then," the Innkeeper pushed Farid towards Onid. "Five gold pieces."

Onid paid her for the food and Farid.

"What are you peddling?" A couple of young men swaggered over from where tankards of strong drink were sold.

Onid turned to Farid, "Open the pack," she waved her hand at a nearby table. Farid put the pack on the table and opened it; the weapons gleamed in the firelight and candles of the dining area.

"Peddle your wares outside!" The Innkeeper waved them out, "I do not want my business dirtied with the arms trade." Farid grabbed the bundle and they went outside.

The taller boy, with blond wavy hair and an air of superiority, grinned and winked at his companion, then followed them.

Then he sauntered over to Farid and pulled a sword out Farid's arms. "I like this one...it is well balanced."

Onid felt as though she had walked into a chill wind from the north.

28

Hania carried another pitcher of wine to the table, the tall maidenhair ferns growing around the spring brushed against him, wetting his leggings. He had to be careful not to spill any of the doctored wine as it may take all of it to put the Bloodstones out of commission.

Raghnall had the Bloodstone out; he and the one called Vritra had their heads together, chuckling. As he came up to them Vritra sat back and smiled as he sipped the wine, shaking with suppressed laughter. He was the second tallest Bloodstone Warrior and his skin was tattooed with pictures of sharp instruments…swords, knifes, axes. His silent giggles making them all jiggle.

Raghnall flicked his hand at the slave pen; Skelly was tossed up and out. With care he got to his feet, a tether and collar flew out of a pack and fastened him to the pen.

"Give him some of that wine," Raghnall nodded at Skelly as he handed Hania his goblet.

Hania walked over, "Are there any silvered weapons left inside?" He asked as Skelly took a sip of the wine.

"No." Skelly looked at him hard as he shuttered. He didn't like fermented wine either.

Was that fear in his eyes or faith. Was he worried about him or for all of the Atwaters?

As he turned back and returned the goblet to Raghnall, he noticed that some of the Bloodstones were already asleep. They had drunk a lot of wine, so maybe Raghnall thought they were just drunk.

Hania waited by the table, the tension in his muscles growing as the full moon climbed into the sky. He filled up every goblet that looked like it needed more; Skelly waited by the pen.

As soon as the last of the Bloodstones had passed out, Hania rushed to Skelly's side. He tried to untie him.

"Don't waste time, we tried that already," Barra spoke from inside the pen.

Skelly turned away; swallowing hard…the gleams of unshed tears in his eye. "Get them out," he slumped against the pen.

"Get the rope out of that pack." Hania told Barra.

Barra tossed the end over the pen's top, Hania tied it to a tree, and after tossing the two packs out, the boys scrambled to freedom.

"Get going!" Skelly said brushing away a tear that had escaped, "And good luck."

"We must stay together, or we will fail," Hania looked at the others. "Who's with me?"

Chval jerked his head towards the Bloodstones. "How long before they wake?"

"Not until morning," Hania swallowed, *I hope.*

Glancing at the sky, Chval turned to the boys. "Go through all their packs…if it is eatable, eat it. Bring everything else here," he pointed at the ground next to Hania.

Barra brought the last of the venison over with some honey cakes, dates, and figs; then he dumped the pack he had under his arm at Hania feet. Only one sword and Barra strapped it on. "I'm better with the sword and you know it," he said at Chval's glare.

As they ate, Hania went through each pack, and the next one, and the next.

Chval went through what Hania discarded to see what they could use to survive, he picked up a knife and headed over to the table.

Hania looked up…he knew what would happen. He watched Chval walk up to Raghnall and stand there, shaking with anger or fear. He raised the knife over his head and with both hands, stabbed down.

He jerked it out and staggered back white faced; he came over to Hania.

"It's like stabbing water." He tossed the knife down and squatted next to the discard pile.

"We have to find something that is silvered." Hania said.

"We've looked through everything," Chval said, "I'm sorry."

Sorry…he was sorry? "I'm not leaving Skelly," he looked over at the Bloodstones.

Chval's eyes followed his gaze. "We'll search the Bloodstones…see if there is anything we can use." Chval headed that way.

Tesar hesitated, "Ah, I'll search over where they were treating the wounded." He grabbed a torch and disappeared.

Hania patted Skelly's big, strong arm, "We'll figure out something." He started to dig through his own stuff to see it there was anything he could use.

"Nothing." Barra had finished searching Istaqa and Zigor.

Dreogan stepped back, "Two more swords...plain, not silvered," he shot a look over to where Tesar had gone.

"Wait!" Chval was looking triumphant as he held Raghnall's Bloodstone aloft. "We'll use this...if it can be used to bind, it should be able to free him."

A chill ran through Hania. "I don't think the Stone will allow itself to be used by anyone but a Bloodstone Wizard."

Chval snorted. "It's just a tool."

"Okay, it's a tool...do you know how to use it? Did it come with instructions?" Hania took a guarded stance between Skelly and Chval trying to keep Chval away.

Chval pushed him aside. "We have to try everything, we just can't leave him here."

As soon as the Stone touched the bindings, they started to contract. No matter what Chval did, the collar got tighter around Skelly's neck.

"You're killing him!" Barra yanked Chval away from Skelly and tried to stop the collar from tightening any further. Nothing worked.

Skelly struggled against the collar, his lips turning blue.

Not thinking rationally, Hania grabbed the nearest thing in his pack, the pot of silver paint. He splashed a handful on the collar, it relaxed, and Skelly was able to breath.

Skelly leaned against the bars massaging his throat. "Thanks," he croaked out.

With all the silver that was on the collar, maybe a regular blade would cut it. Hania pulled out a dagger and sawed at it. Nothing happened.

Dreogan put silver paint on the end that was tied to the pen and tried to slide it up and off the fence. Again, they failed.

Chval put some on a knife and tried again to stab a Bloodstone, the paint just curled away with no effect. The same when they tried it on the collar.

"Just leave me," Skelly wiped away a tear, "I'm strong and I don't mind hard work."

"Skelly, if they give you a mate, your daughters will become concubines or they will kill them." Hania slumped against the smooth bars of the pen. *Please Great Spirit, he prayed, we have tried all that we can do...are we supposed to leave him? Do we kill him? What?*

"Hey." Came a cry from Tesar as he arrived running around the end of the pen. "Their healer left a pack behind...look what was in it!"

He held up what looked like a surgical knife, tiny, sharp, and silvered. Grinning, Tesar walked over to Skelly and hacked layer by layer through the collar.

As the collar fell away from Skelly, they gave a whoop of triumph.

"Quiet!" Chval hissed at them.

"Don't worry," Hania grinned as Skelly hugged Tesar, "nothing will wake them."

Grabbing the blade from Tesar, Dreogan moved towards Zigor. "It's payback time."

Just as he reached him, a sound of snapping underbrush came from the direction of Egil. Chval grabbed one of Dreogan's arms and Skelly grabbed the other.

"Come on...they're coming back...Bloodstones from Egil!" Barra grabbed up the few supplies they had sorted out, and they ran for it!

29

The boys had run for a while before Chval realized that he still had the Bloodstone in his hand.

"Stop!" Barra gasped out, "Take some of these!" He stopped and dropped the bundle of supplies onto the hard packed roadway.

"Sorry, we should have noticed," Dreogan divided the pile up.

"Now what?" Tesar picked out several knives, he was lousy with the bow, and he knew it.

"If we follow this road," Skelly picked a crossbow and bolts; "It should lead us to Bainbridge."

"It should…you're not sure?" Chval looked down, a few arrows and a knife; that was it.

"We just started on the maps of this area," Skelly shut his eyes, "How was Nabi to know we would need this knowledge?"

"Well, what does the prophecies say?" Barra asked, his finger stabbing at the sky as if that could bring forth an answer.

"We can't go back," Dreogan said. "Too many of the bridges are down."

"We go forward," Chval pointed. "We'll see where this leads and then decide." *Strange, I feel calm…is the Bloodstone giving me confidence?*

Hania had his eyes shut and his lips were moving silently. Chval shook his head, every time there was a problem; Hania could be counted on to pray to the Great Spirit.

Gods were for wimps. He looked at the Bloodstone in his hand, and a warrior always makes the best use of what is at hand. He bent down and picked up a pebble.

And a warrior puts forth the time to master any new weapon. He balanced the pebble in one hand and tried to move it with the Bloodstone.

As they plodded along, waiting for their breathing to slow, he slipped on some decomposing leaves, bringing him down on one knee. The sharp pain snapped him upright and then he saw it. The pebble…the pebble had stayed in the air, right where he had been holding it moments before. "Release," he whispered to the Stone, the pebble dropped.

Now, if I knew where the Bloodstones came out of the swamp and in what direction the path needs to go. Maybe it didn't matter…all we would have to do was get to an island…then Tesar could direct us in constructing a raft.

The possibilities raced though his mind as he searched along the swamp's edge, ignoring the pain in his knee. He remembered how the stones of the path lay on the Island of Salina's shore after the rest of the path was sunk.

Come on, come on, his hand squeezed the sharp faceted Bloodstone as he jogged along. The sky was clear and a full moon was helping them to escape; maybe the heavens were with them.

He glued his eyes to the swamp's edge, pausing and examining every promising area.

30

"Fifteen gold pieces," Onid held out her hand her eyes not leaving the arrogant young man's face. She found herself "reading" him, just as Sword Master Eno, had taught her. He was about three inches taller then her, his hair was sun bleached; yet he wasn't muscular. He wasn't skilled, at least not compared to her…but there was something in his eyes, his bearing.

The tall boy walked around as though he owned the town, maybe he did or someone close to him. He wasn't a worker as his clothes screamed out. Expensive. Her sword hand gripped the handle of her weapon.

As Farid rolled up the bundle, Onid saw him slip a dagger up his sleeve, good move. He repositioned himself behind the other boy; there was no one else close on the wide cobblestone street that ran in front of the Inn.

"Well, you see," the taller boy rubbed his chin, "That fifteen gold pieces is the price of duty you must pay to sell here in Dennet…a license fee." His friend smirked, watching her as Farid slipped up next to him.

Out of the corner of her eye, Onid noticed the townsfolk were disappearing off the streets; curtains flickered in the windows facing the road, *know what is around you at all times*, it was the voice of her Martial Arts Master Pallaton, directing her.

There was a smell of fear in the air. The common folk feared these young men.

Farid had a nervous, but determined look on his face, replacing his usual grin.

"You're a thief." Onid pulled out her sword while dropping her cloak; *I've had enough of this oaf and this upside down town.*

She took a relaxed, but guarded stand. As he walked around her, she could see that his training was poor; he had no idea how to hold a sword. After an obvious sign, he slashed out at her with the stolen sword. It was the ornate one, the most unbalance one she had ever hefted; couldn't he see that it was useless as a weapon?

Clang! She parried the stroke, guiding it easily to the ground, it sparked as it hit the stones; she drove her elbow back, smashing into his nose. He sat hard, yelping in pain as his rump hit the uneven surface of the cobblestones before glancing around for his friend, his long blond hair over his face as red started trickling down to his chin. "You broke my nose!"

His brown haired friend was too surprised to move. Farid was holding the dagger to the side of his neck, the point resting against his jugular.

As she held the point of her sword directed at the blond boy's neck, he dropped the handle end of the stolen blade

"You're not skilled enough for a sword...even from the forge of Cerebrus and forget Bainbridge, there you are unworthy to even use a butter knife." She flicked the fallen sword up and caught it with a flourish.

He struggled to his feet, "Let's go," he snarled at the other boy and they left.

Farid rushed over, "We have to go now."

"We haven't finished eating." Onid retrieved her cloak.

"He is going to get the rest of his gang!" Farid yanked on her arm.

That made sense; rats ran in packs. She re-sheathed her sword, "Then call for the sheriff, or whomever the authorities are in this town."

"His father is the sheriff!" Farid hissed as he pulled her across the bridge into the darkness of the woods.

31

"I hope they stop and wait for us." Skelly grumped.

Hania laughed. "Knowing them, they'll be getting into trouble."

"And we will be pulling them out again?" Skelly looked east, "Sun will be up soon. How long will the Bloodstone's be asleep?"

"Not sure." Hania looked back the way they came, trying to think where could they hole up for a few days. Once again he racked his brain for clues to what they should do.

"You're being very quiet."

Hania sighed, "Skelly, I'm worried…are we are up to this? Are we the Spirit Warriors?"

"What else can we do? Become slaves?"

Hania nodded and smiled. "Skelly, you do know how to put things into perspective…and there is something else bothering me."

"What's that?"

"When you go hunting and the prey gets away, do you keep following it? Even when there is easier prey at hand?"

"I see what you mean. Dennet would be easier…much easier."

"They were heading for Atwater." Hania shivered and at that moment he knew what he had just said was the truth.

"Caught up to the boys." Skelly gestured ahead.

Chval was standing off to the side, his back to the road, studying something at the edge of the swamp. The rest were slumped on some handy boulders, they did not look like they were happy to be waiting for them. Why hadn't they just gone on? Who had called for the rest stop?

Chval spun around; he had a triumphant gleam in his eyes, which was a signal to Hania and Skelly that something unpleasant was about to happen. Who else was in on it?

Hania moved closer to Skelly. Keeping Chval in the corner of his eye, he let his glaze flick around the other boys. They looked uninterested. What was going on?

"About time you got here, we were thinking about going on without you," Dreogan glared at them.

"How long before the Bloodstones wake and follow us?" Barra asked. He was working the bolt back and forth on the cross bow he had liberated from one of the Bloodstones. Too bad he didn't have any silvered bolts to go with it.

"I don't know," Hania said, "That is…"

Breathing hard, Dreogan jerked upright. "You don't know?"

"Dreogan, calm down," Chval said, "We're going home, I promise." He leaned unconcerned against a Black Gum tree and grinned over at Dreogan.

Dreogan shot a worried look back down the road. "You didn't go through what I did back there."

"Maybe you are already broken," taunted Barra.

Dreogan jumped at Barra, "Take that back!"

Tesar grabbed at Dreogan trying to pull him off Barra; soon all three were indistinguishable as they rolled around on the ground.

"You know," Chval said scratching his chin. "I have a half of mind to leave them there."

Skelly looked at Hania and Hania nodded; Skelly pulled Barra out of the pile, then Dreogan.

"You sure do know how to ruin a good fight," Chval said.

"If we don't stick together, we will fail," Hania shook his head, "We are fighting the Bloodstones, remember?"

Dreogan looked at Hania and nodded. "I'm sorry Barra…Hania's right."

Barra laughed. "Well, it was a good practice round."

"You're a couple of jerks." Tesar said as he dusted off.

Chval scowled over from the tree; pushing away, he returned to the water's edge.

"We have a decision to make. Stay on the road or take to the hills." Barra said.

"The road is the quickest route to Bainbridge." Skelly bent down and drew a map in the dust. "This way, leads to a wilderness pathway, you have to climb through a high mountain pass."

"What is over that way?" Dreogan hunkered down next to Skelly.

"Dennet is in this valley," Skelly pointed, "And this is Egil."

"Egil is where the Bloodstones are," Barra stabbed the map with a twig he had pulled of a nearby tree, "Egil and Dennet are that close together?"

"Was Egil a Green Crescent Clan?" Asked Dreogan.

"It was a fishing village, the Bloodstones turned it into a slave market. When we drove the Bloodstones out, it became a ghost town. No one has ever resettled there…most say it has a evil feel to it." Skelly added more details to the map as he remembered them.

"What about Dennet?" Barra asked as he twirled the twig between his hands.

"No. Although they fought beside us in the Great War, they have always retained their autonomy."

"So," Barra said, "The choices are, the trail that leads over the pass to Dennet, then to Bainbridge, with luck, shaking off the Bloodstones…"

"Or straight to Bainbridge with the Bloodstones hot on our tail." Dreogan shook his head.

"Or," Chval said with a gleam in his eye, "Straight to Atwater, using the Bloodstones magic against them."

"What are you talking about?" Dreogan asked.

"One of fragments I read said that the Spirit Warriors could turn the magic back against the Bloodstones." Chval had a proud look on his face as he pulled out the Bloodstone.

Dreogan jumped back, repelled by even the sight of it.

"Are you mad?" Skelly blurted out.

Hania stared at it, was it his imagination? There was a halo of darkness around it, pulsating with evil. He swallowed and tried to speak, but no words came out.

"See these stones here?" Chval pointed down at the bank's edge. "This is where they came out of the swamp; we can use the Stone to raise the pathway again." He pointed into the swamp. "It will lead back to Salina; then we drop it and raise the one to Manhood Island."

"Won't they follow us?" Barra asked, "They must have other Stones."

"If we go fast enough, we will be back to Atwater before they figure out where we've gone."

Hania shut his eyes and shook his head to clear his mind; he knew somehow that it wouldn't work. He heard them arguing through the ringing of his ears, it was like he was under water.

"What makes you think you can work the Stone?" Barra asked.

"Just watch," Chval ordered.

Hania couldn't help himself. "Don't use it!"

Chval turned and cocked his head. "Got a better plan? You said we were the Spirit Warriors. Have you changed your mind about that?"

In despair, Hania bowed his head; opening his eyes he looked up. Chval had turned, holding his hand out over the swamp.

"Rise!" Chval ordered. A stone path, like the one that they had crossed to get to Salina arose dripping wet through the surface of the swamp.

Chills caused Hania's hair to rise with the path; this was wrong, this was very, very wrong.

With caution, Dreogan stepped onto the path, "It feels like the one before." He bounced on it before returning to land.

Something was different; Hania struggled to put his finger on it.

"Now watch," Chval grinned, "Lower," the pathway sunk, "Rise!" He turned, eyes triumphant.

"We will be home before nightfall!" Barra jumped onto the path, he hunched down sighting along an outstretched arm. "North east...back to Salina."

"We can't go." Hania said.

"Why not?" Chval turned on him.

"It feels wrong." Hania looked at the pathway, *I know we shouldn't go but I don't know why.*

"It feels wrong?" Chval waved his arm towards the path, "You don't want us to return home because it feels wrong?"

"Of course not. But you can't force the Bloodstone to do good, it goes against its nature."

"Against its nature?" Chval laughed, "It's a tool. You talk as if it were alive."

"During the Great War, our side tried to use captured Bloodstones." Skelly shook his head. "It never worked, something always went wrong."

"Well, I'm going," Chval turned to the others, "Who's with me?"

Barra followed Chval onto the path. "I'll risk it."

Hania turned to the others. "It won't work!"

Tesar and Dreogan looked uncertain. They looked at Chval who was glaring at them to Hania and back. Then the years of blind obedience to Chval worked against them, they moved onto the path.

"It won't work." Hania said as his head drooped; the sound of the swamp seemed to increase in volume, *that was it!*

"Let's get going." Skelly tugged on his arm.

"It's already turning against them." Hania stepped one foot unto the path.

"What do you mean?" Skelly asked.

"Listen."

"So?" Skelly shrugged.

"Remember how quiet it was last time?" Hania took another step as the wake of an anaconda or caiman passed under the path. "Last time, you couldn't hear a thing, it was as if the Stone was pushing the wildlife away from the path."

They both pointed their ears toward the swamp; the sound was very different.

"I don't hear normal bird or insect sounds." Skelly took a step onto the path and dropped to one knee, his sharp eyes probed the water.

"It is as if the Stone is calling the predators towards the path." Hania took another step as Skelly stood up.

Skelly pulled Hania off the path. "They're heading into an ambush and they don't even know it."

"Those boys have been hunting along side their fathers for as long as we have." Hania started pacing up and down the hard packed trail, his eyes glued to the Bloodstone path.

"The Stone may have deafened their ears." Skelly scratched his chin.

Hania stopped…he had made up his mind…he was going to risk his life again. *Why do I feel I have to do this? Was it because it is a way to make my life meaningful? So when I can no longer walk or speak, my clan would want to care for me because I once had been a hero? Or was it something else?*

"Still have that rope, Skelly?" Hania turned and looked around for a suitable tree.

Skelly set down his pack and pulled the rope out. "We're going to save their sorry hides again?"

"Yup." Hania passed the rope around a birch tree that seemed to have been planted there for just this reason and tied one end around his waist.

Skelly stopped him, "That knot will slip," he retied it.

"Thanks Skelly." He looked up at his big friend and gave a weak grin before turning and looking down the path that ran alongside the swamp.

"Looks like a flat run." Skelly tied the other end around his waist. "Well, let's get this over with."

As Hania started down the path of stones leading into the swamp, Skelly played out the rope. At last they had stretched the rope to its full length.

There was no sight or sound of the boys, Hania looked around. The growls and hisses of the swamp predators were all he could hear; even the nighttime owls and marsupials were active. A shadow passed overhead...vultures, owls, and hawks were circling together!

He swallowed as chills crawled down his back; he looked at Skelly, which calmed him. At the first sign of trouble, Skelly would do all in his power to pull him to safety. *But is he strong enough to pull all of us?*

A movement to the right caught his eye, he froze, a lizard's head pushed up out a patch of scarlet Astilbe. A chameleon, he relaxed and turned his eyes back down the path.

He shifted his weight and his foot sank into the fetid water; he looked down in alarm, did that mean the path was sinking? Had they made it back to Salina or had the Stone turned on them...stranding them in the middle of the Swamp?

He turned; ready to give Skelly the signal and saw that he was kicking sprinter holes into the ground, getting ready to run.

A deep snarl to his left made him jump. He couldn't see the puma, but the silent movement of greenery in that direction meant the great cat was stalking near the path.

He stepped back, his foot sinking deeper; the path was, without a doubt, going. He moved back to where the path crossed a small hillock; Skelly pulled up the slack and dug new footholds.

Hania prayed with his eyes wide open, not daring to shut them. Another rustling in the undergrowth; two Gahiji lizards hissed at each other.

This was not the breeding season for the Gahiji, yet the two of them are behaving as if they were battling over some female. The two lizards danced around, hissing and snapping at each other. Their crimson colored ruffs flared out in proud display.

Was this pair the only ones along the path that were acting aggressive out of season? He turned his head in the direction the boys had gone, had they noticed the odd way the swamp predators were acting?

His eyes could only see green; he uncapped and swallowed some Fo-ti juice, the swamp was getting louder. It's as if every predator in the area was making a beeline for the path. Rumbling challenges were coming from every direction. Where were they? Was he wasting his time out here? Had they made it to Salina? Was Chval right? Was the Bloodstone just a tool? *No, somehow I know they are in danger.*

32

Raghnall felt a sharp prodding between his shoulder blades, blinking his eyes he tried to bring them into focus. When they cleared, he saw a pair of highly polished ornate boots. Only Murdoc would wear a pair like that in the wilderness.

He shut his eyes; letting his other senses wake and take stock of where he was. From the feel of cool gritty soil against his cheek, he knew he was lying on the ground like a common drunkard.

He could hear several men clearing their throats, how many men had that dratted Murdoc brought from his ship? Through the pounding in his head, he could hear the snores of his own elite corps of men rise around him.

This did not make sense...there had been only two jugs of wine. That meant no more than four goblets of wine each; that was not enough to cause such a lasting drunkenness.

He pushed himself off the ground as he pushed down the humiliation at being caught like this, might as well get it over with. "Hello, Murdoc." He put his hand into his pocket to pull out his Stone; it was empty. Had Murdoc taken it? He glanced over at his 'perfect' brother. The amusement coming from those coal black eyes galled him.

"Heard you had captured some Atwaters. Had to come and see for myself." Murdoc stroked his well-trimmed goatee.

Raghnall looked at the men that stood around the encampment, some were from his own ship. They looked puzzled and a bit nervous.

"Well?" Murdoc said clapping his hands together, "Where are they? I would like to buy a couple of them myself."

Raghnall turned in the direction of the slave pen; the bile that had been gurgling in his belly was now working its way into his throat. The pen was empty. He turned towards the wine jugs, three long strides took him over to them, and picking one up, he sniffed at it suspiciously. With caution, he tasted it; there was a slight bitterness to it; *why didn't I notice it last night?* He gestured over one of the men from his ship.

"Drink this!" He ordered, "Four goblets." The man did as he was told, none of the men lying around looked dead.

"So, what are you doing in these parts?" Raghnall bushed the dirt from his clothes with as much dignity as he could as another man from his ship rushed over with his ceremonial robe and dagger.

"Curiosity…heard you were going on a raid into Green Crescent lands." Murdoc pulled a chair up with his Stone. "When the men on your ship said you had captured six Atwater bucks, I came to congratulate you and to make an offer."

Raghnall was finding it hard to remain impassive when everything he had been working on for the past ten years, had just disappeared overnight. *All the practicing I've done with the Stones…making them do things they had never done in the past.* He strapped on the dagger as his man draped the robe over his shoulders.

"Well…see for yourself," Raghnall bit out, "The dratted beasts escaped."

"Sit down…relax," Murdoc gestured to a spot in front of him, "Pull up a chair."

Frustration filled Raghnall and he could feel a muscle twitch. The one that had always twitched when they were boys and Murdoc had beaten him at something.

Murdoc was enjoying this; that same little smirk of a smile was playing at the corners of his mouth.

Even Aja was out cold. He walked over and slipped Aja's stone out of his pocket, he won't need it any time soon. He picked up the boy and carried him over to a soft mossy spot under some trees.

Aja's Stone was related to Raghnall's Stone and would work better than any other. Raghnall held the Stone in his hand; Find he whispered, while concentrating on his own Stone.

A flash of red pointed north, along the swamp's edge. So…Murdoc was not at fault…one of those dratted Atwater brats must have taken it. He felt himself relax. Murdoc doesn't know I'm vulnerable.

"So…what happened?" Murdoc called over as the warrior from the ship dropped to the ground.

"It's obvious," pulling up a chair with Aja's Stone, Raghnall sat. "We were drugged."

"How big of a head start do you think they have?" Murdoc flicked a speck of dust off his sleeve.

"I have a couple of ways to slow them down…or stop them cold," Raghnall leaned back. Don't panic…don't let Murdoc see even the least bit of panic. "Want to watch? It may prove to be…educational."

Murdoc stood and yawned. "As entertaining as that might be," He sauntered past the slave pen, his eyes giving it a fleeting glance. "I'll just wait on my ship…hiking was never my style."

Hiking was never my style? Raghnall sneered as Murdoc and his men returned to Egil. Well, that was the truth…he was good at sneaking, cheating, spying, and copying. Actually working? No.

He pulled Aja's Stone out, now to punish the fool that took my Stone.

33

Chval shivered as he strode along the pathway, his heart pounding with excitement; I'm going to be a hero, a hero like my Great Grandfather.

The pathway's stones were wet and slippery, but other than that they were firm. Skelly and Hania, why hadn't they come with us? That part worried him, but I gave them every chance…the boys will back me up; they saw what happened.

As he pushed aside some hanging moss, a lizard dropped from the tree and scurried away. Pride, that was it, Hania wants to be the leader of the Spirit Warriors.

"Ah…Chval?" Dreogan called from behind, "Was the other pathway?…I mean."

"What!"

"It's the wildlife…I don't remember…"

"Remember what!"

"The wildlife is not acting as it should," Barra cut in.

Chval stopped. He didn't want to admit it, but it was making him nervous as well, I hate this whole, stinking swamp!

Barra stepped forward and pointed at the sky. "Owls, hawks, crows, and all of the other hunting and carrion eaters," Barra turned around, eyes searching, "Together at once? And half of them come out only at night."

He clutched Chval's arm, "Look!" He said in awed reverence, "A Thunderbird!"

They all looked up. The rarely seen blue brown giant eagle suddenly dived and then rose with an anaconda in its talons.

"It's a sign!" Smiled Chval. "A sign of our victory." The Thunderbird sailed out of sight.

"But…" Dreogan said peering into the swamp around them, "There are lizards, caimans, snakes, and raccoons all around us…following. And I am sure I heard a puma or jaguar back that way," he pointed.

Chval glared at them, "Have I ever led you into danger?" He challenged both of them with his eyes; they looked down in submission.

"If we just hurry, we will be home before any of them can get near us." Tesar piped up.

Chval could feel the anger rise inside him, why hadn't Hania told us this could happen? "What is it, Tesar?"

Tesar was tugging at his arm; he jerked away from him and turned, there on the pathway, blocking the way was a Gahiji Lizard, a big one. No doubt stopping to argue with Barra and Dreogan had allowed it to get ahead of them.

He glanced down at the Stone, maybe I could use it to push the beast away and any others as well...that would shut them up. Why wouldn't they just follow me like before? Why all these questions?

He held the Stone in front of him; Go away, he ordered with his mind. The lizard hissed and thrashed its tail before lowering its ruff in submission and moving off the path into the undergrowth.

That did it! Now I'll take care of the others. He concentrated hard; go away! He pushed at the predators until the swamp grew quiet.

"Chval?" Dreogan's voice was quivering.

"What now?" Chval turned, irritated with all the nagging.

"The path is sinking!"

Chval standing on a hillock, hadn't noticed, "Oh...okay." Rise, he ordered the path, again it rose and firmed up.

"Let's go." It looks like it is going to be a balancing act between maintaining the path and keeping the predators away; I can do that.

They moved past the hillock and started over what looked like a sluggish river. "How about spearing us some fish for supper?" He called to Dreogan; get their minds on something else...I'll handle the danger.

The Stone in his hand started to get warm. What did that mean? It was getting more uncomfortable and he grabbed a handful his tunic, it was even hotter!

"Hey, the animals!" Barra's voice rang out.

It was like trying to hold onto a burning coal! It seared its way through the cloth, burning his hand.

"The pathway is sinking!" Tesar was backing away.

Chval had no choice; he dropped the Stone. It sizzled as it splashed though the path as if it had been water. "Head for dry land!"

They rushed for the hillock they had just crossed, where the Gahiji Lizard had stood in the pathway. Tesar slipped and fell down.

Chval needed to get where it was safe to put his hand in cool water. "Grab him," he ordered Dreogan and Barra as he jumped over him and kept going. The pathway was sinking back into the swamp…that dratted Hania should have warned us.

Tesar screamed out in pain.

"Kill it, quick!" Dreogan called out.

Chval didn't dare turn back to see…the pathway was getting wobbly…it was all he could do to keep running.

Hania must have purposely kept back some knowledge about the Bloodstones, just to become the leader of the Spirit Warriors; that was it. He wants to be the leader. I've seen it in the looks he sometimes gives Skelly; I bet he's told Skelly more than the rest of us. The two of them are in this together.

Up ahead he could see a figure waiting on the pathway; it was Hania. Waiting for them to come crawling back to him. It galled him to his core, that upstart!

34

Was that a human cry? Hania moved away from the hillock, the pathway was less firm than it had been, what did that mean? He looked back at Skelly, had he heard the cry as well?

He turned back as the first of the boys came into sight, running towards him, he felt a rush of relief. Who was it?

Chval! He bumped into him as he pushed by holding his hand. 'Two injured, staggering back toward land' was in the prophecies, Chval and who else?

Barra and Dreogan came panting, pulling Tesar between them. What had happened to him? Barra and Dreogan shoved Tesar into Hania's arms.

Hania locked his arms around Tesar and nodded at the other two as they moved up the rope and grabbed on.

"Now!" Barra shouted and with three pulling, they were yanked, dripping wet, out of the swamp.

Barra reached the shore, turned around, and fitted a bolt to his crossbow; his eyes scanned the water. Skelly and Dreogan kept pulling as a bolt flew, and with a splash an anaconda turned away from its intended meal.

Dreogan pulled Hania and Tesar higher up the bank, "What is with the swamp animals?" He gasped out.

A caiman launched itself out of the water towards them; Barra's second bolt stopped it.

Dreogan and Hania pulled Tesar farther from the swamp.

"What bit him?" Hania asked as he untied the rope from around his chest.

"Gahiji Lizard." Dreogan turned Tesar around so Hania could see the marks in his leggings where the sharp teeth had cut right through to the flesh, not good.

Barra walked over and stood between them and the swamp, his eyes sweeping the shoreline for any other predators. "Left a spear in it. Didn't dare take a chance retrieving it, the spear, that is."

"Didn't have time," Dreogan panted, "Path was sinking."

Hania split Tesar leggings, exposing the bite; it was already purple and festering, the poison from Gahiji bites always worked fast. The leather had stopped the teeth from making a closed wound. Instead, it would be like two smaller wounds. I won't have to cut out as much. He pulled back the top bite, letting it bleed freely and then repeated with the bottom.

"What can we do to help?" Barra asked.

"We'll need a fire." Hania cut a strip off Tesar's leggings.

"Fire? Build one this close to the Bloodstones? Are you crazy?" Chval was sitting on a boulder rocking back and forth.

Hania fashioned the strip into a tourniquet around Tesar leg and tightened it. "We have to sear the wound, or he will lose his leg. I need the blood from the caiman."

Skelly nodded and taking his knife, drained the caiman into a container Hania tossed him.

"What makes you think you know how to take care of it?" Chval glared over at him.

"Quiet! Both of you," Barra said, "We can make a portable fire." He pulled his shirt off and walked over to the waters edge. "Dreogan!" Dreogan moved over by him and watched the water for any sign of life, his spear ready.

Barra pulled up several handfuls of reeds and laid them on the shirt with two underneath lashing them together with younger more supple growth. Then he dug up some of the drier mud and smoothed it over the reeds. "Portable hearth," He shrugged.

"I'll make a litter to carry him." Skelly moved into the trees looking for a couple of saplings.

"What about me? What about my wound?" Chval held up a trembling hand.

Hania rummaged around in his supplies and found a jar of salve and tossed it over to him.

"What do I wrap it with?" Chval slapped on more than he needed.

"Cut off a piece of your shirt." Tesar said between gritted teeth.

"Do you know how much this shirt cost?" Chval said, holding up a corner of the yoke. "It's silk!"

The looks he got from the rest of the boys told him, none of them cared. He tore off a strip and tried to wrap it around his hand.

With a sigh, Dreogan stomped over and helped him do it right.

Barra was busy lashing together a harness, with whatever he could find, for the portable hearth. Dreogan left to help Skelly make a litter with the rope and two birch saplings.

"Tesar, could you count to ten, loosen the tourniquet, count to five, and then tighten it again?" He nodded; Hania poured half of the blood from the caiman over the wound.

"What are you doing?" Chval shuttered.

"If you had spent any time with your maternal grandfather, he would have told you, caiman blood stops most infections."

Tesar nodded, "I'm glad you're here...and that you know what you're doing."

Hania patted him on the shoulder. "Hope you feel the same way after the searing." He stood, I need moss for the binding; he headed for the trees, passing by Dreogan and Skelly.

"What else do we need?" Skelly looked up from where they were lashing the litter together, "We're almost done here."

"Blue fly larvae," Hania fished through the wilderness kit and found another empty container. "Look for something dead...just follow your nose." He grinned at the look of revulsion on Dreogan's face and returned to his hunt for moss.

The cool shade under the trees revitalized him. It didn't take long to find enough moss; soon his pouch was full. He gazed in the swamp's direction.

The sense of responsibility hit him; I know I can't get them back home without help. He found a secluded spot and knelt down. Father, we need your help...I need your help...he told The Great Spirit what he had planned to do and if that was what he should be doing. I need help with Chval; he makes me so angry. Give me wisdom to know how to treat the wounds and the effects of Bloodstone magic. I have not reached that level in my schooling...he wiped away the tears.

A feeling of calmness filled him; he got to his feet and returned to the group. Tesar was now on the litter; Chval and Barra were ready with the portable hearth.

Skelly handed Hania the container of larvae; Dreogan was washing, whatever it was they had gotten them from, off his hands in a nearby stream. Hania checked Tesar's wound and gathered up the rest of his leggings.

Skelly retrieved the caiman Barra had shot; it would do for supper.

As they shuffled down the trail, Chval whined about his burnt hand. "Why can't you help carry this firepot?" He asked Hania.

"Do you know what wood burns with less smoke?" Barra asked.

He did not answer as Hania darted off the path into the dark of the woods.

Father, please give me the strength to ignore Chval when he…he didn't know what to pray for. He broke off the old dry twigs of the hardwood trees of this area, staying away from the pine as it gave off too much smoke. A tea tree! What a find, the leaves were great infection fighters; shaking with excitement, he gathered the leaves.

Catching up with the boys on the trail, he handed Barra the twigs, and went to check on Tesar, the poison was starting to liquefy the flesh. "It's time," he said, "We can't wait any longer." They set Tesar down while Hania picked out a couple of knives and stuck them into the hot coals of Barra's portable hearth.

"Tesar, the choice is yours," he pulled out the flask of mandrake-laced wine. "I can give you some of this or you can have Skelly and Barra sit on you."

Tesar looked at the flask. "You need that stuff, don't you? I've seen you and Skelly drink it all the time."

"No, this one has mandrake-laced wine. The Fo-ti juice is in the other ones."

"Is that the stuff you used on the Bloodstones?" Tesar gave a weak grin, "What else will it do?"

"If I give you too much, it will make you throw up and give you diarrhea." Hania put his hand on his shoulder, "I have to sear away as much of the bitten area as possible. It's going to hurt a lot, and I can't have you jerking around while I do it."

"Well…" he looked at Skelly and Barra, "I might throw the two of them into the swamp, but if they are willing…"

Hania put the flask away. They moved Tesar off the litter, then Skelly positioned himself at Tesar's feet and Barra straddled the small of his back and grabbed him at the knees.

Hania took a deep breath and said a quick prayer; he picked up a third knife, checked the blade, and stuck it in the coals. He pulled a hot one out, nodded to Skelly and Barra to let them know he was ready to start. They leaned forward, tightening their grip.

He started where the moon shaped teeth marks were the farthest apart. The smell of burnt flesh mingled with the sharp intakes of breath coming from Tesar. He switched knives and kept going.

Tesar was digging holes into the ground with both hands, yet he was trying very hard not to move.

"I'm going…ah…to check our back trail…see if we are being followed," Chval said as he left.

"Coward." Muttered Dreogan as he added more hardwood twigs to the fire and blew on it to keep the coals hot.

Hania kept opening and closing the tourniquet to check his progress. Sweat trickled down his temples and brow that had nothing to do with the heat coming from Barra's fire hearth.

Chval returned. "I don't think they're following…how are you coming?"

Hania removed the tourniquet; there was no seepage. He set aside the knife and checked the wound carefully. "I think I got it all."

There was a collective release of breath. Hania slipped the piece of legging under the wound, packing it with some of the moss. Barra and Skelly got off Tesar and started gathering up their supplies.

Hania walked over to the shade of a tree where he had dropped his pack, retrieving the container of maggots. Chval followed.

"Are you going to leave the wound open like that?"

Hania shook his head; that was rich…it was because of Chval that Tesar had the wound in the first place. He shot Chval a look of disgust.

Returning to Tesar he knelt by his head. "What I'm going to do will seem very stupid, but it will help you to heal." He opened the container of maggots.

"Am I supposed to eat those?" Tesar asked weakly.

"No, they are going eat you…well, they'll eat all dead flesh in and around the wound. They don't bother live flesh, it will prevent gangrene."

Tesar nodded and leaning up on an elbow to watch as Hania dumped the maggots onto the wound.

Hania bruised the tea tree leaves and mixed them with moss and the last of the now sticky caiman blood, then packed the wound with it and bound it up using the length of legging and some thongs.

Chval looked on with shock, "You trust him?" He turned to Tesar, "You might lose your leg, and it will be his fault!"

"If I lose my leg, it won't be his fault," Tesar said as Hania cinched up the thongs, "It will be yours."

Chval turned and stomped off into the shrubbery; Skelly and Barra helped Tesar back onto the litter.

"We better get going," Barra said. "We can take turns carrying him."

Dreogan picked up one end and Barra the other.

Hania checked to make sure they didn't leave anything they might need.

They headed out, Skelly in the lead. The map in his head is the only one we have, I hope Skelly was a real good student and Nabi was an excellent teacher. Chval sulked along at the column's rear.

35

Farid took Onid in a long roundabout way back to the Shrine. He knew of more places to hide as they stayed one step ahead of the sheriff's arrogant son and the others. It was the next afternoon before they safely reached the Shrine. After unlocking the hidden room and entering, he turned to her.

"You told him where you are from?" He paced around a bit before leaning forward against the table, his head down.

"I named two places…what's wrong?" Onid looked at him, his reaction to what happened in the town was puzzling.

"There's no such thing as trade with Cerebrus; they wouldn't even consider it." Farid looked up; there was a tear trickling down his cheek. "The corruption of the people of Dennet goes beyond their using of the Stones, they have lost their souls. Power and profit is all that matters now."

"But what has that got to do with me telling where I'm from?"

"It has to do with appearances. The more they become corrupt, the more they have to put up false fronts of law-abiding exactness, they've twisted the laws until they have driven all the true believers out of the land."

Farid sat and looked up at her. "There are more lawyers in Dennet then the rest of the Green Crescent, doesn't that tell you something?"

"But what has that got to do with Bainbridge?"

"You put up a fight! They will go to Bainbridge and make false accusations, even plant false evidence just to punish you and to make themselves look good."

"Kendra is the judge and record keeper of Bainbridge, she is also a Prophetess, she'll see right though it."

"It's more than that. They over react whenever they lose face," Farid turned around, "They will accuse Bainbridge of deceit and lies. Maybe even go to war over it."

Onid looked down at the solid rock floor, shaking her head, things are getting more complicated. I shouldn't be surprised; the Prophecies said that the split between good and evil would increase.

It looked like Dennet leaned towards evil. Farid raised his hand for silence and moved over to the wall, unlatched something, and removed a block of stone.

She hadn't heard anything, but Farid seemed to be the Prophet of the Spirit Warriors. Whether he has very keen hearing or the Great Spirit warned him of visitors, I don't know, but I'm glad he's on our side.

She moved next to him, they could now see and hear what was going on inside the Shrine. Five young men were searching for them.

"I don't think anyone is here." A skinny young man said as he pushed over a block of stone.

The Sheriff's son hit him across the face with the back of his hand. "That deaf-mute is always coming here," he snarled.

"Now what?" The young man that Farid had held the knife on, slumped down on an overturned statue, "The towns people saw what happened...they are already whispering...laughing behind our backs."

"We need to bring her back in shame." The Sheriff's son turned and glared in the direction of Bainbridge, "Let's go see my father. He'll call up the Brotherhood...they'll know how to handle this kind of mess."

They stomped out of the Shrine and disappeared down the hill.

Onid looked at Farid, "The Brotherhood?" He looked grim as he replaced the stone and locked it back in place.

"The Brotherhood of the Stone," Farid looked at her with a half smile, "It's a secret society. They want to rule the entire known world, for its own good...and their gain."

"How do you know of this?" Onid asked; most secret societies were careful to keep their true ambitions hidden.

"They think I am a deaf-mute," his grin broadened, "Many a time I have served them in the inn's back room. When they are drunk, they talk," then his face darkened. "They have been talking about," he shuttered, "Sacrificing a human, to feed the Stones."

"What have they been using?" Onid wasn't surprised, if it looked like the Bloodstone's were to soon be defeated, the evil one would be looking for a replacement.

"Animals...pigs mostly," Farid looked thoughtful, "You know, I'm glad you came, after all...I think they were planning on using me."

"We can't stay here," Onid started to pace, "And we can't return to

Bainbridge. At least, not directly," that nagging feeling that she had to find the Spirit Warriors was back, she looked over at Farid, I'm sure he's the prophet. Will I have to travel all over the place finding them one at a time?

Back at Bainbridge she prayed at the Shrine's altar and had been led here; but the altar here had been destroyed, its pieces littered the Shrine.

"I don't know where to go next." She admitted to Farid.

"What led you here?" He was gathering up supplies hidden in nooks, under the bunk beds, and even in the ceiling as if this time had been foretold. Perhaps it had.

"The altar isn't out there, is it? It's hidden in here…am I right?" It sounded foolish even as she asked it, yet in her heart she prayed that it was so.

Farid grinned and motioned her to the end of the wooden table. He took the other end, "lift," he commanded.

As the pedestal rose off the floor, the altar appeared, as they set the table aside, tears of relief welled up and spilled unheeded down her face. Chills ran over her skin as she sank in relief to the floor beside it.

Farid knelt beside her, "The Believers saw what was happening and prayed about what to do. Xavier's predecessor saw this day, and had them move the altar into here; then most of them left, with only one family remaining here to prepare for this day."

"The caretakers?" Onid asked.

"They wouldn't join the Stone Cult and they wouldn't leave so…" He pushed away the tears.

Onid understood. Farid was the last of his family, would I have had the courage to carry on without family or friends? But then, she remembered, you are never alone; The Great Spirit, was always with you when you put your trust in Him, and were willing to follow the Spirit…wasn't that what the Spirit Warriors were all about? And wasn't Farid, she finally admitted that he was the one she came here for, and herself part of that?

She put her hand on his small shoulder and they turned to the altar and prayed. Prayed as if the world's fate lay upon it, because it did.

36

Hania looked at the sun. If we don't find some decent shade soon, the fatigue that Skelly and I are plagued with will begin to take its toll.

He stopped short as he noticed a speck of black hovering high in the sky, a hawk or eagle, was riding the thermals; it just hung there, not moving. Thermals this close to the swamp meant cooler air moving in.

Squinting, he looked to the east, a dark line was edging closer. Rain, we need to find shelter soon...all our tents are back on Manhood Island...we'll have to improvise.

Skelly stopped as well; coming back to where Hania stood, he looked east, "Rain?"

"Maybe." Hania put his hand up and shut his eyes so he could feel the air, but what he felt was a whoosh that buffeted his hair, first one way, and then the other.

"Hey!" Skelly shouted, "You dirty, thieving bird."

Hania's eyes snapped open and saw Skelly looking out over the swamp. The eagle had dived down and snatched the caiman from the top of Skelly's backpack.

Dreogan was fitting an arrow into his bow when Barra stopped him.

"It's too late. Besides how would you fetch back your kill?"

"Was that another Thunderbird?" Tesar asked.

"No, too small," Barra stated, "It was a Golden Eagle...impressive wingspan though."

"Well," Skelly mumbled, "the caiman was starting to smell. Maybe we would have all gotten sick eating it."

"If we had, then Hania could have rescued us again," Chval said, his face in a sneer, "Why didn't you tell us the caiman was getting ripe? Or was that your plan all along?"

The accusation was so absurd that all Hania could do was just gape at Chval.

"Just as I thought," Chval turned and stomped off around the next bend. Barra and Dreogan followed, carrying Tesar.

"He acts like this is all your fault!" Skelly shook his head.

"Is there shelter up ahead?" Hania pulled his thoughts away from Chval's attitude.

"Yes, the ancient ones built way-stations, like little inns, all along the old road." Skelly shook his flask of Fo-ti, out of habit, there was no Foxglove in it, and took a small sip. "Some were fancy like the Inn back in the swamp," He jerked his head back towards the swamp, "Others were caves dug next to springs."

They headed along the trail; as they came to a bend next to an outcropping of stones, Chval jumped out flattening Hania.

Punching and kicking, he yelled at Hania for not telling them about the Bloodstones. Skelly pulled him off.

Sobbing, he broke down. Barra and Dreogan put Tesar down and rushed back to see what was going on.

"Why didn't you tell us, why didn't you tell us?" Chval rocked back and forth.

"Is there something you can do for him?" Barra asked Hania.

"I don't want any of his help!" Chval turned away.

Hania felt at a complete loss. I have no knowledge for treating sicknesses of the head...I've heard of them, but was that what was wrong? Or was it a matter of spirit?

Everyone looked at Chval as if he was going mad. Maybe I should talk to Barra...he may be the only one Chval would listen to...but Chval can't see us talking or he will think I put him up to it.

"Take him fishing." Hania mumbled out of the side of his mouth to Barra as he bent down to check Tesar's wound.

Barra went and pulled Chval up, "Let's get some supper," he dragged him over to the mouth of a stream that emptied into the swamp.

The clouds were moving in overhead and a few drops of rain hit the ground. "Let's get Tesar under cover," Hania moved to the litter's foot.

"We will need dry wood for a fire," Skelly picked up the other end, "Just follow us, gathering all you can find." He shot over his shoulder to Dreogan.

They moved off the main trail, following a path along the stream's bank. It led them up a little rise to where a shelter had been carved out of the cliff side. A spring gurgled out the side of the cliff right next to it.

Hania was amazed as they entered it; this is a cave? They set Tesar next to a sleeping platform. Skelly lit an oil lamp and started looking through the contents of a storage room.

A hearth had been carved into one side of the room. Hania stuck his head into it to see where the flu went, there had been no sign of a chimney outside, he could see no glimmer of sky, and yet he could feel a draft.

"Move out of the way so I can build a fire." Dreogan said dropping an armload of kindling; he knelt and started on the fire.

Hania went into the storage room, maybe there were some cooking pots, and we could use some bedding. Skelly had found some sleeping mats and was shaking the dust out of them; Skelly looked at him. "What's wrong?"

"I am worried about Chval." Hania said as opened a chest and searched through it.

"In what way?" Skelly said as he set the mats aside and opened up the next chest.

"He's taking his perceived loss of leadership very hard." Hania pulled out several pots and turned to Skelly. "Is Chval going to do something desperate?"

"To get back the leadership?" Skelly pulled out some pillows and blankets and piled them on top of the mats, some of them showed signs of darning.

Hania nodded. The chests in the storage room were lined with copper; no mice had got into them. A third chest held grain, mortar and pestle, and spices; Hania gathered them up and headed out of the storage room.

"Chval hasn't been the leader ever since we left Manhood Island," Skelly's soft voice stopped him, "It has been the prophecies…and you."

"Me?" Hania turned and looked at Skelly, "I'm no leader."

Skelly gathered up the bedding and passed by Hania on his way into the main room. "You lead by example. Chval is going to be very hard pressed to try and beat that."

"I am not in a contest with Chval!" I don't like where this is going.

"No, but Chval is." Skelly tossed his armload on top of the sleeping platform.

Hania took the pots and stuff over to Dreogan. He took a large pot outside to the spring and watched it trickle full, was Skelly right? Did Chval see him as a rival?

Hania pulled out the wilderness kit and checked the bottle of foxglove; only the smell was left. He left the pot filling and went in search of the fuzzy-leafed plant.

37

Raghnall stomped down the hard packed road along the edge of the swamp with a much larger company than the one he had used on the raid. A full two-dozen men in addition to his Warrior Sons and a like number of slaves, he was hunting this time, a hunt that held a greater prize than just six slaves.

He had emptied his ship of all uninjured warriors; most were green, unseasoned. They had been for show, to look impressive on the ship as he left Cerebrus; but this hunt would do them good, giving them the training they would put to good use on another day. A day when whole clans will be gathered up, slaves enough for his own needs and to spare.

But first these six, they are the key. My honor is at stake and with it, the leadership of Cerebrus. He took a bite of cheese followed by a nibble on the bran cake; the healer said that would help with the diarrhea they got from the spiked wine. He fought down a wave of nausea.

Aja was still out cold and one of the slaves from the ship was carrying him along. I don't want Aja to wake on the ship and make a big fuss over his Stone missing. Not with Murdoc nearby.

I need to find my Stone and return Aja's to him as soon as possible. The red flash pulsed like a heart beat, pointing the way…he slowed…the angle was changing as they moved along.

The Stone was not next to the swamp, but in it. He paused…thinking; had the Atwaters been trying to use the Stone to get home? He smiled and shook his head; I can't believe the audacity of that Atwater buck, attempting to turn my Stone against me! As if he could.

Where were the Atwater slaves now…sitting in trees inside the swamp? Aw, now that would be funny.

He moved to where they left the swamp the day before, Vritra and Zigor high stepping through the tall brush to keep on his flanks. He turned in the direction of Salina; a breeze ruffled the back of his neck, pushing away the swamp's stench. The pulse lined up perfectly. He smiled as he raised the pathway...not all of it, just enough to tempt the Atwaters out of their trees.

He swept down the path, using Aja's Stone to push away the animals and vegetation, *I can hardly wait to punish them. One, I know, will have a burnt hand...he will pay with his life...no mercy.*

He stopped, the pulse was pointing...down? He raised his Stone up out of the swamp and looked around...no sign of Atwaters. He sent a Find Spell out with Aja's stone, his was too weak...*nothing...the headbands of silver paint...I should have removed them.* He sank the pathway from the point he stood towards Salina.

He turned and headed back to shore, his own Stone useless in its pale condition. *Have I stranded the Atwaters in the swamp or were they somewhere else? My Stone was in the swamp...were the Atwater youths cunning enough to set a false trail?*

Getting back to shore, he sank the rest of the path, "Sit!" He ordered the company, "Don't move, and don't touch anything!" He examined the foliage at the point that the path came out of the swamp; a tree's bark showed the marks of being used as a pulley. Footholds for a tall person had been kicked into the path's hard surface...two sets. He put Aja's Stone away.

Interesting, he felt a flush go through him; it was like the war games from his youth. He looked down at his own Stone; *where were they...in the swamp or on the road? If on the road, they were heading toward Bainbridge.*

Should I just let them go? Murdoc would twist that around in the ear of our father...can't control six slaves...that's what he would say. He looked down at his Stone again; it needed recharging.

Aja was stirring. Raghnall took him from the slave, slipped Aja's Stone back into his pocket, and put him down on a mossy spot, taking care not to wake him.

He turned to the slave, tossing his Stone into the air and catching it. The slave's eyes filled with fear as he staggered back; two of the Warriors grabbed the slave's arms, pinning them back.

Raghnall pushed the Stone against the slave's chest. *Feed,* he ordered the Stone. The Slave gritted his teeth against the pain and glared at Raghnall as the Stone drained him of his life; as the slave's heartbeat slowed, the Bloodstone reddened.

Now with a full charge, it beat with a life of its own. The slave's body fell to the ground, drained of life-giving blood; the other slaves in the company shivered and looked away. They knew their place.

Raghnall turned to the north and held out his hand, the Stone warm in his grip.

Aja sat up, "Where are we?" Then he turned and retched.

Raghnall hurried to his side and stood over him, rubbing his back, "Come on, get it all out," *that potion maker will pay.*

Aja moaned as he got up and staggered into the shrubs. He looked pale when he emerged, "What are we doing back here?"

"The slaves escaped last night. What do we do with escaped slaves?" He asked the boy.

"We hunt them," the boy ginned. The excitement that Raghnall felt showed in Aja as well, pushing away the pallor.

This time I'll use my own Stone and a Seeker Spell. "Watch this!" He waved a hand over his Stone. It shuttered as a writhing snake's form arose from it, a Seeker Spell for a certain slave. The tongue flitted in and out of its mouth…testing the air…seeking for the Atwater youth that the Stone had healed. It was a bond that could not be broken by a simple silver band…it would take much more knowledge than a mere potion maker would have…it would take a fully trained healer.

The serpent rose and headed north; they followed. *That will stop the Atwater bucks…they would be begging for mercy as soon as the Seeker Spell reached them.*

Which one of them would he use next to feed the Stone? That sneaky potion maker for one…was he the one that had taken his Stone? It could be another one, the big one that had been tied outside the pen?

It didn't matter; the one with the burnt hand would be the first to die…one or two, so be it. What did matter was that the slaves learned their place…*I'll prove that Atwater is ripe for the picking…then things will be better than it had been before Atwater rebelled.*

I will return Cerebrus to the glory it had held in my grandfather's day, with me in the highest seat, and watching Murdoc turn green; that would be so sweet! Quit dreaming and just do it.

The serpent drifted northward…as if unsure…testing the air, but it did not fade. It was on the trail, unstoppable, and the Bloodstone Warriors followed. Eager for the hunt, they laughed and joked with each other as the slaves trailed behind. This was how it used to be…how it should be.

38

Hania walked back down the dusty path along side the streambed looking for foxglove; there wasn't any to be found. It wasn't surprising; the ground around the stream was too dry and sunny.

Why was it so dry here, when the swamp was so close? Looking around it didn't take long to figure out it was the lake level that fed the swamp. It was like a wide sluggish river, pouring into the Great Swamp.

Closer to the swamp and in the shade of the trees would be a more likely area to search, Hania headed that way.

From the sounds of arguing coming from ahead, Barra was about to toss Chval into the swamp. Hania peeked through the trees at the two of them.

"Hold the net like this!" Came Barra's impatient voice.

"My hand hurts." Chval whined, "and it's not a net, it's just a bunch of branches…it isn't going to work."

"Well, not the way you're doing it!" Barra yanked the branches away from Chval. "Like this!"

Coming up behind Hania, Skelly whispered, "Chval is making record time in angering everyone."

"I noticed." Hania cut across to the swamp without passing by where Barra and Chval were arguing.

He found a patch of Foxglove in the cool shade of a Bald Cypress and searched it for the right age of leaves; Skelly joined him. They tried to suppress giggles as they heard Chval being chewed out by Barra.

Skelly slid down the smooth trunk of a Birch, his body shaking with silent laughter. "Maybe we should just leave them." He choked out.

"Leave them?" Hania fell, hugging his side when the sound of Barra tossing Chval into the water reached their ears.

"Yea. Face it, most of them don't exactly fit the category of Spirit Warrior," Skelly said as he searched through the Foxglove. No further sounds came from where Barra and Chval were trying to catch supper.

Hania ran through the Prophecies in his mind as he got back to his knees and gathered the leaves he dropped when the sound of Chval's unexpected bath had reached them.

He leaned back against a boulder and stretched his legs out, they were cramping again. He took some dolomite powder with a sip from the flask of Fo-ti.

"There is much in the Prophecies that I do not understand," Hania pulled a small pestle and mortar from one of the wilderness kit's pockets. He could see the swamp though a gap in the trees.

"Such as?" Skelly dropped a few more Foxglove leaves in Hania's lap.

"I do not know which of us will be chosen as Spirit Warriors," Hania said, "I…"

"What do you mean?" Skelly sat next to him.

"The Prophecies that I know tell of the Stone Born Maiden and the Prophet or Prophets…gathering the Spirit Warriors out from among the believers of the old lands, the core from Atwater, whatever that means." They got up and started searching closer to the swamp.

"So we are looking for a young maiden and an old man traveling together?" Skelly picked a few more leaves, handing them to Hania.

"The Prophecies doesn't tell the prophet's age." Hania put them into the mortar and bruised them with the pestle, the smell of crushed Foxglove mixed with the swamp's stench.

"There have been a few young prophets," Skelly said.

"Some even younger than us," Hania looked up at the darkening sky. The storm was gathering overhead, once in a while an errant drop of rain would touch them; it was a good thing they had shelter.

"Do we need more Foxglove?" Skelly jumped to a small hillock just off shore, he reached for a wilted looking Foxglove plant laying across the top when a movement in the water caused him to pause.

Hania froze, "Don't move! There's something in the water!"

"What is it…did you bring a spear with you?" Skelly asked out of the side of his mouth.

"No," Hania struggled to his feet and gathered up a bunch of rocks. *Was the large ripple a caiman or anaconda…should I shout for Barra or just yank Skelly out of the reach of whatever was lurking in the swamp's shallows?*

A caiman's snout and head rose out of the surface of the water. Skelly wasn't on a hillock…he was on a caiman nest!

Why didn't we think to bring a weapon? It was a stupid thing to do; we're not at home and we aren't warriors…we are just children play-acting at war games. What should I do?

The caiman was swimming back and forth through the water between the nest and the shore, if Skelly jumped would it attack? If he stayed where he was, it would attack…caiman mothers are very protective of their nests.

I need to distract her! He picked up every bit of stone and wood he could find.

"Hey! You ugly brute!" He rushed the shore and pelted her; she just hissed, jaws open, and moved closer to Skelly.

"I'm going to have to jump!" Skelly shouted over the hissing.

"It will lunge up if you try!" Hania yelled back.

"Pelt her some more," Skelly moved away from the shore inching to the nest's far side, "Pelt her on the count of three." He dug in his feet ready to sprint.

"One, two, three,…" Hania pelted and yelled.

Skelly sprinted up over the nest and launched himself back towards the shore; the caiman lunged for him.

Hania grabbed Skelly's arm and yanked him further up onto the shore, the caiman followed, jaws open.

A flash of light, the sound of a bolt hitting flesh, and the caiman collapsed mere inches from Skelly's leg.

Hania turned and saw Barra standing on the rise, the empty crossbow in his hand; he jogged down to them.

Skelly shuttered as he got to his feet. Hania lay back in the grass; that had been too close.

"Caiman baiting?" Barra teased as he checked his kill.

"Keeps him sharp," Hania said as he rolled over in the damp undergrowth and got to his feet.

Barra jumped over to the nest; he dug a hand in, pulled out an egg, and cut it open. Fashioning his shirt into a makeshift bag, he started filling it, "They're fresh laid."

Skelly recovered, jumped over, and picked up the foxglove; it was too wilted, pulled out of the ground when the caiman built the nest. He tossed it and helped Barra collect eggs.

"You sure were making a ruckus…scared away the fish." Barra grinned over at them.

"Where is Chval?" Hania asked as he took some eggs from Skelly.

Barra shrugged, "Still trying to fish his way. Good thing Skelly was in the mood to play bate."

Skelly grinned, "All in a good cause."

Barra looked over the caiman, "just the tail, I think," he cut it off.

With their shirts full of foxglove, eggs, and carrying the caiman tail, they returned to the shelter.

Barra took the food in and with Dreogan's help, started dinner.

Skelly and Hania went to the spring and put together several Foxglove/ Fo-ti potion flasks. Then they lugged the large pot of water into Dreogan, splashing cool water over their feet.

Soon the air filled with the smell of cooking eggs and roasting caiman; dishes were set out and Tesar was moved over so he could eat.

Chval showed up, wet, and empty-handed; standing in the doorway dripping, he scowled at Barra.

"Any luck?" Barra asked innocently, "Did you catch so many fish that you couldn't carry them all?"

Chval snatched up a plate and went to fill it without answering.

Hania kept his head down and concentrated on eating, he could feel the tension in the air. Chval hated not being in charge.

The eggs needed salt and the caiman was dry, but they were hungry. The spices they had found in the storage room were old and weak; they did little to flavor the meal.

After filling up his plate a second time, Hania went over to the door to eat. The fire had heated the shelter to where it was uncomfortable to him; the fatigue always got worse with heat.

The breeze as it passed the door felt good. He raised his eyes and looked at the clouds boiling overhead; the first fat drops of rain hit the dust, making small craters.

He decided to stay in the doorway smelling the freshness in the air and watching the lightening. Papa called them The Great Spirit's fireworks.

Sheet lightening jumped from one bank of clouds to another, torrents of rain started down, washing freshness over the land. If the Bloodstones were looking for them this heavy rain aught to slow them down a bit.

Another flash of lightening crashed, forking from ground to sky. This time he could smell the ozone in the air, he breathed it in. Healthy air, his grandpapa called it.

There was another flash of sheet lightening; he counted to five before hearing the thunder. Something was moving up in the clouds...another thunderbird? He squinted hard to see what it was.

It's red; I don't see any wings. Flashes of sheet lightning backlit it. Serpentine! Hania jumped back into the shelter, slamming the door shut.

"Skelly! Block the fireplace!" Hania bolted the door and moved over to the only window, slamming it shut and smashing the bar down into place.

Skelly had grabbed the worktable and tipping it up on its side, pushed it up against the fire blocking it.

"Hey! I'm not done eating!" Grabbing Skelly, Chval shoved the table out of the way; Skelly seized it to push it back.

They started to grapple with it; the others sat with puzzled looks on their faces as Hania moved to help. Skelly knocked Chval away and turned to re-block the fireplace.

A serpent's ugly red head pushed its way into the shelter, it's body followed; Chval cried out and scooted back from it. Barra snatched his sword and jumped forward, slashing through it; it was like cutting through smoke.

"I can't kill it!" Barra lunged at it again with no effect.

The serpent tested the air with its tongue; the head weaved back and forth, beady eyes looking them over. Then it struck out, burying its fangs into Dreogan.

He shrieked as the smoky red shape of it entered his body and was gone...he sank to the floor, gasping for air.

No one moved, the flicker of the firelight played over the room. Skelly dropped the table and turned to Hania.

"What was that?"

"I'm not sure," Hania walked over to where Dreogan sat shivering. *Dreogan is close to going into shock, but I don't know why.*

"You called for having the fireplace blocked," Chval glared at him, "So you knew what it was."

"And you stopped Skelly and let that thing in to attack him." Barra said pointing at Dreogan with his sword.

Chval opened his mouth to say something and then shut it.

"I need more light," Hania said as he squatted next to Dreogan; he touched his arm, cold and clammy. Yes, he was going into shock. Barra opened the door while Skelly opened the window. "Turn around."

Dreogan did as asked. Hania fell back in shock; the scars on Dreogan's back had changed, they had turned into snakes. One started to move; it's head sliding under the skin into an area not previously crossed with scaring. Dreogan gasped and reaching back tried to stop it with his hand.

Dreogan is not going to be able to stop those things, he reached out a hand to touch them; *what are they?* Skelly grabbed him from behind and pulled him away just as one of the snakeheads lashed out towards him.

Barra cut down with his sword, beheading the snake. Dreogan shrieked and jerked away from them. The fallen head laid on the floor, only now it looked like a finger; flesh colored and nail-less. Barra rolled it over with the sword; there was no sign of eyes, mouth, or blood.

Hania could feel everyone staring at him, *they want answers; but all I can do is take an educated guess.*

"You're our expert on Bloodstone magic," Chval said, "What do we do?"

"I don't know...this is something new." He stepped toward Dreogan, who scooted back into a corner away from him.

"Something new?" Chval shouted, "When you saw it coming, you knew it would try and get into us."

"That was a guess." Hania went through more of the Prophecies; this was not covered.

"A guess?" Chval moved towards Hania.

Skelly moved between them, "I'll take one of Hania guesses above one of your whiny excuses any day."

They glared at each other; Chval backed down.

"Where did that thing come from?" Barra asked.

"It came from the direction of the Bloodstone camp." Hania looked outside, it had quit raining, the storm had moved south.

"It slithered awful fast." Chval sat back at the eating table rubbing at a spot where Skelly had shoved him into the wall.

"It wasn't crawling, it was flying," *'Flying seeker...' finally a part of the Prophecies jumped out at him*! Hania turned around, that is what that thing was.

He looked over at Dreogan; he could see the fear in his eyes. *This was going to be tricky...how am I going to get Dreogan to co-operate? It was sure to be painful.*

The table? No...outside would be best. They would have to be able to see all sides of him, and to be able to jump out of the way of the snakes.

Hania stepped to the door, the heat was gone; the rain had wet everything down. No dust...the snakes couldn't hide now. He looked around for...for what?

What am I doing? He closed his eyes and prayed; his mind was seeking, pleading for heavenly help. Nothing...no, that wasn't quite right. He felt calmer, but that was all.

He looked...two trees stood along the path...no undergrowth around them. That was the spot. He turned and went back into the shelter, they would need rope, silver...

"It's your fault that thing got in here!" Barra was leaning over Chval.

"How was I supposed to know what was coming?" Chval glared at Barra.

"Would you two shut up?" Tesar was sitting up.

Everyone is falling apart...this has to be part of the Bloodstone strategy...divide and conquer. Skelly looked over at him, waiting.

"I think that thing was a Seeker Spell, a spell meant for one person. To slow down or..." he wasn't about to say kill. Hania walked over to Skelly's backpack and pulled out the rope; he yanked on it, it was strong with little give. But is there enough to do the job...and should we cut it up?

The silence in the shelter was un-nerving; "Is there any more rope?" He asked Skelly.

"I'll check." Skelly pushed himself up from the bench and grabbing up the oil lamp moved into the storage room.

Dreogan wedged himself farther into the corner, "What are you going to do?" He asked through gritted teeth. A snakehead pushed up over his shoulder, still under the skin, that had to hurt.

"We are going to try and remove the Seeker Spell from you," Hania sorted through his supplies. *I have what is left of the pot of silver paint, silvered ointment, brushes, and silver powder. Silver, something about silver...it was the only thing that worked against Bloodstone magic.*

He dipped the brush's end into the ointment and walked over to Dreogan. He daubed the ointment on the snake's head; it lashed back away from it as Dreogan yelped in pain.

"Alright...it doesn't like silver."

"That hurt!" Dreogan rubbed his shoulder.

Hania looked Dreogan in the eye. "You make the choice...stay here and wait for the Bloodstones," He let that sink in, "Or take a chance with me to remove the spell."

"There's no more rope." Skelly reported, coming out of the storage room.

A crash of thunder made them all jump, followed by a rush of wind and the sky dumped more buckets of rain. What else could go wrong? Hania groaned as he walked over to the window.

We'll have to do it inside and on the table; or to be more accurate, next to the table...close quarters. He turned back to Skelly.

"We will need more of those eggs, all you can carry." Skelly and Barra headed out into the storm; Chval sat back.

"What are you going to do?" He asked, "Do you know what to do? Is this more of your 'secret' knowledge?"

"Chval, knock it off." Tesar said from where he lay.

"Dreogan, do you want to end up with burns?" Chval moved towards Dreogan. "I mean...he's just a potion maker, not a fully trained healer."

Hania, shaking his head, went into the storage room; he started to sort through everything in the chests. *I'll have to improvise a basin to hold large amounts of silver salve,* he found a leather apron and set it aside.

Bed linens would do to make bandages. And then he found silver 'rock' in the last chest; it was the only thing to go right this day. As he came back out of the storage room, he glanced out at the storm.

Maybe the storm was not such a bad thing...the Bloodstones would find it hard to follow in such a storm...they would have to hole up somewhere to wait it out.

Dreogan shoved Chval away; he must not have liked what Chval was saying.

"Here, make yourself useful." Hania tossed the sheets at Chval.

"What am I suppose to do? Fold them?" Chval said throwing them back.

"Tear them into bandages." Hania threw them back; Chval went and sat next to Tesar and the two of them set to work.

Hania put together a makeshift pharmacy on the worktable that was returned to its spot next to the fireplace. Skelly and Barra returned, half drowned and grinning; "The rain kept the predators away, so we were able to gather many eggs. It's pouring down now."

They tied Dreogan to the upended dining table and set the leather apron just under him.

"He's ready," Skelly reported to Hania and took over the making of large amounts of silver salve, "Should we give him something for the pain?"

"Not until we are done...we need him to be alert so the silver drink will work." He poured the drink into a beaker and took it over to Dreogan.

"Drink this," Hania held it up to Dreogan's lips; Dreogan pulled a face as he took the first swallow. "Sorry, the "silver rock" wasn't made with maple and we didn't find any honey."

Skelly lugged the pot of silver ointment over. "Should we get more firewood?" He asked as they painted wide bands of salve around the area where the snake scars were slithering around under his skin.

"Why don't we have Barra and Chval do that? They might not understand what we are doing and fight us over it." Hania ladled large amounts salve onto the apron just under Dreogan's back, making sure it was spread far enough on each side so the snakes could not drop out onto the floor.

He was not sure how spell snakes worked, could they live away from their host? He did not want to take the chance.

Chval and Barra left. Chval didn't dare grumble.

They gave Dreogan more of the silver drink and waited. Tesar, now over at the sleeping platform, strained to see.

"How's it coming?" He asked, Hania had almost forgot about him; he left Skelly keeping an eye on Dreogan as he went and checked on Tesar.

Tesar looked anxious, "Isn't there something I could do?"

The pile of torn sheets caught Hania's eye, "Here, roll these up," he gathered them up and dumped them next to Tesar.

"Something's happening!" Skelly was backing away from Dreogan, "What do I do now?"

Hania rushed over with two sticks he had painted with the silver paint.

"Guide them so they will fall into the salve." He handed one of the sticks to Skelly and hunkered down on the other side.

Dreogan screamed out as twisting and jerking, one of the snakes tore its self from his back and fell into the salve. Blood red smoke rose from where it had fallen in and it smelled like burnt flesh.

They guided one after another of the snakes to its grave. The smell was so bad that Tesar hopped, one legged, over to the window and threw up, staying there with his head hanging out of the window until Barra and Chval returned.

The last of the snakes were gone…as they left Dreogan's back, they reopened the wounds left by the lashing the Bloodstone had given him. In fact, it was as if the healing had never happened.

Chval swore when he saw Dreogan's back. "What have you done to him?"

"Shut up Chval," Tesar called over as Barra helped him back over to the bed.

Skelly and Hania untied Dreogan and pulled the table upright; then they helped him lay on the table and set to work dressing his wounds. Barra dumped a couple of logs onto the fire.

"We should get some sleep while we wait for the storm to move on." Barra started to make beds for everyone.

Chval and Barra had to hang their clothes up to dry, they were soaked, even Tesar's head was wet.

Hania gave small amounts of the mandrake-laced wine to Dreogan and Tesar, it was the only painkiller they had on hand. Hania started gathering up the mess left on the floor; he rinsed the apron by holding it out the window.

He had to hold on to it tight as it was like rinsing it off in a waterfall. When would the storm end?

As he hung it up by the fire to dry, he gestured to Skelly, "Look," he whispered and pointed. The apron was scorched as if snake shaped branding irons had been applied to it.

Skelly shook his head. "How did you know the salve would destroy the snakes?"

"I didn't, but since it destroys Bloodstones, I thought..." Hania shrugged.

"Educated guess...better not let them know," Skelly nodded at the others.

After they had knelt and thanked The Great Spirit for the storm keeping the Bloodstone away, and for giving them the promptings and means to get rid of the Seeker Spell, they fell exhausted into bed.

Tomorrow would be another day; they would handle it as it came. Now they needed sleep.

Later that evening, Chval woke Hania up. "I need help!"

"What?" Hania pulled himself upright.

"Tell him to go jump in the swamp," Skelly mumbled and pulled his bedding up over his head.

Hania looked at the window as he got to his feet, the rain had stopped. The sun was going down over the swamp, the glow of it showing through the cracks in the window and door.

"Come over to the window." Hania said as he staggered over and opened it up to let in as much light as was possible; he stifled a yawn.

Chval held out the hand that had been burned by the Bloodstone and Hania unwrapped it. It was raw, weeping, and the hand was hot; he sniffed it...it didn't smell like gangrene.

"I know...I should have had you treat it," Chval was shaking. "My father is always going on about how you should..." His voice trailed off.

Hania knew that Chval hated coming to him. *But why Chval sees me as a rival, I do not know.*

Hania pricked and drained green puss out of the burn. "We have a problem...there is no more silver salve...we used the last of it on Dreogan."

Chval watched as Hania wrapped up the hand in the last of the bindings.

"We need more silver." Hania finished and looked out into silence.

"Where do we go?" Chval asked.

"Call a counsel," Hania said as he tossed the last of the logs onto the fire. Chval got everyone up, "Hania says he needs more silver...any ideas?"

Skelly looked over at Hania; Hania nodded and Skelly stood up. "The cliffs north of here are riddled with mines...if we can find one that is being worked, we have a better chance of finding veins pure enough to harvest raw."

"How do you find out which one?" Tesar asked.

Barra snorted, "Fresh tracks, you dolt."

Chval smiled, "Hania needs to stay here and take care of Dreogan and Tesar."

With a crash of thunder, the wind whooshed into the shelter.

"Shut the window!" Skelly dived forward, "Quick! The bar!" Barra slammed the bar into place.

"Looks like we're stuck here for a while," Tesar mumbled.

What was it about that storm? Then he remembered; Hania looked at Skelly, "Hurricane?"

Skelly nodded. "One must have come ashore."

They went off to bed. They would have to wait out the storm.

39

The next morning Skelly looked outside. *Constant rain...how are we going to find a working mine in this? We'll have to rely on Barra's sharp eyes, but can he see signs of a mine in this?*

"Be careful." Hania called from over where he was tending Tesar's leg, Dreogan was still asleep.

"Let's go." Barra gathered his weapons and exited.

Chval went next, still favoring his hand.

"We'll get back as soon as we can." Skelly ducked through the door into the rain.

Human sign wouldn't be easy to find. They slogged though the rain and mud, climbing higher and higher. The steady downpour made it difficult, but it was the only protection they had from the Bloodstones.

Keep raining, Skelly found himself praying as they trudged along, *but make Barra's eyes sharp enough to find a mine.*

The road divided at the top of a high pass, shallow wheel ruts turning both paths into twin streams. "Which way?" Chval shouted.

Skelly closed his eyes and tried to visualize Nabi's study, mentally placing the map on the table and opening it.

A smell arose around them. "Get down! Lie flat!" Barra dived, knocking them flat into the mud.

With a sizzle and a boom, air rushed over them. Barra started laughing.

"I fail to see the humor in this," Chval said from where he lay, spitting out mud. The green of his silk shirt now covered with the same reddish brown mud that dribbled down his chin.

"That..." Barra chucked, "is the reason so few trees grow on the tips of mountains."

Skelly blinked, they were almost hit by lightening! "Thanks Barra."

"You're welcome," Barra said, "We need to get off this peak before the ground recharges."

"We take the left path." Skelly looked over at the lightening scared tree.

Barra followed his eyes. "See, lightening does strike more than once in the same place."

Barra turned and slid down the pathway to the left; Skelly and Chval followed.

"When can we quit sliding on our rears?" Chval grabbed a handful of mud and threw it at Barra.

Barra looked around. "As soon as we are below the strike zone."

"Are we there yet?" Skelly pushed hard and slid down a rivulet, "I'm starting to feel like an otter."

Barra stopped and got to his feet. "I think we're okay now."

Skelly got to his feet and looked around, mentally comparing the map he studied at Nabi's with the terrain he saw rising in sharp cliffs.

As Barra moved to help him up, Chval cried out, "Not the hand...not the hand."

Barra got behind Chval, wrapped his arms around has chest, and pulled him to his feet; then leading the way he stopped, knelt on one knee, and examined each pathway leading off the main path.

The rain kept coming. "I don't know," Barra shook his head, "This rain may keep the Bloodstones away, but it is making it hard to find any sign of human activity."

Skelly looked at the water streaming over the mud, Barra was right; there was no way to see anything out here. "Let's each take a pathway and see if it leads to a mine...then check inside for signs of recent use."

They left Chval at the next one, then Barra and Skelly each took a path; Barra's led down and Skelly's up. Skelly leaned against the cliff's side as he climbed into a ravine...water ran over his feet, washing away the mud that clung to his sandals and threatened to pull him downstream. He came to a wide fissure and stepped inside.

It felt good to get out of the steady downpour. Was it going to rain like this all the way to Bainbridge?

"And I suppose you came in here to just to get out of the rain?"

Skelly jumped and stumbling on the dusty stone floor, turned around. Where the fissure opened into a cave, an old woman stood next to a small pony laden down with ore.

"I..." Skelly didn't know what to say, *should I be honest? All the Green Crescent Clans were allies against the Bloodstones...so would she help him? It would be stupid to pretend that we were just going for a walk; she would know darn well how long it had been raining and how hard.*

Why was she out in this storm? Skelly took a deep breath, the pony did not smell wet, how long had they been here?

"We need silver," he limped out.

"Why?" Her dark blue eyes bore into him, just like Nabi, and for a woman so old, she had a mass of long blond hair spilling out from under a dark brown headscarf, shouldn't it be white?

"We used all we had for Silver Salve...to fight the Seeker Spell."

"Indeed...the Seeker Spell." She nodded as she sat on an outcropping, as if it were a throne; she patted a spot next to her. "Tell me, how did you come to be so...sought after."

Skelly reported to her all that had happened from the time the Bloodstones had taken them from Manhood Island until now.

"So...you have pricked the pride of Raghnall. Yes, that one has always had a problem with pride." Leaning forward, she seemed to become lost in a memory, an unhappy memory.

"You know him?" Skelly froze, *have I blundered onto another Bloodstone?* His hand slid down to the handle of the knife strapped to his leg.

"I escaped from Cerebrus," she shuttered, "The only one that ever made it back...I knew him well enough."

Skelly stared, was she the one Hania told him about? But she was too old...that one had been a young child twenty years ago...

She smiled at him. "Well, spit it out."

"What do you mean?" Skelly swallowed as he ran his hands back over his head wringing the water out of his hair.

"Ask your questions...I see them in your eyes." She leaned back and relaxed.

Skelly swallowed again. "Hania told me about a woman that returned over sixteen years ago, but she was young at the time."

"So I was. This..." She gestured at her body, "is what the Stones did...aged me 30 years in a single day...almost killed me."

Skelly felt lost. *Here I am, the apprentice to Nabi, the historian, but it was Hania who knew this part...most of this part.* He racked his brain as he sat dripping, *nothing.*

"Are you from Bainbridge?" He was grasping at straws.

She smiled at him and nodded, "How old are you?"

"Sixteen," *What did that have to do with anything?*

"That would fit." She looked out at the storm and stood.

"Do you know..." He stopped and tried to remember whom they were supposed to find at Bainbridge. Oh, yes, "Do you know Gaho…at The Forge, by Bainbridge?"

"I am Gaho." She pointed into the storm. "Bring your companions here…I will guide you to The Forge…there is much to be done and I expect you to help haul ore."

Skelly sat there. *This was too easy.*

"Well?…Get going…I'll be digging until you return." She waved him out.

He slid down the ravine to where Barra and Chval waited for him. He turned and piled up some stones.

"You found a useable mine?" Barra asked, "All we found were old ones; played out."

"I found more than a mine…I found Gaho." Skelly stepped back and fixed the image in his mind. They would not have to struggle to find the mine again. "She will take us to The Forge and give us silver, but we will have to carry ore."

"Gaho?" Chval asked as they started back.

"She runs The Forge by Bainbridge." They reached the pass and Barra kept going; he turned around.

"What's taking you so long?" Barra looked down at them.

Chval looked around and swallowed, "Is it safe?"

"The storm is gone," Barra shrugged and disappeared down the other side.

Skelly went next, eager to be going down hill again; he took another swallow of Foxglove/ Fo-ti potion. He looked up, would there be another hurricane? He was sure the eye of one had passed over the shelter last night. Hurricanes.

It had to do with being near the coast; how often would they end up getting drenched? How did people along the coast keep their clothes dry…or did they just stay wet for the duration of the rainy season?

"We're back!" Skelly entered the shelter; Hania had Tesar and Dreogan on stretchers ready to leave.

40

Hania looked Skelly's group over; well, Skelly looks happy...did that mean they found silver? They didn't look like they're carrying anymore than when they left, except mud.

"Guess who I found..." Skelly grinned, "Gaho!"

"Who?" Tesar asked, sitting up.

"Skelly said she runs the Forge at Bainbridge, but we have to pretend to be pack mules." Barra grinned over at Chval...Chval glared back.

"Well, it beats digging it out ourselves. Or being caught in someone else's mine," Skelly said, "Even if it was for a good cause and where did the other stretcher come from?"

"Behind a chest in the storage room." Hania waved them over, "two to a stretcher."

Chval hesitated, "I can't hold a stretcher with this hand," raising it up for all to see.

"I thought about that." Hania picked up the braided rope he made from the last of the torn sheets; he gestured Chval over and threw it around his neck.

"Just loop it under the stretcher's right hand side and grip the left side as usual." Chval did not look pleased.

He was even more annoyed as they topped a high pass with a lightening charred trunk and started down the other side. But Tesar looked petrified, and Hania couldn't blame him, Chval almost dumped him off as they slid around in the mud left from the storm.

They met Gaho at the mouth of a ravine, four baskets of ore at her feet.

"I thought you said you had to dig more ore," Skelly said as he and Hania set Dreogan down so they could shrug into the harnesses attached to the baskets.

"I may have been a little over ambitious as I waited for the storm to pass." Her deep blue eyes crinkled in amusement as she patted the pony.

As they helped Chval into his harness, Hania couldn't help but notice how Gaho looked both old and young at the same time. And it wasn't just the mass of deep golden hair.

Heading back to pickup Dreogan, Hania had to ask, "Skelly, what happened to her?"

"Bloodstones." Skelly picked up the heavy end of Dreogan's stretcher.

Hania took the other. Could it be…would it be this simple? He stared at Gaho as she headed down the trail ahead of them.

As the trail leveled she moved to the side and let the pony graze as she waited for them to catch up. The slickness of the mud had slowed them down.

She waved Chval and Barra ahead of them and fell into step with Hania, the pony grabbing mouthfuls of grass from the edge of the path as it plodded along. "You've been staring at me."

"I was wondering," *how am I going to ask if she was the one?* "Do you have any children?" His voice cracked.

He turned away from her dark eyes; eyes that held deep pain. *Am I reading more into her than there was?*

"I have…a daughter." She turned as if studying the sky; the tension in the air was a contrast to their conversation.

"How old?" Was she 16? He held his breath.

Gaho turned around and her eyes bored holes into his mind, "I think you know the answer."

"She is Stone Born then," there, he had said it.

"Your friend Skelly says the Bloodstone Wizard that is after you is Raghnall," she changed the subject. It was more of an admission than if she had just said yes.

"That's right." Where was her daughter…was she at The Forge? It just struck him. The Stone Born Maiden had a mother of flesh and blood, a mother who loved her and cared about her. A mother that knew her child was born to fulfill a prophecy…or die trying.

They walked on in silence until they passed through a cleft and came down to a gorge, why had Gaho fallen back to talk to him? She called for the boys to wait.

Moving to the front, she patted the pony. "We will be crossing at the first bridge…we will go first, all the way across, and then each group follows, one at a time."

When they came to the bridge, Tesar gasped, Hania didn't blame him. The bridge was narrow with only one railing and it spanned a gorge so deep it made Hania dizzy just looking over the edge.

Gaho was eyeing them with amusement. "Well, you could take the long way around, of course, but I would hate to walk for most of a day carrying a load of rocks."

I'd be happy just tossing the rocks over the edge…but we need the silver. The Forge is the only place to get silvered weapons and we'll need those as well.

Gaho turned and crossed the bridge, the pony followed without the least hesitation.

Chval opened his mouth…

"We need the silver, Chval," Barra warned and started over; a definite rift was growing between them.

Tesar clutched the stretcher and closed his eyes; "Go slow!"

Hania followed. *Don't look down…It's just a path.* He could feel the sweat trickle down his back and his legs tingled; he promised them a good long rest when they reached the other side.

Out of the corner of his eye, he could see two magnificent waterfalls; they were too far away to let the spray cool them off. *I wish I could hear them, from here it's no more than a muffled roar.* There were buildings between them, crawling up from the bottom of the gorge to the wide gentle slope at the top…Bainbridge?

At last his feet found solid ground…they made it; he let out his breath as they set down their burdens and took a short break.

Gaho was chuckling under her breath; she turned and pushed on a counter weight. As it swung around, the bridge folded up against the tall posts on this side.

The bridge had the same type of lattice type construction along its length as the bridge to the Shrine Island in the Great Swamp.

Tesar stared in awe, "I wondered why there was a tall gate on this side."

"Want to see it again?" Gaho asked.

Tesar nodded.

"My Great Grandfather and Great Great Grandfather built it," she lowered the bridge, "They got tired of going all the way up and over through Bainbridge." She raised and locked it in place.

"Come along, it's just over the rise here." She led on.

Hania got his first sight of The Forge. It was huge…like a small village on it's own; there were smelters, warehouses, workshops, and cottages. Gaho was in charge of all this?

"Who owns this?" He looked over at her.

"Family owned business." She swept her hand across the valley. "Copper mines up there, to the north…coal to the west along the gorge…and sand to the east."

"Sand?" Skelly asked.

"To make glass…and of course, silver," she gestured back at the obsidian cliffs, then started down to The Forge.

But why, if she owned all this, was she digging ore…didn't she have workers to do the hard stuff? Why am I worried about that? If she wants to tell me, she will; I have more than enough troubles of my own.

Would the Bloodstone Warriors follow us here…how desperate was Raghnall to get us back? Gaho acts as if she knows whom Raghnall is. As the maiden that made it back, she must have known him from the time she lived there…I wonder how long she was there…four years?

She guided them to a bin next to a smelter; a curly-haired blond man came to the door of what looked like the office.

"Father, I found some helpers," Gaho greeted the man, he looked younger than her, "What's wrong?"

"Come in here." He stepped back into the office.

Hania turned to the bin and dumped out his ore. Now what was going on…should he eavesdrop? He went to the shade by an open window and sat; as Skelly joined him, he put his finger to his lips for silence.

"What did Kendra say?" Gaho asked.

"She was very serene about it," the man's voice had a touch of…humor? "The delegation from Dennet demanded to search her rooms, even though they were told she hadn't returned. Did you know Onid had gone to Dennet?"

"All I know, is she went to find the prophet…I had no idea which direction she took."

"Well, I can guarantee that we will not be selling many goods to Dennet for a while."

"Why?"

He chuckled. "Kendra asked the young man to describe the stolen sword…in detail…then she asked if it was one of a kind, was there any others like it." He chuckled again.

"I don't think any of this is funny…are you saying that they were trying to frame Onid?'

"After the young man and the rest of the delegation had sworn that that was so…"

"Papa!"

"Sorry," he took a deep breath.

"That's her father?" Skelly looked at Hania, who signaled for him to be quiet.

"Kendra asked him to pull out the sword that was in his bedroll and put it on the table."

"Did he?"

"Well, he was reluctant, but what else could he do in front of half the town?"

"Let me guess, it was the one of a kind sword," Gaho was chuckling now.

"Yup, so they headed back to Dennet like whipped curs."

"What did she do in Dennet?" Gaho sighed.

"She bought a boy, an indentured servant."

"Indentured servant, a deceitful name for a slave. Now why would she do that? Slavery is outlawed here and she has too much on her plate to be going around rescuing people...unless he is the prophet."

"Why did you go to the mine?"

It was as if he knew the answer...it was a challenge. Hania glanced at Skelly, who shrugged.

"Alright...although sometimes I feel like a pawn in a chess match between good and evil."

"I know," his voice showed his tenderness for his daughter.

Hania started to feel uncomfortable; he didn't like eavesdropping and now that he had gotten all his questions answered, it was time to move on. Skelly pulled him to his feet and they went over to where the others were resting under the evergreen boughs of huge Sequoia.

"Well?" Skelly looked at him intently, "Are you going to tell me what that was all about?"

The other boys gathered around as best they could.

Looking around to see if anyone was spying on them, Hania hunkered down. "Gaho is the maiden that escaped from Cerebrus."

Chval opened his mouth and Skelly clapped a hand over it; Chval shoved it away, but kept quiet.

"She returned here about 16 years ago and she has a daughter," Hania swallowed.

"And she said that the Stones made her 30 years older, in a single day." Skelly reported, "That the Stones did it to her."

Chval shrugged, "So?"

"Her daughter, this Onid, must be the Stone Born Maiden." Hania watched the different reactions; Barra and Dreogan both had open jaws, Tesar just paled.

Chval got up and started to pace, "Then we are the Spirit Warriors!" He looked excited.

Hania sighed, "If you want to be a Spirit Warrior, you can't."

"What kind of nonsense is that?" Chval waved his hand in the air, "Either we are or we aren't…who chooses? The Great Spirit? This Onid?"

Hania shook his head. "You have to be in tune with the Spirit…you have to be humble."

His words were ignored; Chval wasn't listening, he was on his knees drawing out a plan to ambush the Bloodstones.

Hania struggled to his feet and strode away. *I must fast tonight and pray. Pray for the safe return of this Onid…pray for our safe return home…pray for our families…and pray for guidance; we'll need it.*

He paced around the well planned out streets of The Forge for a while. Everything was built of stone, which only made sense with the constant threat of fire common to metal and glasswork. He returned to the group by the office; they were now eating.

"Nabi gave me enough silvered weapons for all of us to be armed," Skelly was telling Uaid. He had come out of the office, and they were all sitting under the trees, talking. Some of the trees were Hackberry, just coming into bloom. Scouting bees buzzed around.

Hania was the only one not eating; his stomach grumbled at the smell of the stew they were sharing.

"He said to get acid balls from you," Skelly dipped bread in the gravy on his plate, "Well, actually he said from Gaho."

Uaid looked over the rag-tag group. "What happened to them?"

"What?"

"What happened to all your weapons?" Uaid asked.

"Well," Skelly looked down, "We…"

"They lost most of them in the swamp," Chval broke in, "They should have tied them more securely." He glanced at Skelly.

As Skelly and Chval tossed blame back and forth, Hania got up and left, their bickering not only gave him a headache, it kept the spirit away. Couldn't they see this?

With his stomach gurgling, he meandered in the direction of Bainbridge. *I need to get away from the stew's tempting smell.*

The rolling hills east of The Forge were wooded and cool; even the main road had a lush, green canopy over it. This place is so peaceful, he breathed in the deep earthy smell.

He found a fallen log, moss covered, next to the road. He sat down and started to pray…he told The Great Spirit how overwhelmed he felt, with Chval fighting him all the time and Skelly falling into the trap of arguing with Chval.

He sat, eyes closed, waiting for an impression, for some type of guidance. *I feel warmth…it's intense…it's like the sun was just in front of me. Which is odd…that's north.*

He opened his eyes. A young boy was standing there, his light-brown hair sticking out like a suns cornea; the warmth was coming from him, and then it was gone. What did that mean? They stared at each other; then his eyes moved to the boy's companion.

She was stunning, in spite of the dust covered clothes. She was tall, blond, graceful, and athletic looking; could this be Onid?

Who was the boy? They both look as if they have been on the road for a while.

Hania realized that his mouth was open and shut it.

"Is he a worker at The Forge?" The boy asked her.

"No," Her dark blue eyes narrowed and her hand moved to rest on the hilt of her sword, "Who are you?"

"Hania of Atwater."

She looked him over as her lips moved, reciting, 'and the core from Atwater'

He felt the blood drain from his face; it was getting hard to breath. *The Prophecies are no stranger to her…somehow I know she understands them better than I ever could.*

"Onid." He swallowed.

She nodded as if in greeting, the boy peered at him through gray eyes; it was the kind of look that Nabi had used on him many times. Like Gaho, the boy looked young and old at the same time…but not for the same reason. He couldn't put his finger on it.

"Ah…we met your mother and grandfather," he limped out.

Onid looked toward The Forge, her shoulders slumped. "I better let them know I didn't leave a great impression at Dennet."

"The people from Dennet have already come and gone." *How stupid, now I've done it…when she talks to her family, they will know that I eavesdropped…you muddled up that one but good.*

Honesty…full discloser…nothing less would work, not now. "I kind of overheard you grandfather tell your mom."

"What happened?" She half smiled at him.

"I think your grandfather should tell you," he chewed his lip, "He enjoyed watching it."

He pushed himself up off the log, trying hard to mask the struggle. The three of them turned and headed to The Forge; it was a good thing they had traveled far and were tired, he had no problem keeping up in the coolness of the woods.

Gaho was so relieved to see her daughter and made such a fuss that the youths from Atwater were ignored. Farid was not as lucky, Gaho looked him over with such intensity, that he reddened.

After Uaid had regaled them with the details of Dennet's failed attempt at framing Onid, silence fell. Onid stared at her feet.

Hania looked at Gaho. She knows more about Bloodstone magic than anyone else; he sidled up to her and cleared his throat.

She studied him as she stoked the head of her daughter that now lay in her lap.

"I have much to ask you," he started.

41

Skelly could hear a pounding in his ears and his mouth felt dry; but he couldn't take his eyes off Onid, it wasn't because she was or might be the Stone Born Maiden. She was just so different from the girls he knew at Atwater. Yes, there were many pretty blonds at home, but not like her.

She was lying with her head in her mothers lap; her dark eyes open and focused far away. What was she pondering?

What are you thinking? Skelly chided his self; *she wouldn't be interested in you.* Not that he knew what that meant. It was something his older cousin's said when discussing future eternal companions, as if anyone would ever consent.

He knew that he would never marry. Not with his health problems.

She blinked her eyes and stared at him...he felt the blood rush to his face. Turning, he looked at Farid.

Farid was studying him; his gray eyes had the same intensity as Nabi's, Skelly gave a weak smile.

Without a change of expression, Farid closed his eyes. His lips moved without any sound, praying.

Skelly sighed and turned around to where Hania and Gaho were talking, sitting on a beautifully carved stone bench that circled the trunk of a very tall evergreen. Everything at The Forge was a mix of beauty and practicality. Hania's face was intense, what was she telling him? He was too far away to hear; all he could do was read the body language.

A gray haired woman had come while his attention was elsewhere, settling next to him; she smelled of paper, and burning candles, like Nabi. Was she their historian?

"Yes." She said in a drawn out way as she looked at Farid, now it was his turn to redden.

Skelly couldn't help but smile to himself; then she looked at him with her pale green eyes and the smile died. Definitely, she was another Nabi...this must be the Prophetess Kendra. After giving all the boys from Atwater that same penetrating stare, she stood, walked over, and asked Onid how she was doing, her wrinkled hand resting for a moment on the girl's shoulder. Then returning to his side; sat and smoothed her robes; she surveyed the assembly as if they were on trial.

It was an odd place to hold court; The Forge's central plaza was a well-kept park...in fact, trees grew along every street in this well laid-out village. Foundry work was by its very nature hot; Uaid and his family before him had been wise in providing lots of shade and fountains. Water was not far from any building. Even though most were built of stone with tiled roofs. There were still plenty of wooden objects inside.

"I want to know everything the Bloodstones said or did from the time they snatched you until now." Kendra trained her eyes on Hania and waited.

Skelly slid back against the office's wall until he could feel the rough stonework bite into his back. He wanted to hide...get away from those penetrating eyes.

Chval and Hania talked and Kendra listened while sending looks over at him, sizing him up, sizing them all up. An afternoon breeze played with the trees' branches, causing shadows to dance over the plaza.

Kendra nodded her head and looked at Gaho, "Among these are..." her hand indicated the Atwater youth, "the core from Atwater." Her eyes searched them once again, "But is it all...or just some? Time...will...tell."

Every time her eyes passed over him, Skelly felt two contradictory feelings...excitement and fear.

He turned and looked at Farid; who was staring at him with the same intensity. *The more I learn about the Spirit Warriors and their quest, the less I want do with it.*

Hania and Chval finished their report and Kendra stood up. "Time for the Elders of Bainbridge to be warned...they must choose." She pointed at Chval and Skelly, "You two will come with me."

Why us? Skelly looked over to Hania. Hania, seeing the question in his eyes, nodded him on, "I have lots of things here I must do," he said. That was enigmatic.

He joined Kendra and Chval; they headed for Bainbridge taking the main road. The large oaks that marched along the sides of the road and met overhead providing shade; suddenly stopped, replaced by low walls marking the boundaries of farmer's fields.

It was a warm day and Skelly felt the strength leave his body, why did heat have to affect him this way?

He glanced at Chval; he had his head up and chest puffed out, strutting along. *This is going to be a disaster,* he shook his head and looked at Kendra; *what did she mean...the elders must choose...choose what?*

They came to a high wall with two stone gargoyles guarding the gateway, but the doors were open and unguarded. Entering, they went past homes with small garden plots; as the houses got larger, the gardens changed, less fruits and vegetables and more flowers.

Finally there were only formal patios, some with fountains, sitting in front of large manor houses.

A smile played around Kendra's lips as she hummed to herself; she acted as if this was all foretold, was it? Skelly repressed a shudder.

Crossing over a bridge that spanned one of the twin waterfalls, he let the spray cool his face as the sound soothed him. *I wish I could stay and watch it; let it wash away my fears.*

Kendra led them through a business district to a gathering hall and directed them to a high bench up at the front. Going to a shallow alcove, she pulled on a rope; a bell rang out, calling men from all areas of the prosperous village.

The men trickled in and sat in small groups on the tiered seating, whispering to each other and looking at Kendra with expectation, and apprehension? They sounded like small rodents foraging for grain.

Skelly could smell a nearby bakery, now that was where he'd rather be, with some cheese and fresh fruit juice. A few last men came and slipped into the throng. The tension in the room was almost as thick as the heat, Skelly was glad to be sitting down.

Kendra rose to her feet and the room stilled. "The day we have been dreading is upon us," she waved her hand at Chval and Skelly, "these youth will tell you about the changes in the Bloodstones' tactics." She sat and nodded at them.

Chval stood...he was in his element. With skill born of years watching his father, he wove together what he knew of the prophecies about the Spirit Warriors with what they had seen the Bloodstones do.

After Chval sat down, a man wearing the stately robes of a master scholar got to his feet and shot down almost everything Chval had said.

"The prophecies state, in very clear terms, that The Great Spirit chooses the Warriors," he declared. "They do not choose themselves."

"This one," Another man with plaster dotting his work clothes pointed at Chval. "Has too much pride."

Chval reddened at that, while Skelly fought hard not to smile.

"There are many things the prophecies state has to happen. I do not see that what these boys have been through, although they have behaved bravely, constitutes a fulfillment of the first battle as many of the prophecies declare." A solider in the armor of a captain stated. "A part? Maybe."

A younger man in the clothes of a shop worker popped up. "So far we have heard from only one of them…we should listen to them both." He paled as he looked around at the wealthier men, sank back to his seat, and looked down shivering as he waited for judgment on his rash words.

They all looked at Skelly. Swallowing hard, he stood; *why did Kendra bring me here?*

"I do not know for certain whether or not, we are the Spirit Warriors," he stammered, "Odd things have happened. I do know this, the Bloodstones have returned…they are using tricks and powers that they didn't have before and they will continue raiding the Green Crescent Lands. I'm afraid that it will be like it was before; and somewhere in the Green Cresset are the Spirit Warriors."

"And what else do you know, young man?" A fat baker asked, coming right up to him, the smell of yeast was strong.

"When you fight them. It will be the skills of your fighters, not their silvered weapons, that will matter."

"That is all that will matter at this point," Chval jumped to his feet, "Even as we speak; the Bloodstones that tried to take us are on their way here." He stabbed a finger at the tight fitted stonework of the floor.

Skelly shook his head in disbelief before looking over at Chval.

"What?" Chval asked as they both sat.

A murmur washed through the assembly…then stilled as a man stood; he was dressed in a fine woven cloak with chains of gold hanging from his neck, and even had gold combed into his hair. *He's very proud of his wealth.*

"Get out…leave our village…if they come here, it will be because you led them here." He glared at them. Fear was in the air, it was as tangible as smoke.

Kendra calmly got up and led them back out of the village; she had that same enigmatic smile on her face. In fact, she was humming a battle song under her breath.

"What was the point of that?" Skelly asked her as they reached the top of a knoll.

Chval was lagging behind, sulking.

"The next part, you must do alone." She stopped and pointed towards The Forge, "Go on, your friends are waiting." Humming she walked over to a small house and went inside.

Skelly waited for Chval to catch up, "What do you think we should do?"

"Does it matter?" Chval was more than a little cranky. "All we have to do is face Raghnall in battle," he sighed, "Six untried youth against six or more battle hardened experienced men."

"You won't be alone," said a voice behind them, making them jump. Farid was sitting in the shade of a bolder that sat next to the road.

"Farid, this is not your battle," Skelly said, "In fact, they may have given up and gone back home."

"They haven't, and you know it." Farid spoke this last part to Chval who backed away from Farid.

Farid jumped up, darted forward, and grabbed Chval's wrist. For such a small boy, he was surprisingly strong; he forced back Chval's fingers so Skelly could see his palm. It smelled like raw meat.

The burn pulsed as if it was a heart, not a hand. Skelly stared at Chval, "Why haven't you let Hania see this?"

"You saw what happened to Dreogan; it doesn't hurt, so…"

"They are tracking us with that!" Skelly ran a hand through his hair.

Looking at his hand, Chval pulled it back, "You don't know that."

"Farid knew it," Skelly glanced over at the boy.

Chval snorted, "I will not let my choices be dictated by a slave." He stomped off down the hill, disappearing beneath the branches of the oaks that lined the road.

"He is not one, at least not yet," Farid stated as he turned south. "They are coming."

Skelly looked south, there was truth in Farid's words; how long before they would have to face the Bloodstones in battle? He turned and the two of them headed to The Forge.

42

Hania spent a peaceful afternoon gathering sap to make more Silvered Rock with Farid tagging along with him for most of it. Farid left awhile back; there was something different about that boy, spooky.

The pony was cropping grass, straining toward that which was just out of its reach; the buckets in the small cart would soon be full. Hania laid back and looked into the canopy of new leaves overhead. Bees buzzed around the last remaining blossoms. It was soft, cool, and mossy in here away from The Forge's bustle and heat…it was peaceful.

He closed his eyes. Plop, plop, plop…he could hear the sap dripping into the catch cup while the maple trees' pleasant scent filled the air around him.

Was The Great Spirit watching them? He thought back over the last few days; *it had been a crash course in faith or if you were not open to the Spirit's promptings, such trials could push you to the other side. Even to a disbelief in The Great Spirit…maybe push some back to the pagan gods of the past.*

The dripping slowed; Hania got up, dumped the cup, and heaved the covered bucket into the cart. With the last spot filled, he pulled the spout out of the bark and shoved in a handful of moss.

Taking the brake off the cart's wheel, he turned the pony around and with the pony trotting behind, proceeded to The Forge.

The others were back; Skelly helped him unload the cart as he told Hania what happened in Bainbridge.

"Chval is in a foul mood," Skelly warned him, "Farid…"

"What about Farid?"

"He showed me Chval's hand." Skelly set the last bucket next to a cooker.

"He burned it," Hania shrugged and knelt to start the fire under the cooker. He watched as the smoke curled around the cooker's bottom.

"He burned it with the Wizard's Bloodstone," Skelly poured the pale sap into the cooker's copper basin. "He said it doesn't hurt, but it doesn't look anything like a normal burn."

"I better go and get a look at it…if he will let me." Hania looked out the door, Chval was sulking in the shade, "Keep an eye on this for me, would you?" He nodded at the cooker.

He crossed over to Chval; as the gravel crunched underfoot, Chval looked up at him.

"You're not touching me," Chval tucked his hand into his tunic.

"Would you be willing to have the Bainbridge healer tend to it?"

"It doesn't hurt!" Chval jumped to his feet, "Leave me alone!" He stomped off.

What should I do…ask Uaid to have his men restrain Chval? That would not go over well, Chval's close to snapping, but what else was there? He turned and headed for the office where Onid was just leaving. *Onid…she might get him to listen to reason.*

"Onid!" Hania sprinted to catch up with her; in fact when he did catch up he had to jog along side.

"What is it?" Onid said as they entered the main smelter; the heat and smell of sweat was overwhelming.

"It's Chval."

She looked at him, "Is he still unable to help?" She walked over to where Barra was shoveling coal; Barra grinned and gave him the thumbs up as she marked something down on the wall next to the bin.

"It's his hand."

"I've seen it…does it hurt him? You're a healer, aren't you?"

"He won't let me touch it, says it doesn't hurt."

She looked at him, her head cocked to one side. "What can I do…do you want me to hold him down while you work on it?" She grinned at him, a mischievous glint in her eye.

He didn't doubt that she could, but that would bruise Chval's tender ego even more.

"In a way," Hania smiled innocently.

"Oh…" Catching on, she returned the smile, "I'll see what I can do."

Hania felt the burden shift to her, *now I can work in the background where it's safe.* They started back to the office.

"What brought Chval's hand under your scrutiny?" She asked nodding at people as they passed. People swarmed everywhere and although it looked chaotic, there was an order to the place…and everyone was so polite.

She was matching his speed this time; while it was easier, it reminded him that he had Hesutu.

"Farid was worried and showed it to Skelly."

Onid stopped, "Farid was worried?" Her voice was urgent, "What was he worried about?"

"Skelly said it pulsed…like a heart."

"Did he get the burn from a Bloodstone?"

"Well…yes."

She grabbed his arm and dragged him into a building where Gaho was supervising the making of silvered swords. "Mom!"

Gaho glanced up; she looked from Onid's white face to his puzzled one. She motioned the men back to work and came over.

"Chval was burned with a Bloodstone…can they track him?" Onid asked as Gaho bustled them into a room away from the noise and shut the door.

"Has the burn been treated?" Her eyes bored into Hania.

"He won't let me," he felt like he was shifting the blame.

Gaho paced around the room, stopped, and stared out the window. Her voice was soft, "In Cerebrus, most slaves were branded with an 'S'."

Hania and Onid exchanged looks.

Gaho went on, "When a slave tried to escape, the Bloodstone Wizard whose Stone branded him, could track him down." She turned to them, "He must be treated. Now! Before it's too late," she looked up towards the hills; a flash of worry crossed her face.

"You mean, before they can track him here? I'm sure they have a pretty good idea of where we were headed."

"That isn't all…I've heard stories of the awful things that Bloodstones have done…to discourage other slaves from leaving." She shuttered at the memory.

"Like what happened to Dreogan?" Hania asked.

Gaho shuttered, "Let's just say, that it was usually fatal." She went back to supervising the work.

"I'll tackle him…you get your stuff ready." Onid sighed as she looked out the window; she turned and forcing a smile onto her face, went in search of Chval.

Hania shook his head; *I like Onid. She is a lot like my older sister, firm and gentle at the same time.*

He gathered his things and waited by the bench under the Sequoia in the main square. What would happen to Chval if he didn't get his hand treated…did Chval deserve to have something bad happen to him? Part of him said yes, let him suffer, the other part said no. He remembered the snakes under Dreogan's skin and shuttered.

He heard voices, arguing, as they got closer.

"I was just worried what kind of Seeker Spell he would use on you." Onid's face showed extreme concern.

Chval shoved his hand at him, Onid, her arms crossed, stood behind Chval and winked at Hania. Hania couldn't help smiling.

He took the hand, pulled his instruments close, and inspected the thing that was Chval's hand, and not his hand.

43

Raghnall relaxed in the shade of a Live Oak where a stream dumped into the swamp; a pathway meandered along the stream up into the hills. Noticing fresh foot-traffic on it, he had sent a small exploratory group to see where it went. The main path continued towards Bainbridge.

The Atwaters were more slippery than he had first thought…who led them? Was it the rock thrower or that potion maker?

He pulled out his Stone, drawing his finger over a trace pattern of white marring the deep crimson, lines that squiggled and crossed. What did that mean…was the Stone losing its power? It should have lasted a lot longer; it had a full charge and was ready to go after feeding off the slave.

He turned it over, a white edged circle, about one quarter of the stone, beat like a heart under the faceted surface. He stared at it.

A shout from the right pulled him out of his contemplation.

Aja scampered back to him along the pathway between the trees, the sun overhead made shadows dance over him as he ran…Oh to be young. "We found a shelter!" He panted out.

Now they find a shelter…why couldn't they find one last night? He had to use much of his Stone's power to erect a primitive shelter…had that drained the Stone to the point that it was on the edge of failing…had a Stone ever failed as long as there was blood to feed it?

He and his entourage followed Aja along the path climbing away from the swamp's stench; Aja bounced along the path jabbering like the usual eight-year-old. "Istaqa thinks that the Atwaters sheltered in it." He picked up a stick and started swatting the undergrowth, "They left the place a mess."

"Indeed. What do you think they did while they were there?" *The sooner one started to read what prey did before you got there, the better…a skill too many thought useless.*

"They cooked a meal…caiman and eggs," Aja looked thoughtful, "And slept."

"Anything unusual?" They had reached the shelter, ducking, he entered. Very interesting place...the stone and woodwork, he ran his hand along the mantle over the fireplace. Edur was already making good use of the fireplace and setting out what looked and smelled like a feast...food from the ship, complete with un-doctored wine.

Aja ran over and grabbed a leather apron that had been hung by the fireplace, "Look at this," he laid it out on the table's edge.

Raghnall felt a chill run through him...the pattern of lines on the apron matched his Stone.

"What caused that?" Aja asked, "It looks like someone did a bad job branding it."

Raghnall shoved his Stone deeper into his pocket, Aja's sharp eyes or one of the other men might see it and he did not want them asking questions that he had no answers for. Besides, who knows when we'll find shelter again...we'll rest here for the rest of today and start fresh in the morning.

But what had happened? He ran his hand over the apron where it was rough, was that silver speckles trapped in the groves? He looked at his hand...little silver glints; he went and washed it off. Silver...must be that potion maker again.

He walked over to the window; looking down he saw silver glints among the foliage. *Soon, potion maker, soon I will have you.*

He could feel his Stone beating against his leg, what did that circle mean? With his back to the others, he pulled out his Stone and stared at it...it just sat there, beating. *What if I fed it...would that fix it?*

When they got closer to Bainbridge, he would sacrifice another slave, and then he would use the Find Spell...to indicate where the Atwaters were hiding. No need to deplete his supply of slaves any faster than he had to. He slipped the Stone into his pocket and turned to the table to eat.

44

Hania examined Chval's hand, turning it so he could see one side and then the other; Chval trembled as Hania turned it burn side up. While Chval's hand was warm to the touch, the burn was ice cold.

The burn's edges were not loose, with no sign of healing. He touched the silvered surgical knife blade to it; smoke rose wherever the blade's tip contacted the burn, yet there was no heat.

He drew his finger across it, "Did you feel that?"

Chval shook his head, "No."

He pulled the knife's un-silvered handle across the burn, pushing hard. "Do you feel that?"

Again Chval shook his head, worry glistened in his eyes as his body shuddered; Chval bit his lip and took a deep breath, fighting the fear.

Skelly called from the cookhouse, "It's getting thick!"

Onid rushed into the smelter, emerging with two men carrying a small pot into the cookhouse.

"Come on," Hania said as he pulled Chval over to the cookhouse.

Hania checked both pots and supervised the last part, the pouring of liquid silver into the thickened sap. After that, they poured the silvered sap into molds to cool; soon it would be ready to pull. He turned to Chval, wiping the sweat out of his eyes; his back and legs ached and he wanted to stretch out with his feet up. No time for that…or any kind of rest, except sleeping at night.

I wish we could have made some of that sap into syrup, what a shame to have to make it all into Silvered Rock.

He fished out some old Silvered Rock he got from Gaho from a pocket of his wilderness kit, "Eat this," He tossed it to Chval and leaned against the door jam, *I need to get way from this heat.*

"That's it?" Chval looked at him, "All I had to do to get rid of this thing is to eat some Silver Rock?"

170

"Let's hope so," Hania said as he bent down and held his hand over the silvered candy to check the temperature, at least his sweat tasted like maple candy.

"What do you mean, hope?" Chval yanked him around to face him.

"So few have been touched by the Stones," Hania tried to explain. "We don't know for sure what will happen in each case…but it does react to silver."

Chval stared at the Silvered Rock in his hand, holding it out like it was poisonous.

"It's the same stuff they dust birthday cakes with," Hania said, "It won't kill you."

"It hurt Dreogan," shuttered Chval trying to hand it back, "It made those snake things."

"It did not make the snake things, the snakes were already under his skin before he had any."

Selective memory…Chval could be so…he could feel a tension headache coming on. He half closed his eyes, trying to relax by taking deep breaths…the air in the cookhouse was humid with the moisture boiled out of the sap.

"We are trying to keep what happened to Dreogan from happening to you." He said as calmly as he could.

Onid was watching them, leaning against the wall, waiting for Chval to eat it.

Chval looked at the determination in her face, popped it in his mouth and chewing, went to sit in the shade waiting for something to happen.

"What is it about silver that affects the Bloodstones?" Hania asked Onid as they joined Chval, it was a lot cooler under the trees and a fresh breeze brought with it the smell of something baking. *I hope it's for us.*

"Farid told me…it's because silver is pure," she shrugged.

"I was looking at the acid balls…isn't there something we could pack them in so they won't break?" Hania asked.

"Sand," Onid watched Skelly cross over to the smelter.

Hania watched him go in, *how can he stand the heat?* The doors shimmered as he passed them.

"Sand is kind of heavy."

"Silicon sand," Onid leaned back against the tree trunk, drew her knees up, and rested her arms on them.

"Where can we get some on such short notice?"

"The catacombs."

Hania turned to her, shocked that she would steal from the dead, "Used or un-used?" His voice quivered slightly.

"Un-used," that smile was back, "Skelly and I can get it. I'm sure he can carry all that we would need."

Hania looked from her to the smelter where Skelly was working, *was she interested in Skelly...or was she just pulling on Chval's chain?* He glanced over at Chval; he was scowling at them.

She got up and brushed off her leggings, "I'll go see if he's free," she strode to the smelter building. *She is treading on...*

"Hania...something is happening," Chval's voice quivered. With Onid gone, he set aside his bravado.

Hania pulled a small pot of silver ointment over to Chval, not only was he shaking but holding out his hand as if something foul was in it, straining his head away as far as possible.

The burn quivered as if it was alive, but it smelled dead and like it had sat in the sun awhile...funny that no flies came near. Hania positioned the pot of silvered salve under the burn and brushed the ointment around Chval's wrist.

"Cut it off!" Chval was panicking.

"Is it hurting?" Hania spread the ointment to the burn's edge, covering his fingers, wrist, and back of his hand.

"No," Chval whimpered.

"Then don't look at it," Hania held the burn over the pot, was it going to drop off like the snakes? He jiggled the hand.

Chval was panting.

"Take slow, deep breaths."

"Okay," Chval complied; his eyes squeezed shut.

Hania watched as Skelly and Onid left the compound, they waived as they started to climb towards a structure that was halfway up a tall hill. *This is an interesting place; some of their structures...some other time*, he chided himself.

Both Chval and Skelly are good looking young men and I can see why Onid would find both of them worthy of her interest. Would they start a rivalry?

We don't need that...we need to fight the Bloodstones, not each other.

He turned back to Chval's hand just in time to see the burn slide into the pot with a hiss...it was gone except for a foul smelling smoke curling into the air. A tender, pink patch of skin was all that was left.

Hania dressed it with silver salve from a fresh jar; the smoking one was contaminated, and wrapped it with a clean strip of linen.

Chval stomped off, throwing dirty looks in the direction Onid and Skelly had gone; then turned and went into the smelter.

Hania sighed and gathered his stuff; *this day has been long and hard.* He rubbed at the sore ache in his back; *my bedroll is going to feel so good.*

45

Skelly followed Onid up through the thick trees; the trail they took was wide and beaten smooth by the passage of feet over the years. He could feel the effects of working in the smelter's heat start to ease off…shade, wonderful shade.

He didn't have fatigue as bad as Hania, but he had to be careful, stress and heat could trigger a seizure. Onid stopped in a clearing at the edge of a cliff, acting as if she was contemplating something as she looked down into the valley; he took a quick swallow from the Foxglove Fo-ti flask.

"Last time I was up here," she said as Skelly caught up, "was for a cousin's funeral."

Skelly turned to see the full view of the valley. It was so different from Atwater. There were waterfalls, many waterfalls…fields of grain next to pastures of cattle, sheep, and other grazers; above that, woods marched up the slopes of mountains. Real mountains, not like the rolling hills of Atwater.

Onid sat down on a log, "I sometimes come up here to ponder why I have been given such a task. It helps."

"Are you?" Skelly waved off a bussing fly.

"Am I what?" She pulled her knees up to her chest, hugging them.

"You know, " he shrugged, not wanting to come right out with it as she stared at him, "The Stone Born Maiden…I mean…we are preparing as if…" He let it trail off as he settled on the log next to her.

She tilted her head back and looked up through the canopy of leaves, green light speckling her tanned face. "I…Kendra is sure. She is quite sure. Farid, too."

Skelly moved back along the log, being this close to her made him nervous. "So…what do they think of us? I use to think that it would be grand to be one of the Spirit Warriors, but now that I've been given a taste of what may be involved, I'm not sure…I would want the task."

"They are sure that the core from Atwater is here," Onid started unpacking a late lunch she had brought.

So this was not some spur of the moment thing...that both thrilled and scared him.

"Some of us that are here...or all of us from Atwater?" He took a napkin full from her and sat on a nearby boulder.

"She says, time will tell." She watched him closely as she ate the dark bread with sliced cheese and honey.

He found it hard to swallow the bite he had taken. "Farid said something last night."

"What did he say?"

He looked out away from her; *I hope this doesn't sound like I'm gloating.* "Chval is not one, at least not yet."

"You do not seem thrilled by the chance that you may be a Spirit Warrior." She said quietly.

Skelly shook his head, "I'm not strong...I could never be a warrior." That sounded dumb, he knew what he looked like. He was built like a warrior, but the Lise's hidden weaknesses could pop up at the most dangerous and inopportune moment.

"There are warriors and there are Spirit Warriors." She took a few bites of her lunch.

"What's the difference? I know that Hania says there's a difference," He felt so strange. *This is not where I expected to end up,* "I'm training to be a historian. To record history, not make it." *On the other hand, having a knowledge of history would be of great use to the Spirit Warriors, I could tell them what had not worked in the past.*

They finished eating without another word. As she gathered up the lunch things, Skelly shivered, *have I done something wrong...have I just failed a test?*

She did not speak again until they reached the catacombs. As they reached the opening she turned, her dark eyes bright with tears, "I don't like being the Stone Born Maiden...I want to be like other girls. But I'm not!"

Skelly stood there shocked, as she turned and entered the caverns, *she doesn't have a choice. Do I?* He blinked; *she feels the same way about being different as I do...as Hania does.*

He ducked and entered as well. After a few feet, he could stand upright again; Onid lit a torch and headed down a passage, Skelly following.

This place is different than the caverns on Manhood Island; there you have to be careful of sloping floors, fallen rocks, and holes waiting to injure the unwary. And low ceilings...his hand reached up and touched the tender spot on his forehead where the bump once was. *These floors are smooth, flat, and swept clean. Someone cared for them as they would a home, or a temple.*

He was glad Onid knew where she was going; there were so many passages and rooms. Deeper and deeper they went. He looked up at the high smoke stained ceiling, how long had this place been in use?

Onid paused, stepped back, and waved him close. Looking at her, he saw her finger was up to her lips in a caution for silence. She pointed further into the passage; stepping aside he peered around the next corner and noticed there was a pool of light coming out of an opening, spilling into the corridor.

They were not alone. Onid pulled him back, "We aren't supposed to be here..." she whispered, "Technically that is...stay here." She stuck the torch in a wall bracket and pulled out her dagger.

She moved on ahead, not making a sound. He left the pool of light and slipped up behind her, not wanting her to face danger alone, *why do I feel this way?* They crept closer to the slit of light spilling out into the corridor from a room to the right along with smell of an oil lamp, the sound of scraping came from inside the chamber. Was it a thief or a worker? Pressing themselves tight against the wall, they sidestepped in the direction of the light.

46

Hania wiped the oily sweat out of his eyes; the heat in here was almost more than his Hesutu could take. He took a long drink of Fo-ti juice and dropped the flask back into the bucket of water sitting next to the bench. The rack of Silvered Acid Balls gleamed with the reflected light of the kiln.

"Done." He eased the funnel out of the last ball, dropped it into a bucket of soda water, and watched it fizz as he pushed himself up from the workbench. Gaho inspected his work and nodded in satisfaction.

A worker dipped a rod in and out of the kiln, the molten glass at the end glimmered. He touched it to each ball sealing the openings, inserting it into the kiln as needed.

Hania and Gaho watched from the doorway. Hania took a wet towel from the vat by the door and wiped it over his head and neck, removing the tartness of the acid. The touch of soda in this water felt good on his skin.

"Are you doing okay?" Gaho asked.

"I'm fine." *Why had she asked that...did she know about the Hesutu...does she think I'm a weakling, too?*

Ambling off, he went to check on the 'Silvered Rock'. He needed a break from the heat and took a roundabout route through tree-shaded paths, stopping long enough to scratch his back on the rough bark of an old oak, *ah that's better.*

Uaid's workers, wearing thin, fat covered gloves, were pulling the almost cooled silvered sap, taffy like, into long shimmering ropes. There seemed to be plenty of them, so he headed to the nearest fountain to get a drink.

The water was so cool and refreshing that he dunked his whole head in, *I wish Skelly were back, a water fight right now would be welcome.* He looked in the direction Skelly had gone; someone was coming, but it wasn't Onid and Skelly. He pushed the water from his hair as he stood.

A group of men were coming from Bainbridge...they did not look happy.

Uaid came out of the office with a look of concern on his face; he sent for Gaho and joined Hania.

"Don't they even read the prophecies?" Uaid mumbled to himself.

Gaho arrived; "I knew this was going to happen. Ever since they elected that idiot to head the counsel." She nodded her head at the men marching into the square.

Hania looked the group over, which one of them was the idiot? It didn't take long to figure it out…the man had more gold hung around him than most families made in a year. Even his outrageous hair had liberal amounts of gold dust combed into each meticulous lock, it had to be a wig, there was no way you could sleep on it.

Why they were coming here? Hania glanced at Gaho; she was ridged, her arms crossed in front, and eyes thinned. *I'd hate to have her look at me that way.*

The look on the face of the 'idiot' changed from composed to uncertain to self-righteous. He tore into Gaho as soon as they walked into the shade of the trees.

"We, the Counsel, have come to a decision," sniffed Gold-hair. "We understand how kind hearted you can be. But these youth are putting our town, our way of life…" His voice took on an air of pleading, "in greatest peril."

"And?" Uaid waited, the air in the square crackled with tension…Hania almost expected lightening to strike.

"The Atwater youth must leave," Gold-hair bristled, "First thing in the morning." The men around him looked uncomfortable, faces averted as Gaho's gaze touched them; none would meet her eye.

"Think about your workers, their families," Gold-hair whined.

"Oh, I don't think our families are in any peril." One of Gaho's men stepped forward, the edge to his voice as sharp as the fine, silvered sword at his hip.

"They must go." Gold-hair snarled back and turned to leave, the men from Bainbridge slipped into his shadow.

"You think that will keep the Bloodstones from your gates?" Gaho called out and then turned. "Idiots," she looked at Hania, "You're not leaving until you are ready."

Chval stepped out from one of the buildings, "We don't stand a chance."

Hania sank to the lip of the fountain, his hand dangling in the water, *was Chval right?* A breeze tore through, splashing spray on Hania, and then it struck him, *why not put Chval's talents to work? It would give him something to do…and help his bruised ego.*

"Do you have maps of the area we have to travel through to get back home?" Hania asked Uaid.

"In the office," Uaid nodded towards the building.

"You?" Chval snorted, "Now you're going to plan our flight back home?"

"You think you could do a better job?" Hania needled him, *would he take the bait?*

"In my sleep," Chval walked over and looked down at him.

"Fine, you do it!" It had worked, relief flooded through him as Chval and Uaid went into the office.

"Nicely done," Gaho said from behind him…she had seen right through it, "Where did you learn to do that?"

"My dad and Nabi." he grinned, "They do that with Chval's father, when necessary." But it was getting less often…Chval's Paternal Grandfather had been a much better leader.

Gaho chuckled as she put her hand on his shoulder, "We've got a lot to do tonight."

"And we need to help," Dreogan arose from a litter lying in the shade of a tree, "I can't stand laying around any longer."

"I second that," Tesar limped from around from the tree's other side. Standing on one leg, he showed them the crutch he had spent the morning making, "Point me in the direction of a task I can do."

Hania put him to work breaking up 'silvered rock'; sitting with his injured leg up on the bench, Tesar put his pent up anger to good use.

Hania looked at Dreogan, *what could he do that would not hurt his back?* He put him to work supervising the making of six bundles of weapons, one for each of them.

"Work out what we'll need with Chval."

Dreogan looked uncertain, his eyes flicked over to the office.

"Remember the war games?" Hania looked into Dreogan's eyes. "Chval always won, because he had the best strategy," the worry left Dreogan's face and he grinned.

Relief again flooded Hania, *or was it something else…Peace? When we are in the biggest jam we've ever faced? Odd.*

The sooner we get home, the better, more of Gaho's workers showed up to help them. *Was it because they were in a hurry to get rid of them or did they want them to be as prepared as possible before the counsel of Bainbridge made them go?*

47

Skelly and Onid reached the doorway where the scraping sound came from, Skelly peered in as Onid slipped like a shadow into the room and ducked down next to a crate that was being used as a table. She was good!

An oil lamp sat atop the crate threw flickering shadows as it added smoke to the dusty haze caused by the silicon sand harvest. Onid signaled Skelly to go one way as she crept to the other side.

Skelly moved behind the person that was kneeling down, filling bags with the off-white crystals scrapped from the wall. Silence was tricky as the floor was covered in loose crystals. He had to pick his way over as sweat trickled down from his temples, gumming up as the moisture attracted the drying dust that filled the room. He suppressed a cough.

The person was small, *but that wouldn't matter if they were trained as a warrior.* Swallowing, Skelly nodded at Onid to move around the table. She was the bait. "It's okay," she called out as her body relaxed and straightened, "It's just Kendra."

"It's just Kendra?" The woman lugged the bag of crystals over to the crate. She had a cloth tied over her mouth and she tossed them each one, "I was wondering how soon you would show up," soon they all looked like roadside bandits.

She turned and looked at him, disapproval flickered in her eyes before she could hide it. *What's wrong...what did I do to displease her?*

"I understand you had an interesting run-in with some folks from Dennet," Kendra said as she and Onid started to tie bags shut on the crate. Skelly listened as he filled bags and carried them over.

"What did you do to that young whelp?" Kendra looked at Onid, her eyes crinkled.

Chuckling, Onid told her.

Kendra sighed, "It is only going to get harder; I know you have read all our

Prophecies. Pick your companions carefully," she looked at Skelly again. "One from Dennet; how are you coming with the core from Atwater?"

"Well there are six from Atwater here right now." Onid dragged Skelly next to Kendra, he didn't want to go, but what could he do…run? "I'm sure his is one of the core."

"Um…yes, you were at the council."

"You had me go," Skelly said…*why doesn't she like me?*

Kendra looked him over, "And are you trained as a warrior?"

"No," Skelly shivered, *why did she ask that…should I have been trained as warrior?* "My father has a fishery…I'm a student of history…Nabi is my mentor."

"Oh! I must say…you don't look like a historian." Kendra's eyes changed and with a big twinkle in them, she warmed up to him, "And how is Nabi doing…did he tell you about the Spirit Warriors?"

Skelly, taken aback, started to think about that last time he had been with Nabi, "He told me very little. He just mumbled parts of our Prophecies as he was giving me the weapons we would need."

"Tell me again, what did he give you?" Kendra started to pile the bags of crystals into his arms; she was now beaming up at him like a long time friend. For some reason that made him more nervous.

"Swords, spears, sling-shots, bows, and arrows…all were silvered." He looked at Kendra; she was waiting for something else. He shut his eyes and dragged the memory up out of what felt like the far past. "Knives and he said to get acid balls from Gaho…Oh, yes…a cross bow and bolts."

"What did he say…what were you to use?" Kendra's bright eyes bored into him.

"The cross bow." *What did it matter?* But Kendra seemed happy with his answer…very happy.

Kendra led the way out of the caverns, turning to them as they reached the mouth. "Much of what has been prophesied has yet to come to past." With a deep sigh, she looked over the valley, "You are up against a very dangerous man."

"His name is Raghnall," Skelly said as they shed the bandit look, handing the cloths back to Kendra and brushing the silicon dust off their clothes. The air of early evening smelled of night blooming flowers, a refreshing change after the stuffy air of the catacombs.

"Raghnall, yes…Gaho told me." Her gaze passed over Onid before it returned to Skelly; "Has Gaho told you anything about him?"

"Isn't he the one that gave Mom the Bloodstone Seeds?"

"Yes, one of the elder Wizard sons of High Wizard Quinn," Kendra looked at the sky, "We have much to do, much to do. Come! They are waiting."

They headed down the hill. *What was it that Gaho knew about Raghnall...should he ask...and what did it have to do with Onid?*

Kendra said he was dangerous...no kidding...we've seen what he is like.

"Onid," Kendra stopped and turned, "You must be very careful. Raghnall is extremely dangerous, but he is more dangerous for you than the others. He will kill you instantly if he ever gets his hands on you. Watch your back!"

They reached a fork in the path; Gaho turned and handed the bags she was carrying to Onid. "May The Great Spirit watch over you and guide you," she pressed her wizened cheek to Onid's. Then she placed her hands on Skelly's shoulders and gave him a small shake, "You will do." Turning, she headed towards her own home.

"She will be praying all night...I know her." Onid proceeded on to The Forge.

Skelly felt a tremor go through him, *I will do? Do what?* He felt very inadequate over the whole Spirit Warrior thing...but...watching the end of Onid's golden braid brush at her waist, he decided. *I will protect her...Raghnall will never get his cold hands on her.*

48

Hania stood and stretched the kink out of his back; he couldn't remember such a long day. He was fatigued, but as he looked over the piles of weapons, he smiled. This was the first time he had felt the least bit prepared to face this adventure. *The Manhood Trip of this group of Atwaters certainly is earning its place in the Atwater Clan's history...if we survive it.*

He turned as Chval came out and looked over the weapons, there was a frown on his face. "You and Skelly have enough Fo-ti juice?"

"I think so," Hania looked at him closely, "We won't let you down." There was something about the closed look on Chval's face that bothered Hania, *just nerves...but were they his or mine?* With relief he saw Skelly and Onid return with the crystals from the catacombs.

"Any problems?" Hania asked them.

"No, just a warning," Skelly said.

"What kind? And from whom?" He turned from Skelly to Onid.

"It was Kendra...she wants us to be careful," Onid went into the building where the Silver Rock was cooling.

Hania followed as Skelly lugged in the bags of sand, "Who is this Kendra? Was she the woman that talked to you earlier?"

"Yes," Onid opened one of the cheesecloth bags and started filling it with the crystals, "She's a prophetess...her husband was the Prophet of Bainbridge. The Great Spirit told him that the mantle of prophecy would not leave his family, until Bainbridge fell." Onid's eyes filled with sorrow, "They had only one child, and she died in Cerebrus, after giving birth."

She picked up the bag, tied it, and dropped it in another bag filled with chunks of silvered rock. She stared at it as she continued, "My mother said she had bore a Stone Born Maiden. They sacrificed the babe to the Mother-stone...the main Bloodstone...their Idol," She couldn't hide the bitterness in her voice.

"I don't understand," Hania and Skelly started filling bags.

"Kendra lost her only child to the raid that took my mother. Then…" Onid shivered slightly, "her husband died a few years later. She was the only one left in her family. Xavier was told by the Great Spirit to give her the mantle of prophecy, to fulfill what the Great Spirit promised and gave her the strength to see, with courage, the past, present, and future. She is to watch over the people of Bainbridge; her calling will end with the fall Bainbridge."

She turned. "The only reason my mother lived," she sniffed, "Is that Kendra was told, in a dream, how to keep her alive after my birth."

Hania did not know what to say…He and Skelly just stood there, absently stuffing bags, and staring at her.

"It still almost killed her…Kendra brought me forth and proclaimed to the people of Bainbridge that I was the Maiden." She stood there breathing hard, fighting for control; she turned to them.

"I have been plagued with dreams ever since I came of age," She hugged her arms to herself to quell the trembling, "Our whole civilization…is in my hands. I do not feel capable; I am so weak."

Skelly stepped forward and gave her an awkward hug; she clung to him and sobbed. Hania patted her on the back.

"We'll help you." The words just came out…no thought behind them, *have we just signed a contract in blood?*

Skelly was nodding his agreement over Onid's head.

Hania sighed and walked out into the night, *I need sleep.* He walked over to a fountain and washed the stickiness of the silver rock off his hands…even the taste of maple as he splashed water on his face was not enough to dispel the gloom hanging over him, *what a day this has been.*

Chval was there. "I can't see why they can't provide us with porters," He was saying to the other boys, "I can't carry stuff…Dreogan and Tesar are wounded as well."

"If your ego wants a honorable place in history, you will do what needs to be done." Barra growled at him and giving his bedroll a shake, he climbed in.

Chval glared at them and took his bedroll off to another patch of grass and climbed in, "You will all go into history as just another Bloodstone raid," He tossed out and turned away.

"Onid and I are going into Bainbridge to see if we can't get some of the younger warriors to join us…even if the older men…" Skelly's voice trailed off.

Hania watched as they left; was it his imagination or had Skelly appointed himself her guardian? *Oh, Skelly…do you have any idea of the pain you will suffer if you take that roll?* It was one that Hania knew he wasn't willing, even though that trial would not happen until the third and final battle. *Watching the one you loved most...*

"You will need Heaven's help, Skelly, but we all need that...if we are to make it." He prayed before climbing into his own bedroll, and then drifting off, had bad dreams.

49

Onid and Skelly strolled towards Bainbridge; cool mountain breezes came down off the hills and played with the strands of hair that had escaped her braid. The moon providing plenty of light, but she was in no hurry. She looked at the tall young man walking next to her; he was a paradox…strong, and weak…and strong. Odd feelings ran through her, *I want to be protected by him and to protect him.* She shook it off, *we have a job to do and I'd better keep my mind on it, or we will fail.*

As they passed Kendra's place, she stopped. *The House of Records…was there anything about him…*she grabbed Skelly's hand and dragged him in with her; the almost full moon shed enough light to read.

"What are we doing here?" Skelly asked.

"Shush." She warned him and looked over the walls…they were gone, every one of the scrolls having anything to do with the Spirit Warriors.

"They're gone," she told him.

"What's gone?"

"The Spirit Warrior scrolls." Who had taken them, Kendra or the fear filled council of Bainbridge? They left the records building and headed on to Bainbridge, it took some time before she realized she was still holding his hand. A hand as rough and callused as her own, she let it drop, *I can't lead him on…there is no room in my life for romance; it just isn't going to happen…not yet…*

Clouds crossed over the moon, they stopped and sat on a grassy knoll, waiting for the moon to return. In stories…this was where the hero kissed the heroine, a tear escaped her eye and she was glad it was dark.

"Was it hard for you?" Skelly asked, making her hurry and wipe the wetness of the tear away…*quit feeling sorry for yourself.*

"Was what hard?" She plucked at the grass.

"Growing up knowing what you were?"

Onid thought back, "Not really. Other than having more training in weapons, marshal arts, survival, and rock climbing, it was no different than any others." *Any other boy, that is.* She pulled up one leg and rested her cheek on the knee then grinned at the dark shadow next to her, "What about you?"

"What do you mean?"

"There is something different about you and Hania. You seem to be more…I don't know, more like…religious."

Skelly laughed.

"What's so funny?"

Skelly sighed, "I wasn't much different from the others until three years ago."

"What changed?"

"An accident. I almost drowned, it caused me to have Lise," Skelly shifted in the dark.

She felt him move away from her, "Go on."

"My father is quite wealthy; he owns fleets of fishing boats, a couple of marinas, and warehouses. I was to learn the fishing trade and take over from him."

"And?" She prompted.

"Could you just see me?" He chuckled, "Passing out and falling overboard? They could lose a day's catch trying to pull the captain out of the water before he drowned."

"So what happened?" She looked up, the cloud cover was denser, and it looked like rain. *Well, it is the season.*

"My father took me to Nabi to see what could be done."

"Nabi is?"

"Our prophet. My father did not like what he said…so he took me to see Xavier."

"The Xavier?"

"Yes. And when he sat with me, it was odd," Onid could hear him shift again.

"Odd in what way?"

"I've never even told Hania about this. Xavier stared at me for a long time, then he looked into the sky…his eyes darted back and forth as if he was reading something."

Onid could feel a prickle at the back of her neck.

"Then he smiled at my dad and said that I was blessed. My father asked if that meant that I was cured…and Xavier told him, no and refused to say any thing else."

His voice holds no sorrow, no resentment; what does that mean? "What did he do?"

"He took me to every soothsayer and charlatan he could find...using a third of his wealth."

"He must love you."

"He does...nothing worked so we returned home. Hania's family are healers and they have done much to help me," He stopped as the clouds drifted aside and let the moonlight touch his face. He looked towards heaven, "Hania and his family taught me how to pray...how to be grateful for every day."

In the moonlight he almost glowed...unbidden the memory of him holding her...She got to her feet, *forget it...it isn't going to happen...not for me*...Onid led the way down the path. *I'm sure he is one of the core Spirit Warriors from Atwater...which one?*

Instead of going into the town, she headed to the old mill. The boys she trained with went there to practice the martial arts and sword work; it was like a clubhouse away from the parents.

Going in, she stopped short. A few of the boys were there, but so were some of the fathers.

"What are you doing here?" Julian's father growled, "Get out! And take the Atwater with you."

"The Bloodstones have returned," Skelly's voice was unruffled, "and they are more powerful than before. Making us leave will not keep them from you."

"We know how to take care of our own."

Skelly stepped forward to challenge him.

Onid grabbed his arm, "It's not time yet," they went back outside. *It had happened...just like in the scrolls.* They started back, *how soon? How soon would?*

"Onid," the voice hissed out from behind some rocks.

"Julian," *Is my life no longer mine? Am I preprogrammed to perform as written in the scrolls?*

Julian, grinning stepped out bushy brown hair and all. "A group of us will meet you at the lower gate...first thing in the morning, before the folks get up."

"Your father is..."

"I know. Go!" He ducked out of sight.

"Come on...let's get some sleep. We are going to have a very busy day tomorrow," they walked in silence back to the Foundry.

She felt comfortable with him…no, that wasn't it…safe? No, it just felt…right. *Drop it! Get your mind on tomorrow*…"Go to that spot Chval marked on the map. I'll get there as fast as I can, with as many as Julian can get from Bainbridge."

As she watched Skelly join the other sleepers from Atwater, chills ran down her arms; *would I have the nightmares again tonight?* Reluctantly she headed to her bed.

50

Hania wasn't having any luck sleeping on the uneven ground; a tree root was under his left shoulder; a crunch of gravel announced Skelly's return. As Skelly slipped into his own bedding, Hania moved around, adjusting his sleeping mat to turn the offending root into a pillow. "How did it go?" He whispered, not wanting to wake Chval, and then he remembered that Chval was sleeping elsewhere.

"A few are coming."

"How many?"

"Don't know...I think as many as can sneak away and join us. The adults don't want anything to do with it," Skelly sighed, "They want the prophecies to come to pass, but without them getting involved, without it endangering their lifestyle, livelihoods, or families."

"It will involve them anyway, I fear." Hania turned and looked at the sky, "The Bloodstones will not let them off."

He looked up through the overhead branches of a hackberry tree; the stars were playing peek-a-boo with the leaves. Why was it so peaceful up there when everything down here was falling apart?

"Where do you think they will attack first?" Skelly asked, bringing Hania back to earth.

"Atwater."

"Why Atwater?"

"We were the first to rebel...revenge," Hania put his hands behind his head.

"How soon?" Skelly moved closer.

"When the rains come...so they can use their boats."

There was silence, except for the gurgling of the fountain and Tesar's snoring; they both got lost in their thoughts. *This is one of the reasons why I like Skelly; he doesn't go for idle chatter.*

"What if?" Skelly mused, "We fixed some nets under the water that they needed to cross? There are only three main channels they can use. Well, actually two, the third breaks up into a bunch of un-navigable streams."

"Entangle their boats?" Hania pondered as he watched the shadow of a barn owl dive to the ground, with a snap of wing, it purchased air and disappeared into the trees. "They could use magic to get rid of the nets."

"Not if the nets had silver woven into them."

"We can give the elders some our insight when we get home." *Home...that is what I want more than anything...I want to be home...safe...with life back to normal.* He yawned, breathing in the pine fresh air; sleep was coming; his eyes drooped, and then snapped open. *Going home won't make it all go away.*

It was still dark when Hania woke to angry voices. Chval and Onid were arguing; Chval wanted Onid to come with them; Onid was going to Bainbridge and wait by the lower gate.

"Fine!" Chval yelled at her retreating back, "They won't show...Bainbridge men are all cowards!"

Chval turned around, "What?" He had caught the look on Hania's face.

"She is not our enemy, the Bloodstones are." Hania turned and gathered his bedding, shaking out the pine needles.

"If she walks out on us, than she is..."

"She went to get us more help," Skelly cut in, "I was there when arrangements to meet them were made."

Chval snorted and stomped off, Hania didn't want to admit it, but he felt the same way about most Bainbridge men. But this Julian seemed willing, if he brought friends...Uaid said the men of the Forge would set up a blockade first thing in the morning; by mid morning, no Bloodstone could follow them.

After everyone had eaten and made their quiet good-bys, they shouldered the weapon bundles and headed into the mists of early morning. At the lower bridge, they gathered around Chval as he pulled out the map Uaid had given him. It was hard to see in the dim light of dawn, they chose to leave early so that they didn't have to travel in the heat of the day.

Hania and Skelly didn't do well when it was hot.

"We should be able to make it here before nightfall," Chval pointed at a spot on the map.

"Onid said she would meet us here, at this cleft." Skelly pointed.

Hania was sitting with his back against the raised bridge as Tesar was getting a last look. "Fascinating," Tesar mumbled.

Farid, hauling a bundle of weapons, panted up to them, set down his load, and put a water flask to his lips. He put the stopper back in the flask and froze, staring across the mist filled chasm.

"What is it?" Hania asked him.

He blinked, "Something dark and evil is coming." He squinted to the south, "He will catch us."

Hania looked across the gorge a shiver going down his spine, was it a reaction to Farid words…or something else? He closed his eyes, and felt out with his spiritual sight; asking The Great Spirit. A weak burning in his chest was his only answer.

"Chval, how far is the next town?"

"Three days hike. Why?"

"Farid says the Bloodstones are not far behind." Chval looked at Farid, Hania could see the wheels turning in his head, should he act on Farid's words or not.

"They have to get to this side of the chasm," Chval said.

"They used magic to get through the swamp…you think they can't get across this?" Skelly swept his hand in the chasm's direction.

"You have to work together or you will fail," warned Farid.

Chval looked across the chasm, nervously chewing his lip, then he looked down at the map. It was as if he was coming to a conclusion.

Hania crossed his fingers and prayed, hard.

"Onid said she was going to meet up with us here. There are several caves," he turned and looked north.

Skelly nodded, "You have an idea?"

"The Bloodstones are arrogant; they would not expect us to make a stand." Chval knelt and spread the map out on the ground.

Using small stones, he showed them a plan; Farid nodded.

Hania pulled himself up and took a drink from the flask of Fo-ti and Skelly did the same with the Foxglove-laced Fo-ti that he carried. They were both feeling the pressure.

Chval stood and rolled up the map, "Let's move out. When Onid catches up, we want to be in place."

Skelly reached down and took one end of Farid's weapon bundle as Farid took the other, "What have you got in there?"

"Stuff for Onid," Farid shrugged, "I'm not much of a warrior."

Hania gave one last look across the chasm as a shiver ran through him, down to his core. *Yes, I'm scared…I hope they don't catch up in the heat of the day...I don't know if I could handle the Bloodstones and fatigue at the same time. Would Uaid's blockade be set up too late...will we have to fight the Bloodstones alone? We'll just have to face it...if it reaches that point.*

51

Onid sat on the smooth back of one of the stone gargoyles that stood on each side of the gate. She reached down and plucked a sprig of lavender, pulling it apart, letting the smell soothe and calm her as she waited; it was odd that the gate's guardians stood in a patch of lavender, but maybe they needed calming as well. She smiled at her little fantasy as she strained for any sound that would mean someone was coming, all she heard was the twin falls crashing to the chasm's floor as they had for hundreds of years. She looked at the sky and frowned. Was Chval right…was Bainbridge no more than a town of cowards, hiding out between the twin falls?

She jumped when a helmeted and armored Julian touched her arm; while her heart slowed back to normal she looked around at the three young men. Was this all? Then another nine appeared out of the gloom and pride touched her heart, all the young men that she had grown up with, trained with. Tears threatened her eyes and her throat was tight with emotion, she couldn't speak; Chval was wrong.

They walked away from Bainbridge in silence…as if they were ghosts walking in the mist. They cut through an orchard that was so heavy with blossoms they could almost taste it; the bees would return with the sun, but for now it was quiet. It wasn't until they had gone past Kendra's home that they broke the silence.

"My father was in rare form last night," Julian said. The other's agreed.

"What did he have to say?"

"The usual…Kendra is too old…she can't tell the difference between a vision and a dream."

"What do you think?"

"Well, if she is wrong, we will have had a good hike through the countryside."

"And if she is right?" Onid waited.

"If I have the choice between becoming a slave or dying in battle?" Julian scratched his chin, mimicking his father, "Well, in battle there is always the chance you live."

It was a choice with these youth; I was never given that choice. But that's not right...I could have taken some of my family's wealth and headed north.

It was a choice for all of them...to choose to leave or choose to fight evil. She looked to the east; what choice had the people of Dennet made? They were enslaving themselves to a false god who would abandon them at the first crises.

They walked through the dew damp undergrowth, their tall well-oiled boots keeping them dry as they pushed on into the dawn.

52

Hania watched Farid, he seemed nervous. It reminded him of a rabbit he had once seen. The trap had been set with Skelly waiting up in one tree and he in another.

The rabbit would come close and just tremble; it was caught because it did not run when it had sensed the danger.

Farid was twisting around and staring behind them. Looking up at Hania, he pled, "Don't you feel it…the evil…the darkness?"

Hania did not want to say no, *what could I say?* "I'm too tired to feel anything," he sighed, turned around, and squinting his eyes he looked for some sign of the evil Farid felt.

Nothing, but Farid was near panic or was he spiritually sensitive. The pink tinge of dawn gave way to the gold of a new day as Hania took a small sip of Fo-ti and looked around.

They were heading into wilder country. No more farms here with neat rows of crops…no cattle grazing inside sturdy paddocks…no barns, no silos. They continued to climb.

It was desert land, what large trees there were lined up along the creeks. Most of it was dry and sandy with little shade; the road was built of blocks of raised limestone, with sand blown up against it. A high pass was ahead according to Chval's map and lots of limestone and old quarries, the roads were good; they would need to be to transport the rock.

Was this where the stone to build Bainbridge came from? Probably, maybe stone from here could be found as far away as Pendragon. Pendragon, the island home of the head Prophet Xavier, was he mindful of us…praying for us? I hope so.

A dark ridge along the east appeared to be volcanic in origin…rough and sand scared; it threw jagged shadows over the paler land beneath it.

The sand piled against it; to the west a long leaf pine forest was gaining ground, younger trees and shrubs in front, such a desolate place.

There would be cool shade under the trees, but the diamond back rattlesnake loved that habitat. He looked a little closer along the road where sink holes full of spring rains were pooling, fragrant short-lived flowers raced against time to set seed before the dry season. "Chval!"

Chval stopped and came back, the others gathered around. A look of irritation flitted over Chval's face, "What is it...do you need a rest?"

"Look around you," Hania waited.

Chval gave a cursory glance in all four directions, "So?"

"Coastal desert...rattlesnakes."

Chval almost leaped onto the nearest boulder. Barra burst out laughing, "They're lethargic this early in the morning. Besides, unless we go into the forest, all we have to worry about is the pigmy rattlesnake...painful, but not deadly."

"Just use your walking stick to probe beneath the sand in front of you before you step." His face became stern as he watched deer disappear up a draw, then Barra looked skyward, "I don't like this."

Hania glanced up, even the hawks were leaving the sky; it was an eerie replay of the swamp.

Barra dropped to his knees at the road's edge, his trained eyes searching for something, "Look!" He pointed at an indentation in the sand that led into salt grass alongside the road.

"We won't need to worry about rattlesnakes," he frowned up at them, "It's like in the swamp. The animals are fleeing."

Animal often sense danger before man, they were escaping; but was it from them, or did they feel something else?

Did they know the Bloodstones were coming?

Hania looked at Farid's pale face, and swallowed his fear, "We have to keep going." Wind began to blow, at least the sand was damp from rain or we would have had to take shelter in the forest or didn't Chval say there were caves?

The air smelled fresh, rain-washed; he looked up and saw a bank of clouds against the peaks of a tall mountain range to the north. "Barra, do you think we are in danger of a flash flood?"

Barra looked around shaking his head. "See no sign of flash floods, been too wet for the wind to erase it...I'd say no."

That was a relief. It was safe to go on, so they did.

53

Raghnall stopped on a hilltop, breathing hard. He hated hiking, hated the sweat trickling down his back, hated being thirsty, and hated the blisters forming on his feet.

The narrow pathway they had been forced to take had switch-backed all the way up the face of a cliff riddled with mines. Silver mines. Being this close to silver made him nervous, *silver here is as common as water, I'll have to destroy the mines, bury the silver.*

Again he glanced at the stone, the part that had beat like a heart was now solid white. There was no doubt the Stone needed recharging.

His men were disgruntled; he had made them get up early. He wanted to cut the lead of the slaves. How far ahead of them were the Atwater slaves…had they stayed in Bainbridge, sending word to their sires that the big bad Bloodstones were after them? What if he took some Bainbridge youth as well…umm…that sounds good.

Aja was skipping down the path singing songs, dancing around in circles. The hike was a grand adventure for the boy, such abundant energy, even slipping in the pathway's loose gravel only made him look up and grin. *What I'm doing is for him, for his future.*

They entered a narrow cleft; Aja gazed in wonder at the height of the cliffs that rose on both sides. A moist breeze flowed through, the path flat and smooth, slightly damp…silver glinted in the stone face on both sides, he shuttered.

Taking a long drink from the water pouch a slave handed him at a snap of his fingers, he pondered, *how many of the slaves should I use? After we are finished with retaking the Atwaters, I could use any number of captives; no need to be stingy at that moment, if I have to use all of them, I will. Though I would hate to lose this one, he is well trained.*

But a fear nagged him, what was happening to his Stone? Once again he stuffed it down into its pouch.

He exited the cleft and the dawn sun's direct rays hit, almost blinding him, but at least he was no longer surrounded by silver. The path made its way down to a gorge; the sound of a waterfall shaking the wall of stone behind him and a misty breeze from the deep valley enticed him to move on.

Vritra ran back. "Lord Raghnall, we have found where a bridge crosses the gorge."

"What kind of bridge?" He followed Vritra down to where a path ended at the gorge's edge and looked across. An odd contraption was wedged against the other side, beneath it mist from the gorge bellowed, scented with pine.

The Bloodstone Warriors waited as Raghnall pulled out the Stone. "Bring me a slave, a young one," he wanted his Stone to be strong.

After the Stone had fed, he whispered his questions. Fingers of energy flicked over its surface, a surface showing only a vague image of the marks that once marred it. The Stone was picking up three traces of Bloodstone magic.

He sent out the Seeker Spells. Two headed straight across from them before fading away...healing had taken place. The third one pointed to the mountainside above a village; it died as soon as it left the stone, never really taking form. It touched something dead or something that was under the influence of another's Stone. Now that was odd.

He looked up the gorge to where Bainbridge was nestled between two widely spaced waterfalls; the desire to own it, to possess it...rushed through his veins. From here it looked impenetrable, it would make a worthy home. His eyes traveled over the valley...farms...vineyards...he caught himself drooling and wiped his mouth. *I'll return soon,* he promised it; *you will be one of my possessions.*

Vritra grinned, "What do you want us to do...shall we take it now?" The light of desire gleamed in his eyes, Vritra wanted to own his own place; that was good; greed and desire worked to motivate as much as power and position did.

"We are going after the Atwater slaves, we will take Bainbridge the next time we come." Raghnall pointed the Stone at the contraption on the other side, the bridge lowered and clunked onto the pathway. "Let's go," he nodded away from Bainbridge in the direction the Stone indicated the Atwater bucks had gone.

If the rumors of Bainbridge's defenses are correct, they'll be an admirable foe...but I'm here for the Atwater slaves. I have to keep my mind on that. If I want to become the High Wizard, I will have to keep my mind on what matters, but it is hard to pass by Bainbridge and not test the waters.

Making hard choices was part of it…yes; Murdoc would claim that he was afraid to attack Bainbridge, thinking of Murdoc made his stomach twist, pushing bile up into his mouth. He took another drink to wash it away while pushing Murdoc into the back of his mind.

When I get home, I will immediately ask permission to take Bainbridge. Prove that I am willing to take any chance, make any sacrifice to make Cerebrus the shining gem it once was.

Aja started across the bridge, he stopped and looked down. "Wow! Look at the rainbows!" He pointed down to where the dawn light touched the rising mist.

Raghnall looked over Bainbridge with an eye to owning it, "Yes…they are quite beautiful." His heart felt great longing as he watched the rainbows dance above the early morning mist.

54

Onid led her small group through the lower orchards' cover, in about an hour this place would be swarming with bees, now it seemed unnaturally quiet and thick with the scent of apple blossoms. If the sentinels atop the towers of Bainbridge saw them, the boys' adventures would end. She guided them to where she had stashed some bundles of silvered weapons.

Everyone seemed lost in their own thoughts as they strapped on the weapons, wasting no time with bravado. With a nod, they moved out.

As they topped the rise, Onid froze...the bridge was down. She signaled the boys to hang back while she checked it. Hunkering down next to the bridge, she saw many sets of prints had moved off the bridge and headed in Florete's direction, the same direction the Atwaters had gone. The tread was unfamiliar, it was hard to tell how many and mixed in with them were the prints of bare feet...warriors and slaves? This Raghnall had brought a small army with him.

She turned. She needed to check the other side, unsheathing her sword she crept onto the bridge. It swayed with the morning breeze, but not enough to use the handrail.

Reaching the other side, she found a body. She shivered and closed her eyes...*okay; this is why your teachers always had you help with the embalming of the dead...so you could handle death when you saw it.*

Re-sheathing her sword, she dropped to one knee to examine the corpse. Bloodless eyes stared out at her and again she shuttered. She had heard of this, read of it, her mother told her about it...but this was the first time she had seen it. It was a boy's body, about 10 to 12 years of age; why kill one so young?

With trembling fingers she touched a wrist, not that she expected a pulse; it was out of habit and training more than anything. No pulse, but to her surprise, the body was still warm...the Bloodstone's must have just left.

She glanced across the gorge; the boys were still there...waiting for her.

She searched the ground around her, chiding herself for not doing so earlier; the Bloodstones had all gone across the bridge, no strange tracks headed for Bainbridge. Releasing her breath, she turned back to the task on hand.

The boy was dark skinned and rather stocky; a race she was not familiar with. The skin didn't have the blue tinge of death, or the pink of life. He was bloodless.

Fine, straight blue-black hair was pulled back into a short braid. Dark eyes, a little large for his face…too young to have facial hairs…hooked nose and high cheekbones. He had on an old tunic, thread worn…but expertly darned…it was torn open at the chest and there was a perfect oval shaped mark over the heart.

That must be where the Bloodstone Wizard had placed his Stone. There were indentations on the upper arms as well…the boy had struggled.

If she failed, this was going to be a common sight. She shut her eyes. *I must not fail.* She opened her eyes and gritting her teeth, picked up the body; it hung limply over her shoulder, hardly any weight…she fought back the tears; they wouldn't help this poor child. Neither she nor the Bainbridge boys had ever taken a life before; they could not hesitate when the time came. Seeing this body should give them the knowledge of what they were fighting and the resolve to do what needed to be done when the time came.

Onid turned. The boys had not come onto the bridge, the fact that it was down spooked them,…or were they just following her orders? *I hope it's the later.* She returned to them, this time using the rail, and dropped the body down in front of them…most of them recoiled back; Julian and two others stepped forward and examined the body.

"So young," Julian turned the body over, a small bundle of thread and needles fell out of a waist packet, "Such a waste of talent."

Julian had not missed the needlework on the old, worn tunic.

"There are many Bloodstone Warriors heading towards Florete following the Atwaters and a good number of slaves." The boys tore their gaze from the body and swallowed.

"What's the plan?" Julian stood, brushing off his leggings.

"We were not planning on a group this large." As she stood there biting her lip, trying to decide her next move, a gust of wind threw a cloud of mist over them; snapping them back to the reason they were there. "We need further supplies, those best with rock climbing skills, will come with me along the high ridge. The rest of you gather silver headbands and extra weapons. Julian, take this spyglass and follow them now…see which slaves are disgruntled."

Julian's hazel eyes stared at her, "I don't understand."

"I've been trying to put myself in the Bloodstone Wizard's place...I am entering a place where the people know what silver will do." She began pacing.

"And he has with him, slaves that..." Julian nodded as he looked north, "Some of them, if they could protect themselves from the Sleep Spell and get their hands on silvered weapons, would turn."

"If I were Raghnall, I would use the Sleep Spell to keep the slaves out of the way during the battle...then dispose of all silvered weapons before waking them." She raised the bridge, relocking it into place.

Julian pocketed the spyglass before looking up; "I should be able to spot the ones that would be willing to fight if given the chance. I'll look for disgruntled body language from a safe distance. Let's give them that chance."

As Julian followed behind the Bloodstone war party, the rest of them turned and hurried back to the Forge to gather further supplies.

She prayed they'd make it to the Atwater youths in time to help. As they slipped into the packing shed, she kept seeing in her mind one of the Atwater's more than the rest. Skelly. For some reason, she felt the same concern for him as she did for any member of her family.

She didn't know why, *but bless Skelly. Please let me get to him before it's too late.* As her group strapped on mountain climbing equipment, early morning light peeked through the slats that formed the shed's walls, the others packed up silver headbands, shields, and swords.

"Where is my nephew?" A gruff voice came from the doorway.

Onid whirled; Pallaton, her martial arts master, was standing in the door, shaking in rage. She was confused; of all the men of Bainbridge, he was the least likely to stop them.

"The Bloodstones have crossed the ravine and are on their way to Florete, following the Atwaters." She swallowed. "Julian is following them at a safe distance to see which slaves will join us, should the opportunity arise."

Pallaton looked them over, his eyes missing nothing, "What are your plans?" He switched to from concerned uncle to schoolmaster at the revelation of the danger.

Onid was used to the speed at which his mind could jump from one subject to another. "These five will follow the Bloodstones' trail, catching up with Julian, and waiting for the Bloodstones to use the Sleep Spell."

Pallaton nodded as his eyes brightened, "Yes...that may be the Bloodstones' fatal flaw."

"These six will come with me along the high ridge, we will try and get ahead of the Bloodstones. Then challenge and attack from the high ground."

Pallaton turned, "I'll get my cart, we'll load the swords and shields into it. That will be faster than carrying them."

"You're going with us?" Volny, the youngest boy asked.

"Wouldn't miss it," Pallaton grinned, "Besides...someone in the family should be supportive of Julian."

Gravel crunched and Pallaton turned, it was his son, Kajika...Onid took her hand off the hilt where it had lit at the sound...they were all jumpy. Kajika was a year older than Onid, with a smile he nodded at his father.

Pallaton turned to Onid, "Take all the boys with you, Kajika as well. I have other help coming," he looked at his son, "Watch over them...follow your captain," his nod indicated Onid.

Kajika helped the other five boys into climbing gear as his father left.

"Other help?" She asked him as she gathered together spears and extra arrows for all of them.

"You think the ones my age want to be left out of this?" He smiled at her as he tossed bags of silver acid balls to each of the boys.

Pallaton...that sly fox...he must have guessed what was going on when Julian disappeared...sent his son to round up help and then...he wasn't shaking with anger when he challenged me...it was suppressed laughter. She shook her head, *I should have known.*

But again, the older boys would be bigger, better for hand to hand. Plus they would have had one more year of training, yet they would still be single...not worried about leaving behind a widow and children.

Onid, hearing Pallaton returning, remembered her mother's words. She rushed outside and tossed him a bag of silvered rock. "Have the slaves each eat a piece to protect them from a seeker spell. Also, there's a dead slave by the lower bridge, a young boy. The Wizard fed his Stone before crossing."

Onid's group left for the high ridge; she felt she had left the operation's other half under wise leadership, in fact she couldn't have chosen a better leader.

But if we don't get to the Atwaters before the Bloodstones, she did not want to think about that.

They climbed to the top of the ridge, Kajika helping the less experienced boys, and gaining the upper pathway...ran with the clear morning light showing the way.

55

Later that day, Hania wiped the sting of sweat out of his eyes and looked over the rise to the top of the next pass. According to Chval's map, it would be followed by a shallow valley that bumped up against a sheer wall of stone with a cleft that led through to a long gentle slope leading onward to Florete. There they could get passage on a boat back home.

He struggled to the top and turned to wait for Farid to catch up as he rubbed the tingle out of his legs. Farid had stopped and was looking back they way they had come.

"Are you looking for Onid?" He asked the boy as he gulped in the cool morning air.

Farid climbed up to him and turned. His eyes focused on something behind them on the trail, "It's not Onid."

"What is it?"

"Something dark…evil."

Try as he might, Hania could not see anything moving along the trail; something dark would have showed up against the off-white dolomite rocks behind them. His eyes scrutinized every foot of the trail…nothing.

"It shimmers…it bends the light," Farid shivered.

Hania pulled the spyglass out of the wilderness kit, "Where is it?"

"One third of the way down into the valley."

Hania trained the spyglass on the spot. At first he thought it was just a heat wave, *but it isn't hot enough for a heat wave and heat waves don't move down along a trail like that.*

"What is it?" Hania was at a loss as he lowered his arms.

"A tall man…he holds a stone, black with…" He broke off.

Hania was almost too late catching him as he fell. Dragging him back into the shade of a boulder away from the top of the pass, he slapped his face. "Farid! Wake up!"

Farid groaned as he sat up, he looked at Hania. "It tires me to look at him."

"Don't look at him anymore," Hania put a sympathetic hand on his shoulder.

"I think…he's a Bloodstone Wizard." Farid coughed as he got to his feet.

A weary sigh escaped as Hania gathered up the stuff he dropped when he caught Farid, "More than one?"

"No…just the one…he stopped, like he was resting…he may be waiting for his men to catch up. I wonder how many he brought?" Farid gathered up the stuff he dropped. Adjusting the straps of the makeshift pack Barra had fashioned for him. "Have you ever heard about them being able to be invisible?"

"No." Hania shook his head, "But there is nothing about them being able to raise pathways or pulling stone walls and stuff out of the ground."

"We better not assume what they can or cannot do to us," Farid started down the path, "Does silver still work?"

"That still works." *How can we make the Bloodstone Wizard show himself? What would disrupt his power, this spell he is using?*

"We need to set a trap…make him come to us on our terms, not his." Farid said.

Chval and the others were waiting for them, the map spread out on a boulder, had they reached the spot where Onid was to meet them? If so, it was time for a war counsel. But no, Chval rolled up the map and nodded to the top of the next pass. "We meet Onid in the next valley," he looked at Skelly, "That is…if she is coming."

Skelly's jaw tightened, "She'll be here."

Hania looked back, would she make it here before the Bloodstones caught up? He looked at Farid…his eyes were closed, lips moving, praying; Hania added his own prayers. How far behind the Wizard were his men? They gathered their stuff and moved towards the next pass as the shadows in the valley shorted while the sun climbed overhead. Time was not on their side.

56

After moving to this side of the valley next to the cleft in the tall basalt ridge, they waited in the heat as Chval paced back and forth. Chval pulled out the map, looked at it, and then scrutinized the terrain around them. He frowned and then nodded, muttering to himself.

It was a wide soft scoop of a valley with smooth round boulders and many smaller stones of white dolomite scattered across the path of a small stream; the sparkling water of it meandered around the stones before disappearing into a sinkhole. Willows struggled to mark its path.

The road builders had removed any stones in their way, heaping them up in two long rows alongside the path. They had used some of the stones to build a bridge over the stream, the only sign that civilization was once here.

Why was it so barren here? Hania took out the spyglass and followed the stream back to where it entered the desolate valley. It was like a small river as it entered, but disappeared into the valley's stony floor…the valley was a giant sinkhole. It gave him the shivers; he liked plants, lots of plants and only willows lived here…except for the ferns that grew in the lava flows' deep cracks and a straggly scrub oak forest that covered the hill coming down from the pass. It ended where the valley's floor began.

The cleft was no more than a break in the solid wall of a lava flow. You could see where the lava had met a glacier by the odd sharp edge pushed up by the steam as well as caves that looked like the pocketed air bubbles found in candies made on ice slabs in winter. Wind poured dust through the cleft, dark against the dolomite.

Another flow of lava was on the east, pointing like an arrowhead at the cleft. It too, showed the markings of its violent creation.

"Should we make a run for it?" Barra asked, drawing Hania's attention from the valley's violent birth to their possible violent death. Would this thirsty ground swallow their blood just as it did the water?

"Most of us can't move all that fast," Dreogan glared at Barra, "You want to explain to our folks why you abandoned us?"

"The people at Bainbridge know we all left together," Tesar added as he turned his gaze on Barra as well.

Barra blushed, "I meant, that one of us could run to Florete…get help." He sat on a bolder, checking the workings of his crossbow; head down, not meeting their eyes.

Chval raised his head from the map he had spread out on the top of a boulder, "This is the spot where Onid was to meet us." He slapped his hand down on the map, "And the best place to lay an ambush." His eyes had the same fanatical gleam Hania had seen at the war games back home…but the flame was brighter, this was no game.

"You're still going ahead with the ambush?" Tesar shook his head, "We are not warriors…we're boys, untried boys!"

Chval turned to Hania, "Does it say in the prophecies, the age of the Spirit Warriors?"

"Sixteen." Hania said as he took another small sip of Fo-ti, *it is getting warm, too warm for Skelly and me, we need shade and soon.*

"See?" Chval glared at Barra and Tesar as he nodded at Hania, "Now if you want to run off, get going…the rest of us know what is at stake here."

Barra didn't move. "Well…you need me here."

The decision made, the boys gathered around the map as Skelly came over to Hania, "I'm feeling fatigue already…what about you?" Skelly looked up to where the sun was burning high overhead.

Hania nodded as he placed his hand on Skelly's shoulder, "Do your best." They both knew the Foxglove-laced Fo-ti juice didn't stop seizures, just cut down on the number and duration. He could see the anxiety on Skelly's face; it was on his mind as well.

Chval looked back the way they had come, a look of worry crossing his face; it was followed by one of determination as he reached down and scooped up a handful of pebbles.

Chval pointed, "There is a cave at the point of that ridge, inside that crevice; it's high enough for a man good with a crossbow to get off a clean shot. Skelly, you will be our back-up," he placed a pebble to mark that spot.

Hania watched Skelly climb into the thin opening, disappearing from view.

"The coolness will help him…right?" Chval asked Hania.

"If we fail…" Hania looked him in the eye.

208

"We won't fail." Chval cut in as he placed two stones at another spot, pulling Hania over, "And you go over there, in that shade, with Farid."

Hania picked his way over to the spot, pausing as he reached the path. *What would reveal the Wizard?* As he pondered what he had that was silvered, a small dust devil moved past him, making him sneeze; the pathway was covered in dust. As the wind left the cleft, it created small, swirling dust devils. Bit by bit, the darker dust was scattered across the valley floor until it reached the stream.

That was it! The ground here is very dusty... if I add silver to the dust... He pulled some of the silvered rock out of his pack as another dust devil came through.

He ground up the biggest piece of the silvered rock he had and sprinkled it onto the dust following the dust devils' path between the two large rows of boulders that bordered the path.

Farid's shaking voice quivered out over the next dust devil, "He's coming."

57

Raghnall strode along the pathway; sensing movement to the side, he turned and stared, an animal? No, every creature within one days journey would have fled, must be human...and banded. It was near the next pass...along the top of an old lava flow. He continued up the steep switchbacks, keeping an eye on the lava flow's top; *why am I worried? They can't see me.*

He looked at the Stone...it was so dark, almost black...he had force-fed it on two more slaves and now it was far more powerful than before. Yes, the Seeker Spells still died soon after leaving the Stone, but they were more defined. *I'm not that surprised...when I ordered the Stone to make me invisible, it had happened in a flash.*

Should I, after becoming High Wizard, let select others know that forcing the Stones to feed gives them this kind of power?

Why not...weren't most of the Stones' uses discovered by accident? Was this not just the next step and what about some of the Stone Born, the ones that were touched in the mind? There's a good number of them...wasted; now just locked away...useless.

The path, which had been going away from the lava flow, turned and climbed toward it...where was the top of the pass? His foot slipped, sending gravel rattling down the path behind him as he froze; again he caught movement along the ridge to the east, someone was up there...did they notice the gravel?

A breeze came down off the pass, it carried the scent of pine; shade waited just over the next rise. He wiped sweat off his brow before moving on.

Careful not to slip again, he climbed the switched-backed path all the way up. Gaining the top, he stopped to rest, it was quite the climb...*I'm getting too old for this*; he again mopped his forehead as he stepped into the shade of the woods that grew on this side of the pass.

Looking down between the trunks, he felt he was being watched…then it was gone. What a strange sensation, he put a water bag to his lips.

He shrugged and started down the hill. Again that feeling…*someone is watching me*. He slowed his descent through the coolness of the trees. *I don't like this…I don't like the movements on the lava flow…I do not like the unknown*. The pathway was covered in wild mint; the smell grew stronger with every step. He stopped; *I am a Bloodstone Wizard…the entire world is at my feet*. With that he raised his chin and finished the decent into the valley, the last half through short trees with little shade.

He stopped…across the valley he saw four boys gathered around a boulder, he took another step, this time to the edge of the last switchback. At last, he was out of the trees, now he had a clear view across the valley; but then the boys straightened, they turned and looked towards him!

They scattered, as if they knew he was coming…how could that be? Again the feeling he was being watched, it couldn't be, he pushed it away, even other Wizards can't see you once you vanish.

Back to the boys…four, the other two must have stayed in Bainbridge…well, four is better than none. *So, I will have to hunt them down one at a time,* he gave a shrug, *let the games begin.*

As he sat on a boulder waiting for his men, he looked again at the ridge to the east, something about it nagged at him. There, another flash of movement. He raised the stone, *what if I give it a little shake…nothing…idiot, it's basalt…must have silver in it.*

Again, he felt like someone was watching him…he shook it off and smiled as his men caught up. He became visible causing some of the younger ones to jump.

As he stood, a lance flew through the air from the ridge.

"Shields up!" Istaqa jumped protectively in front of Raghnall as Zigor did the same for Aja.

"You," Istaqa pointed to a young Bloodstone Warrior, "retrieve it!"

His men made a barrier of shields as the warrior crouched down and scuttled forward to snatch the spear.

Istaqa turned, concern on his face, "Any idea on who is up there?"

"Two possibilities," Raghnall frowned, "the two that were with them when we recaptured them the first time…or Bainbridge sent a group to keep an eye on them just in case we showed up." *This is not what I had in mind…these Atwater brats had better be worth it.*

The warrior sent to retrieve the spear handed it to him; on the side, in letters of silver, was a warning to turn back. *Turn back? After all I've gone through, I will not turn back. Besides…it doesn't look like there's any easy way down off that ridge.*

He tore his eyes away from the ridge, "We will have to be careful and use the shields…grab the Atwaters, then go. No one is going to tell a Bloodstone what to do!" He turned and sent a Sleep Spell to keep the slaves out of the way.

Raghnall turned his gaze to where the Atwaters had disappeared; he signaled Istaqa and Zigor to him. "I will go on ahead," Raghnall put his hand on Aja's shoulder, "Zigor you will stay with Aja, and Istaqa you will lead the assault as soon as I become visible. Keep an eye on that ridge…it is from there they will launch the first attack."

Aja did not look happy, "I want to go with you."

Raghnall knelt next to the boy, putting his hands on his shoulders. "This is a battle, I want you safe." He wiped away a tear that had escaped the boy's eye, "There will be other raids…better raids, you'll see."

Rising to his feet, he turned and walked over to where the spear had struck the ground, then with a look of defiance at the ridge, he made himself invisible and stepped over the mark that was left in the path.

58

Skelly slid deeper into the cave and looked around, his eyes adjusting; at the mouth was a boulder of dolomite, sealed in place by the lava; he was in a long glassine bubble formed into a low flat cave behind it. Hunkering down he turned to face out. *Can't see a thing, I'll have to depend on sound and move out to shoot when the time comes; at least my ears are good. Is this the best place for me? It is nice and cool; I just wish the opening were wider.*

On the other hand, Chval did know how to place people to get the best from each and he was the best shot with the crossbow.

Now, trust your ears...don't look out! He could hear the movement of someone climbing behind that pile of stone just below him, Barra or Dreogan judging from the clatter of stones.

Some heavy breathing and a shadow, wrong...it was Tesar who limped inside, "I think he wants me out of the way," Tesar wiped away the sweat on his forehead. "Huh, you wouldn't believe this was here from the outside," his eyes traveled to the back of the cave where a crack disappeared into the gloom.

Skelly rolled over onto his back into the sparse light filtering in through the opening. He checked the workings on the crossbow, the soft dust and sand that had blown in over the years was cool and smooth; it was a relief after the heat of the outside, even if it lacked the earthy smell of the caves on Manhood Island.

He felt conflicting emotions, both excitement and worry; he was worried about the Foxglove laced Fo-ti juice, with the extra stress and the heat, would it be enough to stop a seizure? He remembered the look of worry on Chval's face.

It is a bit too late, Chval; too late to change anything, at least you thought to put someone with me, just in case I pass out. If we fail, Raghnall may not allow you to live; I'm sure he's angry over you taking his Stone...is that what's bothering you? Let the chips fall where they may...it's too late to change anything now.

He heard footsteps coming from the direction of the pass; this was it! He rolled over and sensed Tesar stiffen, as they both listened hard, piecing together what was going on outside the cave.

Then it happened...the feeling he was about to split in half, not now! He reached for, grabbed, and guzzled down the rest of the Foxglove Fo-ti juice, was there enough to stop it? He bowed his head in frustration; Tesar's hand was on his shoulder. He looked up into his worried eyes, "When I wake up, just tell me what to do...tell me to shoot! Just shoot Raghnall!"

59

Hania waited behind the last boulder on this side of the pathway. It was so quiet, just as it had been on Manhood Island and in the swamp…the only sound was their own breathing and the wind whistling through the cleft behind them.

He leaned against the cool smoothness of the boulder, ears straining for the footsteps of the Bloodstone Wizard that Farid said was coming…was it Raghnall? He could see Chval trembling at the end of the paved part of the path, right where the two long rows of stone ended.

He could see the paler of Chval's face…he was scared, in spite of the fact he had his sword out, his fingers tight on the hilt. He had never seen such determination; in fact he was seeing a side of Chval he had never seen before, that of a noble leader. Was it courage that drove him…or fear of failure…or was it the very thing that had caused Chval's Great Grandfather to defend his wife and people against the Bloodstones years before?

Whatever it was, it felt right. Chval had come a long way; he had left behind the childhood bully and now he was facing the test that would prove if he was a warrior or a coward.

It is up to the other side to make the first move; all we can do now is wait. No, that isn't all I can do; I can pray…I hope The Great Spirit, doesn't mind me praying with my eyes open.

What made me think that we might be the Spirit Warriors? Right now, I only hope that we survive to see another day; he shivered in spite of the heat.

Where was Onid? Would she and the boys from Bainbridge get here in time?

Speed their feet…bring Fo-ti juice…bring weapons and trained warriors. He never felt more inadequate.

"He is almost to the rocks," came Farid's whisper, he sank back next to Hania after popping up to check. "He is invisible again," he closed his eyes. "He ignored the warning."

"Warning?" Hania didn't understand.

"The warning spear from Onid's group; they're on the ridge." Farid unpacked the sword and shield and set them out in front of him.

Chval swallowed, took a deep breath, and tightened his jaw; he had heard Farid's words.

Hania was praying harder than he had ever done in his life as he slid his sword out of its sheath, his hand felt odd gripped around the roughness of the hilt as if it did not belong there. He shook it off, whether he liked it or not, it did belong there today; *please let the dust do its work.* They needed a visible opponent.

60

Raghnall felt a snap as he reached the halfway point between the cleft and the small stone bridge he had just crossed, he was no longer invisible. How? Looking down, he saw silver glints in the dust, that sneaky potion maker...a dust devil had blown some of it onto him...he was exposed.

He would have to figure out how to keep that from happening when he got home. He glanced back to see his men surge forward...it was too soon! Silver glinted off spears and arrows raining from the ridge; some of his men fell.

Anger flashed though him as he turned to confront the white faced Atwater youth; it was the rock thrower.

"So...you're the leader," he smiled through gritted teeth as he glared at the boy, who was standing there defiant...as if he were an equal. He saw the bindings on his hand, so this was the Stone stealer as well.

"Now!" The boy shouted.

There was movement on the left and right, Raghnall tossed dolomite boulders at the sides of the cliffs on each side of the path. Muffled cries from both sides told him; he had guessed right.

"You thought you could be the Stone's master?" He smiled regaining his composure, "Now you will pay."

He sent streamers of power to grasp the boy, then shook him hard and threw him against the cliff face. Scooping up several rocks with the Stone's energy, he dropped them one at a time on the rock thrower, what was his name...Chval, that was it. Chval, bruised and bleeding, struggled to his feet; he had lost his shield and sword.

Now what should I use next? Using the Bloodstone, he gathered up some more large rocks. This time he made them shoot towards Chval like they had been launched from a sling, a very large sling...the boy ducked and darted, so Raghnall sent two at once, a crack announced the cur now had a broken arm.

"My Stone uses a special type of wine," Raghnall smiled, "You will be squeezed to provide it."

217

Reaching deep under the earth, he pulled a slab of dolomite out of the ground and used it to press Chval against the cliff wall.

Thirsty? He asked the Stone…soon you shall feed.

61

Onid raised her hand, this time those who were good with slings prepared to drop acid balls on the Bloodstone Warriors. Her archers were ready to fire the instant the shields were raised overhead.

She signaled and the silver spheres arched up and dropped with accuracy, these boys were good. The shields raised, bows snapped, and six more Bloodstones were meeting their demon.

The remaining Bloodstone Warriors snatched up the shields of their fallen comrades. Onid's group could no longer hit them, but the Bloodstones could not weald a sword either, they had done all the damage they could from up here, it was time to move.

She looked over to see what Julian and Pallaton's group was doing; Pallaton was killing a slave...*a fake slave? Yes, I would have put one in with the slaves.*

Another older man was there, Eno the sword master? He led the charge of Bainbridge's older boys, his strong hulking body hefting his battle sword high overhead. War cries echoed through the valley as the Bloodstone Warriors turned in surprise; the two groups clashed together and soon she couldn't tell them apart; not even which group was gaining the upper hand.

Just then a strong hefty built boy she had never seen before came running up, his skin was dark, like the child the Bloodstones had murdered by the lower bridge. This older boy must be from the same tribe as that poor child, he had the same large dark eyes, she shook her head in wonder; he must have scaled the cliff in record time.

"I come to help..." he panted, "I very good with spear." The boy, a just freed slave grinned with excitement as he pulled the silver band down tighter on his head, "I called Zaki." He turned and threw a spear with deadly accuracy and strength. Another Bloodstone was gone in spite of his shield.

"You go...you go...I good help," he threw again.

That he was. She had them give the remaining spears to their new backup and got ready to drop into the battle with swords and shields. Just then, a sword and shield disappeared down a crevice, the boy looked up and showed her his battle-axe; he was still going.

They tied off their ropes to the sun heated jags at the cliff's top and dropped over the side; as she reached the bottom, she stopped to access the situation.

The Bloodstones or Pallaton's group drew the battle away from the ridge. She sent her group to assist after giving her sword and shield to the one who had lost his, *Farid has another set and my new friend Zaki is the only backup I'll need...I hope.*

Where is Raghnall...is that him? A blood-red braid...it must be him. She didn't see any of the boys...Raghnall was pushing a slab of stone up against a cliff, why? Then she saw a hand; someone was being crushed!

She ran hard, jumped over a line of rocks and slipped a little on the gritty sand as she gained the pathway; recovering, she rushed at Raghnall, tackling him from behind so hard that she rolled up and over past his head.

Sliding to a stop at the pathway's edge, she regained her footing just as the slab fell away from the cliff, revealing...Chval. He gasped for breath, cradling a broken arm; where was Skelly?

She whipped around to face Raghnall, the man who tried to kill her mother. Kneeling, he snarled and pointed the Stone at her, a red band of energy shot out at her and shattered as it reached her; a silent explosion.

The only sound was his gasp as he jerked back, his blue eyes wide in shock, "You're...Stone Born...a Stone Born Maiden? Well, you have met your match," Raghnall glared at her with a mixture of anger and fear on his handsome face as he rose to his feet.

Some of the prophecies must be known among the Bloodstones...that must be why Stone Born Maidens are killed.

She heard movement from the side and flicked her sight to the sound and back, then she leaned down, determined not to take her eyes off Raghnall again, not until it was over. Farid slid the sword and shield into her waiting hands. In spite of all that was happening, he had remained calm and did what they had planned, Hania was with him...where was Skelly?

Raghnall sent several dolomite boulders crashing above the spot behind where Farid and Hania were; she found it hard not to look. She did not dare take her eyes from Raghnall.

With her eyes locked on Raghnall, she slid her arm into the grips on the shield; spinning the sword around into a battle grasp, she took a step towards him. He gestured and pulled the ground out from under her. She fell on her back, hard...but years of training paid off. She flipped up and onto her feet, landing even closer to him. She slashed out with her sword, pushing him back.

He gestured again, but this time the ground did not move, there were flecks of silver underfoot, he was going to have to try something else.

He pelted her with loose stones, but they just clanged as she deflected them with the shield. *Now I see why my family had me practice the marshal arts until I was good enough to teach.*

Fear was growing in Raghnall's face as his eyes darted around and landed on a small boulder. He picked it up with a band of energy and slammed it into her.

Over and over he hit her with it, pushing her back until she reached the cliff; the shield and sword had no effect on it.

She was pinned. She couldn't pry it off with the sword so she dropped it and pushed at the boulder. It shifted, but she was still unable to get the shield's edge under it, *have I made a fatal mistake coming after the Wizard without the boys?*

Raghnall leaned, panting against one of the larger boulders, "So, Maiden...how did you end up being Stone Born?" He mopped at his brow with the edge of his cloak. *Using the Stone's power must be tiring.*

She glared at him as the pressure increased. *He is concentrating so hard on me; he isn't paying attention to how his men are faring behind his back...I need to keep his attention on me; a Wizard alone would be easier to defeat than a Wizard with men.*

"Well? Answer me," he waved a hand and small white stones gathered into the shape of a chair and he sat, as if they were the only ones there. He increased the pressure; it was getting hard to breathe.

He wants to know how I became Stone Born? I could let him know all at once or draw it out...draw it out. "You did it," Onid watched his face turn from puzzled to angry.

"I asked you a question," he snarled and pushed with the boulder.

"I answered it...if you don't...want to know...fine...finish it...kill me," she gasped out, where was her back up? She glanced up at the ridge; Zaki and a Bloodstone were battling it out on the top. And to make matters worse, one of the Bloodstone Warriors had broken away from the battle by the trees and was marching this way; *I'm on my own.*

"I get it, Rodor's concubine," he looked thoughtful, "The fool put a child in her to prolong her days."

Onid could feel the anger grow inside her; her mother was not a concubine.

"My niece, the Stone Born Maiden." He thinned his eyes as he cocked his head; he relaxed the pressure on the boulder, "You look a lot like her. Did she suffer much during the death from the Stones?"

"She still lives. It is the Stones that died," Onid felt sick and it had nothing to do with the rock pressing into her belly. *This monster thinks my mother was no more than a concubine and that my father had only been trying to postpone her death?*

"You put the seeds in her," Onid gasped out as he increased the pressure, "Out of jealously, and spite." The Bloodstone Warrior was still coming.

"And he created you to…"

"I was already with her when you put the seeds in the food…this is all your doing." The fight had moved into the trees, she could no longer tell what was going on or who was winning, *please let it be our side.*

Raghnall snorted unwilling to take any blame, "Enough of this. I have a batch of Atwaters to round up."

"You will fail," a small voice said from the side, Farid's voice.

"Fail?" Raghnall put out another band of energy catching the boy and shaking him; Farid had scooped up the fallen sword. He tossed it behind the rocks, why had he come out here?

"Watch me write my name in her blood." Raghnall began to push her with the stone; the cliff's roughness digging and scraping at her back…the fabric of her tunic tore away. "R…" his voice seemed far away as she struggled to breath. The Bloodstone Warrior had reached the bridge.

62

Hania yanked again at his leg trapped between the two boulders, it was pinched so tight that his foot was falling asleep. Dust filled the air, obscuring everything; he looked around, where was Farid?

What have I done...how many will die because of my pride? But they will be the lucky ones...the rest will be slaves. Tears pricked at the corners of his eyes, *stop*, he ordered them, *you don't have time for self-pity.*

He could hear Raghnall's voice, spelling out his name with a slow drawl, "R...A..."

He strained towards the sword Farid had tossed to him; it was just out of his reach. He pulled at the rocks and boulders trying to stretch far enough; stopped, and took off his tunic, twisting it into a thick rope with a rock weighting one end; he tried snagging the sword. Success! He grabbed it and wedged both swords into the space next to his leg; he pushed one up and one down with all his might; the weight shifted and he pulled himself free. As he did so, one of the swords snapped and the boulder fell back into place. *What was I thinking...that we might be the Spirit Warriors? Look where that had led us.*

Chval collapsed, maybe dieing? Skelly, Barra, Tesar, and Dreogan; where are they...buried under rubble...now what? What a mess.

He flexed his foot around while feeling the ankle, sore but nothing broken.

He untangled his tunic and slipped it over his head as he got to his knees and rose up for a quick look over the smoothness of the boulder's top. He could see two white faces peeking from around other such outcroppings; okay, they were fine for now.

He slipped his arms back through the sleeves as he glanced up at the cave where Skelly and Tesar were positioned; the opening was gone! Had they survived...can we get them out? First things first, he put it out of his mind as he pulled the tunic back down in place and picked up the unbroken sword. *Onid, Chval, and Farid are in danger of being killed.*

Onid! She had arrived, but where are the Bainbridge boys that were supposed to come with her?

He looked down at the sword in his hand, *were we all that were left?* He had to do something...gritting his teeth he lunged out, *this has to be the stupidest thing I have ever done. Is it going to be my last?*

He cut through the energy strand holding Farid...it shattered; he stared as Farid dropped. Stunned silence filled the ravine...it was as if all nature had stopped to watch...even the wind had stopped blowing dust around.

"Attack!" Chval croaked out, it might as well have been a shout. The air filled with acid balls, how had they survived the landslides?

Raghnall grinned as he put a barrier of spinning stones around himself; his eyes gleamed with madness. He threw more boulders at the cliffs trying to hit the boys or bury them; the boys lurched around, scarcely keeping out of the way.

Hania cut the band holding Onid's boulder; she slid down, shoved away the boulder, and using the shield, pushed herself to her feet.

Raghnall sent out another band, picking up a different rock and slamming her again; she caught it on the shield. She could not last much longer.

"No!" Hania darted around, cutting energy bands as fast as he could; the heat was taking his strength, *how long before...I collapse?* Cold anger kept him going, stumbling on.

As acid balls hit Raghnall's shell of small spinning rocks, some of the acid would reach the thin power barrier holding the stones causing the ones that were affected to fly off, taking the acid away from him. It splashed and sizzled as it hit the dolomite boulders, etching odd patterns as it trickled down to the ground.

The shell was like a tornado, gathering every loose stone into itself, protecting Raghnall from the Acid Balls.

Through the gaps in the pillar, Raghnall kept picking up boulders and tossing them at Onid and the boys. How long could they keep this up? Boulders, bands of energy, acid covered stones...a cry marked that Raghnall got one of them, which one?

With an oath, a Bloodstone Warrior raced towards the sound; swords clashed from that area as Barra leaped the path, rushing to Dreogan's aid. Raghnall turned his attention back onto Onid...throwing one stone after another as Hania tried to stop it; he was getting weaker, where were Skelly and Tesar...trapped?

63

Skelly coughed as he sat up...*where am I?* The air was full of dust and there was only a small sliver of light, stabbing like a long thin blade into the gloom. *I'm in a cave*...he racked his brain...*what am I doing here?*

The blade of light was growing wider and there was the sound of digging. Tesar was at the opening, crouched over at the handle end of the blade of light, digging, pushing, and mumbling under his breath.

"Tesar?"

Tesar jumped and hit his head on the top of the cave, causing more dirt to fall away from the crack. "Skelly, you're awake!"

"How long have I been out?"

"No time for that, just follow my instructions...first, we have to dig ourselves out," Tesar had his dagger out, using it as a digging stick."

Dragging his weary body over to look out, Skelly's hand brushed over a crossbow; *we were hunting in a cave?* No, that wasn't it...we were escaping, his memory was coming back in a rush as he reached up and fingered the band of silver that matched Tesar's. He turned to the crack...he could hear more than he could see.

A landslide had blocked most of the opening...*it doesn't sound like we are winning.* He sat the crossbow out of the way and pushed at the dolomite boulder as Tesar kept digging. He stopped; *I hate being so weak, I can't do it alone...even with Tesar's help I can't do it*...he knelt weeping, *please, please Great Spirit;* he turned his eyes upward.

Surely this was not an unrighteous desire. He put his hands on the boulder again; a sound of feet limping past below was followed by a jolt and the sound of another landslide; the cave filled with dust, blocking the light.

Skelly found it hard to breathe as coughing he pushed again. This time the rocks moved, falling away from the opening almost taking him with them as the remnant buried Tesar. Scrambling back, he pulled Tesar out from under the dirt and stone. He grabbed his crossbow…only one bolt was in view through the swirling dust.

Grabbing it, he looked at Tesar, "What am I supposed to do?"

Tesar sat up, spitting dirt, "Shoot Raghnall!"

There would only be the one chance. He looked out as he slid the bolt into place, where was Raghnall? Hania was darting around cutting at bands of energy…Chval and Onid were at the cliff's base, Onid standing.

The sound of swords clashing drew his eyes to the path's other side where Dreogan and Barra were in a sword fight with, was that Vritra? Every so often a flash of red would get in their way, but where are the flashes coming from? Then he saw it, every time they cut a band, a new one replaced it. All were coming from the same point, a spinning pillar of stones. Farid sent an acid ball at the pillar, some stones flew off, leaving a gap in the pillar, and revealed that Raghnall was in the pillar.

It was inching towards Onid, with Hania standing, sword drawn, before the stone pillar, shielding Onid.

Skelly began to pray, harder than he ever had his whole life. *Please bless this shot…make it true…help me save her life.*

"Tesar, do you have any acid balls left?"

Tesar climbed out of the cave and perched next to Skelly, he had his sling already filled. "On the count of three."

The pillar was slowly inching closer to Hania, Chval, and Onid. Skelly took careful aim.

"One…two…three." Tesar's sling snapped.

Skelly fired.

The acid ball hit the pillar, stones flew off leaving a gap, the bolt slipped in, and then the pillar collapsed in a shower of stones, revealing Raghnall standing with shining stones piled up to his knees. The last few stones bounced off his shoulders and head. No more energy bands came from him. The bolt had struck him in the back…he just stood there.

Skelly scrambled out of the cave, sliding down the rubble that now banked against the cliff face, Tesar followed; *a lot has happened while I was in Lise's grasp.* He helped Tesar to his feet and they turned to face Raghnall.

64

Raghnall stood in shock; with a snap the stone barricade he had put around him fell, rattling into a pile around his knees…it hurt to breathe and the stench of acid lingered in the air. He looked down, the silvered point of a crossbow bolt protruded from his chest; it had missed the heart but not the lungs. *I lost…no…I'm a Bloodstone…we never lose.*

Raghnall clutched the Bloodstone with both hands, ordering it to heal him; instead, blood stained his hands and ran from the Stone onto the rocks, it sizzled as it mixed with the acid from the silvered acid balls. *I haven't lost…I'm still alive.*

The Atwater bucks and the Stone Born Maiden gathered around him. Two of them dragged a body over and dropped it at his feet…it was Vritra; *are all my men dead?*

"Onid, how bad are you hurt?" The big one with the crossbow asked the Maiden as he protectively touched her arm.

*Onid…Atwater…the prophecies…*he could feel his own blood rise in his throat, making it harder to breathe,…*how could this happen…where are my men?* He looked back over his shoulder…some men were coming, but they weren't his. He looked back at Onid, the Stone Born Maiden…*my creation…my fault?*

"Do you know what happened to the Stones from my birth?" Onid asked him as with shaking hands, she opened a bag and poured sliver ointment out, covering the Stone.

A putrid, burnt smelling, green smoke boiled from the Stone and from his chest. *No…no…this can't be…*He retched several times as he sank down onto the stones, he could smell the acid burn him, but he was past feeling…past feeling.

65

Was it over...was it really over? Hania looked around at those who entered this first battle. They look awful, and beautiful, he felt a lump form in his throat and he shivered; there are so many wounds to dress...need to get to work.

The group from Bainbridge struggled over, they looked tired, some walked over and looked down at Raghnall and Vritra. Dreogan reached down and dipped a handful of water from the stream; he lifted it to his lips then spat it out, "The water's bad!"

"Where's the nearest spring?" Hania asked Onid, she shook her head.

Chval turned. "Get the map from my backpack," he said from between gritted teeth.

Hania pulled it out and looked, the stream was called Bitter Creek.

Using the map, he located a spring called Sweet Water at the forest's edge but away from the battleground, they started to limp towards it; those who could move helped the others. Chval refused any help; he was very quiet as they went.

Onid turned to the man who came with the boys from Bainbridge; "Pallaton, what happened?" She nodded in the battle's direction.

"Eno showed up just as we finished loading the cart; his grandson, Dyami, was among the boys coming with us. He joined us," Pallaton put his arm around a pale-faced boy who must have been the grandson.

"We caught up with Julian...he pointed out the ones that he was sure would fight with us; we waited. As soon as the slaves were put to sleep and the Warriors had moved away, we slipped in and put silver bands on the chosen ones."

"When the Bloodstone's moved to attack, so did we...much to their surprise. An un-banded slave jumped up and killed one of the banded slaves, a plant."

"I saw that from the ridge," Onid confirmed.

"Eno led the charge, the plan was to engage and then lead them away from you and the Atwater boys, denying the Wizard his men."

Hania paused as he reached the woods, then he realized he could hear the forest coming back to life.

Pallaton forced his sight away from the battleground, "I was going to send Julian to help you, but Zaki said he was a boar hunter, so I sent him instead."

"Good choice," Skelly helped Onid up the stair-stepped rocks to the spring's edge.

"The rest of us joined Eno's group, then Onid's boys came…the battle was ferocious; we lost Eno and two other boys, Jadar and Rigal. Also, all the slaves we freed except Zaki."

"How did Eno die? Even at his age, he was a remarkable fighter," Onid sat on a stone next to the spring and braced herself for the cleaning of her wounds.

Dyami sat next to her, he turned to her as if telling her would help him grieve and give honor to his grandfather, "After we engaged the enemy, we broke into back to back battle formation. Jadar and Rigal were paired, Rigal was pitted against a rival too great, and Grandpa sent me to help as he thought he could handle the two we were fighting."

All gathered to closer to hear what happened.

"As Rigal fell, Jadar moved around his opponent so they were both in front of him; Rigal's opponent shoved his blade through his fellow Warrior into Jadar, killing him."

Pallaton nodded, "We will have to remember that their blades have no effect on their fellow warriors."

"I killed Rigal's opponent," Dyami shook his head in wonder, "the other one, with the blade still stuck though his chest, turned and lunged at me. I side stepped him…at least my silver blade was effective."

Dyami took a deep breath and went on as if to purge his memory, "I turned to see if my Grandfather needed help, he had killed one and had just taken the other on his blade," he stopped and shuttered. "The Bloodstone Warrior ran up the blade, grabbed my grandfather by the neck and…" Dyami broke down unable to finish.

Pallaton picked up the narrative, "He bit Eno on the throat, tore out his jugular. We will have to add something to our armor to stop that, in case other Bloodstones have been trained to do that as a final act."

Pallaton stared at the battleground, shaking his head, "All of the un-banded slaves have disappeared, and we don't know what happened. Maybe when Raghnall died, so did the sleep spell and they ran off."

Dreogan started a fire to heat water and Hania began dressing wounds. Onid did not have a cracked rib…she did, however, have a bruised abdomen and most of the hide scrapped off her back.

Chval just sat, staring across the valley. He did have a cracked rib and a broken arm…and more scrapes, cuts, and bruises than the rest of them. Hania's wilderness kit was almost empty; he looked around at the forest, *I may have to glean raw supplies soon…I wonder what grows here?*

Barra returned from the battlefield and gave his report. "Zigor and the boy, Aja, are not among the dead, Zaki told me that they were here just before they were put to sleep." He tossed a couple of packs to Hania, "Here, you'll probably need these."

They were healer packs; Hania couldn't help but grin up at Dreogan. It was taking a long time, even with Skelly's help, to treat all the wounds. Pallaton pitched in after the cut on his forehead was taken care of, he had been lucky, no…blessed that the blade that grazed him had been dulled by an earlier errant blow.

Chval didn't even wince as he was sewn up and his arm set. It was like his mind and emotions were miles away.

Onid sat, looking at the fire, "He killed so many…and for what?"

"He what?" Hania was making some more silvered salve as Skelly cleansed dirt and grit out of the wounds on her back with warm water.

"Raghnall, he killed at least…" She looked over at Pallaton, he raised three fingers, "three slaves to build up the power of his Stone, he used the youngest ones." She told them what she had found at the bridge and Pallaton told them that he had found two more bodies of young slaves on the trail here.

"He…" Zaki swallowed, "at bridge…my cousin." Silent tears formed in his large eyes and ran down both cheeks as he sat against a tree, "my cousin and my friends."

They sat in silence as the woods' cool, pine-scented air calmed them, helping them to recover from the day's events. Hania looked at Chval, something about him had changed. Chval kept looking across the valley then at Hania.

Chval got to his feet, walked over to him, and sat; he turned and after several failures, blurted an apology.

"I am so sorry Hania, I planned badly…I should have put Skelly in a different cave. The Spirit was prompting me…and I ignored it. Thought I knew better, because it looked like it was the better spot. I planned for me to be the big hero, so I could be the leader of the Spirit Warriors."

"Only The Great Spirit can choose the leader of the Spirit Warriors," Farid said from where he was grinding up the last of their silvered rock and adding to a jar of ointment from the Bloodstone packs.

"I'll never be a Spirit Warrior," Chval sighed, "I don't have what it takes. I should have listened to the promptings!"

Farid jumped to his feet and stared in the direction of the battlefield, then raised his eyes to the top of the pass and gasped.

Skelly leapt up and jerked him around, "What did you see?"

Farid was shaking so hard that it was difficult for Skelly to hold onto him.

"Deep breaths, take deep, slow breaths," Hania told him as he finished wrapping Onid's wounds.

Farid looked at them, "It was another one, a Bloodstone Wizard." They all grabbed weapons.

"Where is he now?" Skelly let go of him, "Just take a quick look and tell us what you see."

Farid looked back and forth from Skelly's face to the top of the pass.

"He's leaving!" Farid gasped out, "He is very powerful, a boy of about eight and a large Warrior with a whip are with him."

"Zigor!" Dreogan jumped to his feet.

"We're not in danger." Chval shivered as he slid his sword back into his scabbard. "Not at the moment anyway."

"They're gone," Farid sank to the ground; his ability to see what others could not was spiritually draining.

"Looks like this is just the beginning," Barra said as he sat down and finished cleansing the small gash on his leg; one of Raghnall's stones had grazed him.

Hania knew he was right. He sat going over what he knew of the Prophecies; Barra is dead on. He remembered the Shrine in the Great Swamp, were there other Shrines with hidden weapons? We may need them.

He sat up…they had forgotten something. "We need to give a prayer of thanks, that we are still alive."

Farid volunteered. The young prophet from Dennet had a clear, strong voice.

66

"It's okay!" Uaid called from the clearing's edge by the spring, as he stepped out of the trees, he re-sheathed his sword. Men from the Forge and Bainbridge melted out of the trees, a runner was sent back over the pass.

Hania's heart settled back into his chest and he turned back to his work.

"We saw your wood smoke from the pass. We were worried that we may be too late." Uaid grinned as he nodded at the battleground, "Looks like we were. Julian's father was against us coming until he found out Julian was missing. Not that any of the other boys fathers were listening to him."

"Did he come with you?" Pallaton looked around.

Uaid shook his head in disgust. "His gout was bothering him."

Pallaton reported the losses and Uaid started the supervision of the burial detail as others arrived, Gaho and Kendra among them. They had brought medicine, bandages, clothing, and food.

Kendra was chiding Gaho for worrying so much, "I told you that Onid would be fine."

"You call this fine?" Gaho knelt at Onid's side taking her hand; she cupped Onid face with her other hand, as tears rolled freely she whispered, "Thank you, Great Spirit."

"We won, ma-ma," Onid smiled guiltily at her.

Bainbridge's healer checked Hania's work, nodded his approval, and got to work on whoever was left. Soon they were all bandaged up, clean clothing, and with food cooking.

Hania's stomach growled, when had they last eaten?

Zaki was the hardest to clean up, "I want big scars…to show my bravery…I helped defeat the Dream Stealers." After being told he would have plenty of scars, he let them treat him.

"What are Dream Stealers?" Hania asked him as he dumped an armload of wood next to the fire.

"Every year that it floods," Zaki looked the sky," there comes a night of deep sleep. Even the village guards fall asleep and in the morning the village wakes to find many young ones gone; never to be seen again."

"The Sleep Spell," Hania nodded.

"This white metal...it stops the deep dreams?" Zaki touched his headband.

"Yes, and it can also kill them," he nodded at the battleground.

"I must find my way home, take this metal to my people." He looked sad, "But what can we trade for it? You have much, we have little."

"We'll think of something, Zaki," Hania stared into the fire; this had been such a long day.

It was not over for everyone; the families of Eno, Rigal, and Jadar were sorrowing, grieving as they built litters to carry them to Bainbridge's catacombs.

"What shall we do with Cerebrus' dead?" One of Bainbridge's warriors asked Uaid.

"We'll take the slaves to the catacombs," Uaid looked around, the soil here was too shallow for a grave, "But the Bloodstones..."

Skelly pointed across the valley, "What about one of the caves? A deep one, then we can fill in the opening with stones."

Kendra nodded her approval.

A part of them left with the honored dead; the Bloodstones, including the plant that Pallaton had killed, were stacked in a cave and the entrance filled with stones.

Finished, they sat around a large fire going over the day's events. Something was bothering Onid and she turned to her mother.

"Raghnall said he was my uncle," Onid waited.

Gaho started to giggle; "Now that is a tale of royal intrigue if ever there was one," silence fell as Gaho told the story.

"Every year, High Wizard Quinn would come to the slave township and send four slaves to the Temple of The Stone. Each year, he selected two couples with the female with child."

Hania felt himself blush, good thing it was a dark night, he moved back into the shadows.

"One was very beautiful and had spurned Quinn; refusing to become one of his concubines. I think that is why they were chosen," Gaho looked up at the stars, lost in her thoughts.

What she must have gone through, Hania shuttered.

"After the Stones killed them…"

"Are all the Stone Born?" Skelly stammered, "Are all the mothers, all the workers, given the seeds?"

"Yes."

"And they all die?"

"Yes…the Stones kill them…then their priests kill any girl child, sacrificing her to the Mother Stone."

Skelly sat there, stunned.

"After the Stones killed them, one of Quinn's concubines brought a baby boy to the girl's parents to raise. The concubine was supposed to raise the Stone Born one, but she had switched them. They were raising their own grandson and didn't know it. They were good people and did not blame the child for their loss; they loved him and taught him about the Great Spirit…even though it was forbidden."

"The concubine had switched them? How was it found out?" Onid frowned.

"The boy the concubine raised couldn't do magic and when the one the slaves raised could…well, Quinn was very angry. The concubine was sent to the Temple to die and Rodor was taken to the palace; that is where I met him."

"What was the fate of the concubine's son?"

"He was made a Bloodstone Warrior, which is where he was supposed to be anyway," she sighed.

"They are truly evil…they have turned from the Great Spirit to His opposite."

There was a cry from one of the guards; it was the one guarding the road towards Florete. "People coming!"

Hania, one of the few that could still move, limped over to see. "It's alright, they're from Atwater."

The families from Atwater were so happy to find their children alive; speech was difficult. They just stood around crying as they hugged their loved ones.

"Figured you'd head for Bainbridge." Nabi wiped his tears away with both hands. "It's not in the prophecies, but a good guess?" he nodded as he hugged Skelly.

In the jumble of folks, Hania saw Kendra bend down to Farid, "What did you see today?"

"I saw them, the dark ones…is that what you meant? They couldn't hide from me."

"They?" Kendra asked.

"Raghnall and one that was watching. The watcher…" Farid looked up at Kendra, "He was…darker…more…evil, I could see it."

Kendra stood and sighed; "Yes, I saw him far off in the distance as we came here. Becoming invisible must take a lot of power…we found many dead slaves on our way here. So we fight on."

Nabi, Kendra, and Farid gathered together with Onid…after a few nods of his head, Nabi stepped forward, "Sit…sit…it is time! The Great Spirit has chosen the first of the Spirit Warriors."

Everyone gathered around as if it was some kind of game, this is no game; Hania shook his head.

Chval's father stood tall, he expected Chval to be not just one of the chosen, but the leader. Chval shook his head as he looked at Hania; Chval believes he is no longer worthy. *Yet…wasn't it he that said they were not in danger from the other Wizard? I wonder what Nabi thinks?*

"Farid is the Prophet and Warrior," Nabi put his hand on the young boy's shoulder. "Onid is and always has been, the Stone Born Maiden."

Onid looked at Kendra, then back at Nabi. Nabi nodded at her and Onid stepped forward. "The core from Atwater," she bit her lip, there were tears in her eyes, "Are Skelly…"

Skelly stepped forward and took her hand, "The protector of the Maiden." She said that part in almost a whisper.

Hania exhaled a breath; *I've just lost my best friend…he will go off on big adventures…into history.*

Farid stepped forward, "The next is the leader of the Spirit Warriors."

Chval's father looked ready to bust, Hania looked at Chval; he was looking at Farid, shaking his head.

Farid turned to Hania, "The Leader of the Spirit Warriors is a potion maker…soon to be healer…it is you, Hania."

Hania felt the blood drain out of his face…how could this be? He glanced at Chval's father, he was standing stock-still, conflicting emotions crossed his face as he frowned at his son.

Nabi stepped forward, "The Prophecy's first part has taken past. Now we must prepare for the next part and to do that, we name the rest of the core from Atwater," he turned to the group.

"Chval!"

Chval rose to his feet, a look of stunned disbelief on his face. Nabi smiled at him, "You are to go north to where your maternal Grandfather will start a training camp. You are to be the leader in the fight to keep the Bloodstones contained. Your job will be to protect our borders, keep them out, and if the opportunity presents itself, rescue captives. It will not be easy…when it starts, you will be in constant danger, but only if you listen to the Spirit, will you succeed."

Chval nodded, he looked thoughtful…it was a different look then he had when he was planning the ambush. His father had backed into the shadows, nursing his disappointment.

Nabi tuned his eyes to the next one, "Tesar, you are to go to Pendragon…there your talents will be used to design new weapons."

Then he turned to Dreogan, "You always wanted to work with animals. You will go north with Chval. Horses from Lapis will be your first duty and other creatures, as they are needed…you will learn to care for them, how to train them and prepare them for battle." Dreogan nodded.

Finally he turned to Barra, "You are also to go with Chval, but you will not train with him. You will teach other young men how to track, how to survive in the wilderness; for they will often have to live off the land as they guard our borders," Barra looked relieved by his calling.

With a smile, Nabi turned to Zaki. "You too, Zaki are a Spirit Warrior. At first, you will go with Chval. You will teach others how to use the spear."

He put his hand on the boy's shoulder, "At least until we figure out where your homeland is. Then you will return to them and help them learn to fight the "Dream Stealers"."

Zaki nodded his head; he had the same solemn look as Chval.

"Others will be called as needed." Nabi stated to the group. "From all the clans and other groups of Believers."

"Your people are Believers?" Hania asked Zaki.

"We have prophecies and a prophet." Zaki looked sad. "But he old."

It was too late to return to Bainbridge, so they slept out in the open. Hania, as usual, found it hard to sleep though the night. He sat looking at the stars, rubbing at a knot of muscles in his calve, and pondering what Kendra, Nabi, and Farid had said.

We fight on. And now, I know; I am a Spirit Warrior.